Eos

Jen Guberman

ISBN: 9781089216964

Any references to historical events, real people, or real places are used fictitiously. Names, characters, and places are products of the author's imagination.

Author photo by: Steep Creek Photography

Printed by KDP Amazon in the United States of America

Second printing edition 2019.

Edited by Amy Guberman and Shelby Brown

www.UberGuberman.com

For mom, who has read this book more
times than even I have.

CHAPTER ONE

Click.

After weeks of careful observation, I felt like I was actually going to get away with this. I moved out of my crouch for a moment and peered one more time over my shoulder, checking the dark barroom. I squatted and turned back to the ancient brass lock underneath the bar counter, once I was certain I was alone. Removing the lock carefully and silently, I placed it gingerly on the dingy red and white checkered tile floor beside me. The cabinet let out a quick squeak as I opened it, revealing a few palm-sized liquor bottles filled with caramel-colored liquid. *Jackpot.*

For the past few weeks, I had spent my nights watching this bar from across the street, studying when the barkeeper would typically lock up and leave for the day. I knew that every day during the earlier hours of the night, he would leave for a while to go home to his family. He would always return late at night to spend some time tipping back the bottle himself before he would eventually lock up. At this point, I was certain of when he would be gone for the night and I knew it was my chance. I have gone in the bar before—I'm an in-city messenger. Within

1

my city, Rockhallow, I'm hired out, typically by government officials. They pay me to deliver letters, documents, packages, or whatever else throughout Rockhallow, wherever they need me to go. I'm too young to be a cross-city messenger; the roads to the other few remaining cities in our country have become fairly dangerous since the war. The last time I was sent to deliver a letter to this bar, I overheard some men discussing some very old, very expensive liquor. I immediately wanted it.

I'm underage, but only just. Rockhallow follows the laws of our country's past in regards to alcohol, and we are not legally able to drink until we turn 21. I'm 20. I've only had a few drinks before, and always in secret. This time would be different—this liquor was special, from long before the war ever destroyed most of the country. These few bottles are some of the only remaining ones, and are said to be some of the sweetest rums that were ever made. I figured, if I snagged two bottles, I could drink one myself, and save the other for when I become a cross-city messenger at 25 to barter in one of the other cities. By then, no one should be looking for a little bottle of rum, but it could easily earn me a wad of cash.

I wrapped my fingers around the first bottle I saw—a short, round bottle with the shape similar to that of a clamshell. It was full about three quarters of the way, and the caramel liquid sloshed as I stuffed it in my coat pocket. Just as I was reaching for the second, I heard the crash of a door being thrown open.

"She's behind the counter! I knew someone has been watching my shop for a long time now! I knew it was a thief!" a clumsy man with a red, bulbous nose shouted while stumbling into chairs as he made his way into the room—the barkeep.

I swore under my breath, unsure of what to do. As I

tried to scramble behind some of the boxes concealed by the counter, I heard two more people enter the bar as the lights flickered on, illuminating the room in an amber light. One of the newcomers, a thick-set man with close cropped black hair and a crooked nose, stepped behind the bar just as I was trying to wedge my way between two crates. He grabbed my arm with a strong grip and dragged me out of my hiding place, sending the crates around me crashing to the ground as I flailed my legs. The other newcomer, an unusually muscular woman with frizzy brown hair and a wide jaw, joined the man at his side. She tugged at my other arm, causing me to slide significantly faster than I could scramble away. Once they got me out from behind the counter, the woman reached into a pocket on her security vest and pulled out a syringe, jabbing me in the neck with it before I could even utter a word, sending me into blurred darkness.

When I began to regain my vision, I could begin to make out the figures of my parents. They were talking to someone. *Who are they talking to?*

"Mom... Dad?" I grumbled quietly, blinking through the bright fluorescent lights of the room. *How long was I out? There's sunlight… Where am I?*

My vision gradually grew clearer, and I could make out distinct voices. I was in a courtroom, that much I could tell. I could see the sparkle of white marble columns and floors, oak seats surrounding me. There were very few people in the room with us: me, my parents, the barkeep, and a handful of whom I could only assume were government officials. And then there was Redelle. Patrick Redelle, our city leader, was a man of average height, average weight, and above-average intelligence. His hair was a chestnut brown that grew no more than an inch above his head and was always styled and gelled without a hair out of place. He had a strong face, with what seemed to be a permanently stubbly goatee. Redelle was always fashionably dressed, and today was no exception. His brown suit was free of any blemishes or specks of dirt and was perfectly pressed as he stood stiff at the head of the room.

"You've obviously made a mistake!" my mom shouted at the barkeep, her green eyes wide and reddened, filled with tears. "My daughter would never steal from anyone! Especially not rum! She's too young to drink!"

"We can reimburse you for any stolen or damaged goods, we just ask that you please give our daughter another chance," my dad bartered, a stern but pleading look on his sharp face.

"There's nothing we can do," Redelle replied, from his position in the room. "She is no longer a minor, and therefore must be tried as an adult and unless substantial evidence is provided in her favor, she will be sentenced to exile to Avid."

"Avid?" I spoke up, trying to prop myself up, only to jerk forwards and find out I was handcuffed to a bench. "You can't do this!"

Ever since the four cities were built after the war, people began devising new ways to deal with criminals. It began with the old prison system, only to find out they couldn't contain all the prisoners. Eventually, the exile system was put into place. Towns were developed for different crime groups, spread over a small region of the country, considering most of it was left in too much of ruins for even the criminals to live. Because of this, criminals were exiled from their cities into the appropriate towns.

The thieves are sent to the junkyard town of Avid.

Even though this was about to become my new home, there was very little I knew about it—people never really talked about what the exile towns were like.

Those with violent habits are sentenced to the caverns of Bellicose. These include your murderers and psychopaths, but it also includes those who pick a lot of physical fights with others. Their caverns are located the furthest from any of the cities because the people in them are considered the biggest threat to the safety of the citizens.

I knew a guy who used to be in my class when we were young who was fairly recently exiled to Delaisse because he was caught with a stash of drugs in his apartment. People who are vandals or drug abusers are lumped into the same group because of the statistical links between the two at the time of the group's creation, and these people are transported to the industrial fields called Delaisse.

Extreme liars even have their own exile group in the heart of a forest somewhere around a lake. It wasn't as if the cities would banish a person for telling a few white lies, but when lies get out of hand and drastically disturb a city, these people are exiled to the town of Equivox. Few people live in Equivox, but those that do are some of the most coldhearted liars that ever walked.

As for the last exile group, there's Clamorite. These "noise polluters"—rioters and general nuisances—are sent to live on a mountain. These people are treated the best of all the exile groups, with larger monthly rations delivered to them because their crimes are considered the most innocent—they simply caused too much public disturbance, often receiving complaints from citizens.

"You can't send me to Avid!" I protested, struggling

against the cuffs. "I'm your messenger! You know me better than that!"

"I'm sorry, but we don't have much of a choice—there were witnesses, and Mr. Cantrell has a solid case against you. He has spotted you watching him closing his bar for the last couple weeks, and he notified me when he saw you picking his lock. I sent some of my officers to check it out immediately, and when they came back with you sedated claiming you were resisting arrest…well, you can see where my hands are tied here," Redelle eyed my cuffs apologetically.

A rail of a woman with short greying hair and spectacles grimaced at me before turning to Redelle.

"Can we please proceed with the trial, Mr. Redelle?" she croaked.

"Yes, yes, sorry Esther."

"Daughter of Mira and Troy Dawn. Twenty years of age. Accused of theft by a Mr. Grod Cantrell," Esther read from a file. She clicked a button on a tiny remote in her palm and a large projection flickered into the middle of the room. I was staring into my own pale green eyes on the image. My fair skin and countless dark freckles, framed by my long black and platinum blonde streaked hair, displayed in an emotionless photograph of me in front of the people that were undoubtedly going to cast me out of the city I had grown up in. As I stared at the projection, Esther continued to read off the details of my crime.

"Are there any council members or witnesses present who are able to provide evidence to prove the innocence of the accused?" questioned Esther.

Silence.

"Eos Dawn, you are hereby sentenced to exile to the

town of Avid," Redelle began, followed by the wailing cries of my mom as she threw herself at me, sobbing onto my shoulder as I squirmed uncomfortably, crushed by her but restrained by the handcuffs still. "Your exile is due to take place in three hours. You have this time to spend with your family and friends, as well as to pack five items you are permitted to bring with you to Avid. During this time, the same officers that took part in your arrest will accompany you. After your three hours have expired, you will be escorted to the city gate, where further information will be given to you before you depart."

At the word "depart," my mom slid back onto her knees and looked me in the eyes, covering her mouth and nose with both hands, a look of surprise, shame, and disbelief on her face.

"Mom, I'm so sorry," I said.

"This isn't you," she sputtered through sobs. "My E would never do something so stupid…"

"Mom," I started.

"Stop. Please, honey. Just…let me go on with the image of my sweet, innocent little girl. I can't be around you… I can't have my last memory of my daughter be of a thief," she sighed shakily as she stood unsteadily to her feet, steadying herself with my free hand, allowing her grasp to linger for a second before she gently squeezed my hand and pulled away as she turned and walked out of the courtroom doors.

"Mom! Mom, come back!" I shouted in vain.

"You know we both love you, Eos," my dad said calmly. "Your mother is just in shock. She'll come around before you leave. I'm going to try to catch up with her and keep her around the house if you want to spend any of your three hours with us. Don't forget to pack your things before you have to go."

He walked out of the room without waiting for a response. City officials began filing slowly out of the room after the chitchat began to die down. When the two officers were the only other people left in the room, the woman who injected me with the tranquilizer pushed a miniature key into the lock of the cuffs chaining my arm to the bench.

Click.

CHAPTER TWO

I made my way to my house on the eastern part of the city. Rockhallow isn't the biggest of the four populated cities—it ranks as the second smallest: Fallmont, Eastmeade, Rockhallow, and then Nortown. In Rockhallow, I can easily cross from the western side to the eastern in about an hour by foot, despite the fact that the city is on hilly terrain. Luckily for me, considering my limited time, the courthouse happens to be located near the city center, so my walk didn't have to use up too much of what little time I had before I would be forced to leave my home forever. Exiles aren't given a second chance.

By the time I got to my front door, I was already fed up with the officials following me. They hadn't said much on the walk, aside from a few friendly greetings with other citizens they passed along the way—friendly, as if they weren't playing a role in destroying my life.

I wrapped my fingers around the knob of my front door and gave it a twist. The knob made a quiet *thunk*. I tried again. *Thunk*. I reached into my coat pockets for my key, but came back empty-handed. Great. They not only took the rum, but they took my keys and my parents locked me out of the house. Considering my parents left quite a while before I was even uncuffed, they should have made it back by now. I knocked on the door and waited patiently. No response.

Knock knock knock.

"Mom? Dad?" I pressed my ear to the door and listened intently.

I can hear you! Let me in! I thought, my face growing warm.

I could hear muffled voices, but I couldn't tell what they were saying. Frankly, I didn't care. They didn't want me in the house, and no words would have meant anything to me at that point.

Turning to the officials behind me, I asked in a snarky tone, "Does it count as stealing if the items belong to me? Or are you going to stab me with another needle?" I glared at the female official.

"We'll see," she said, her grin rubbing her undeserved power in my face.

Letting out a frustrated grunt, I turned on my heels and walked around to the side of the house. It was only ever my parents and me that lived at home, so we had a simple ranch style house. Fortunately for me, I usually kept my window unlocked for easier access in and out of the house without alerting my parents. I didn't sneak out often, but when I did, I always came back with something—jewelry, money, and other little trinkets. I never stole anything that would draw attention to myself. *Until now, apparently.*

I opened my window with ease and hoisted one leg over the windowsill, followed by the other in an almost fluid movement. I grinned to myself when I tried to picture the two large officers attempting to replicate the motion. To my surprise, they both stayed outside the window without even trying to step inside.

"So, there's some trust here?" I asked sarcastically as I began to dig through my desk drawers. You never really think about which five possessions in your life are most valuable until you have to pick or have them taken forever. This made me wonder what my parents would do with my other stuff once I was gone. *What to bring...what to bring...*

While rifling through my belongings, my eyes met a shiny ring—the one my best friend, Fabian, gave me before his parents made him move with them to Fallmont about a year ago. Fabian's father was asked to move for some work-related thing. He never really talked about his dad's work, but we talked about practically everything else. We had been best friends from the time we could walk, and were nearly inseparable until he moved. The day before he left, he gave me a ring he bought from the market for me to remember him by—it was copper, twisted into an intricate design set with a stunning sapphire gem fixed in the middle. I slid the ring on my finger as I have countless times, with the same result.

Clunk.

The wide ring fell back into the drawer, off of my thin finger. Considering I didn't foresee the officials counting the clothes on my back in my item count, I was hoping it would fit just enough to wear instead of having it count as one of the five items. I had been meaning to get a chain to wear the ring on my neck. *I guess it's a bit late for that now.* I dropped the ring into my coat pocket.

I wonder if Avid has any kind of marketplace...I assume it would, so I had better bring some money. Unscrewing the lid on my glass money jar, I turned to the officials at the window.

"If I took all of my money, would that count as just

one item?" I asked with genuine, innocent curiosity.

"Yes," replied the man, leaning his head further into my window.

At this, I stuffed what money I had into the other coat pocket. That's one thing I've always loved about my black coat—it has two external pockets, and four internal pockets I tend to stash stuff in. I could try to slip something extra into my hidden pockets in hopes that I could skirt the rule, but if they found out, they'd probably just take everything from me. I can be greedy at times, sure, but I'm not stupid. I couldn't resist though. I grabbed for my grandpa's old pocketknife on my dresser and slid it quickly into my sleeve, pretending to be moving things on the dresser top around. Holding the knife in my palm, my hand shrunken back into my sleeve enough for the knife to be out of sight, I scratched a fake itch on my chest and let the knife fall into one of the hidden pockets.

I still needed three more objects. I looked around my room. My eyes immediately went for the picture frame on my bedside table. Holding it at eyelevel, I made out the familiar figure of younger me riding piggyback on my dad, a frozen expression of laugher on both of our faces. My grandpa stood in the background, a goofy look on his face as he was caught in mid-bite with his hamburger from the annual summer barbeque my family hosted. I have always been closer to the men in my family, particularly my dad. I removed the picture from the frame and carefully tucked it into the same pocket as the ring from Fabian.

I always considered myself a fairly realistic person, so the next thing to come to mind was a small fleece blanket. Obviously, I had no idea what I'd gotten myself into—I didn't know what to expect in Avid. Nobody ever talks about the sleeping situations in the exile towns, and for all I know, I might be sleeping on the dirt outside tonight.

One more item. *This is it.* Luckily for me, I was able to think of something that was both sentimental as well as practical—my leather satchel. When I turned 18 and was hired as an in-city messenger, my parents rewarded me with a real leather bag large enough to hold a package and some letters. This bag was the first expensive thing I had ever been given, and my parents saved for months to buy it for me. It was a symbol to me of a new level of independence—that job gave me my first taste of adulthood, and that bag was a vital part of my success at it, as simple as it was.

Emptying my external pockets into the bag in obvious sight of the officers, I hoped they wouldn't check my hidden pockets later. I shoved my blanket on top of the other items in my bag; I then lifted the long strap over my head and let it rest on my shoulder. I began to make my way to the window when I stopped for a moment. Should I try to talk to my parents; at least to say goodbye?

No. If they cared enough to say goodbye, they wouldn't have locked me out and ignored me at the door. I turned back around and made my way back out the window, sliding it shut behind me.

"You have one hour remaining before we have to make our way to the city gate," the male officer notified me.

Without a response, I walked away from the window, never turning back.

CHAPTER THREE

With my last hour, I decided it would be best spent roaming the city—it would be the last time I would ever see it. I didn't have any close friends to say goodbye to—Fabian was the only person I ever considered as such. It isn't like I could go visit him.

While thinking about my old friend, I wandered around the main city street. This street ran directly from the east side to the west side and through the city heart itself. I passed one of the few letterboxes located in our city, giving me an idea.

"Do you have any paper and a pen?" I asked the officials.

The woman pulled out a stationary pad and a blue pen from a little bag on her belt and handed it to me, crossing her arms and watching me. I began to scribble frantically,

Fabian,

I just wanted to let you know, there was an incident back home and I'm being exiled to Avid. See if you can get some of my stuff sent to you—my parents won't need or want any of it, but I want you to

utter a word, Redelle slammed the door shut behind me. Redelle, the officers, and the senior officer all stepped back as the driver started to drive the truck past everyone witnessing my exile. As the truck began to roll away from my city, I scrambled in my seat to turn around, just in time to see the last of the brass city gates with their fancy lettering.

Rockhallow.

CHAPTER FOUR

I turned back around in my seat. About ten or so minutes into the drive, it was still silent. *Well,* I thought. *This is sufficiently awkward.*

"So…" I said, trying to break the tension. "Which city are you from?"

"Eastmeade."

"Cool," I bobbed my head in an exaggerated nod. "Got a family?"

"No."

"Alright. That's cool too. How often do you drive these trucks?"

"Often enough."

I didn't know how to reply, so I just sat there, even more awkward than I had been in the original silence.

"Well you're quite the talkative one…" I muttered under my breath.

He grunted.

"What's your name?" I asked.

"You ask too many questions," he complained, looking at me in the rearview mirror with deep-set hazel eyes and notably bushy eyebrows.

"Just making conversation…"

"Well don't."

I sighed in frustration, slouching back a bit in my seat and pushing my feet against the passenger side seat, diagonal from my seat behind the driver. May as well get comfortable; this is clearly going to be a long drive.

"Get your feet off my chair," he growled.

"Are you kidding me right now?" I hissed. "You won't answer my questions or talk to me, the least you can let me do is prop my feet up!"

"We aren't going on some kind of 'trip!' This isn't a *vacation*. You're a prisoner—you're *scum*—and you're going to an exile town. Do you really think you have any right to say what *I* owe *you*?" His eyes glared angrily at me.

"Fine," I pouted, taking my black boots off the seat.

After about a half an hour of sitting with my hands in my lap, quiet and anxious, I couldn't help but to speak up.

"Sir?" I asked, hoping overdone politeness would warrant a better response.

"What?" he grunted.

"Have you been to all of the exile towns before?"

"Yes. I don't go much past the main gates though."

"What's Avid like?"

His eyes met mine again in the mirror, but this time he almost had a look of sympathy as his gaze softened.

"It isn't the best of the towns, but it isn't the worst. The Bellicose exiles literally live in caves," he let out a brief, deep laugh. "From what I've heard, the cities threw the brutes in caves, calling them barbaric cavemen. The founders had a sick sense of humor."

"Do you know why they picked a junkyard for Avid then?" I asked, my curiosity growing.

"I'm not sure about that one. I haven't driven many of the Avid exiles. I know that the exiles in Clamorite were put on a mountain because there's a giant waterfall stuck up on it, and I swear you can barely hear your own thoughts there, let alone the noise of the exiles. And the liars in Equivox are around a lake because some symbolic crap about reflections and transparency. I never quite understood that one," he pondered as he rubbed a stubbly black goatee.

"So, do you mind me asking what happened?" he asked, his tone significantly lighter than it was at the beginning of the drive.

"Uhh," I started. "I stole some rum."

"Is that all?" He let out a booming laugh. "I hope you got a good swig of it before they got ya."

I let out a half-hearted chuckle.

"I didn't. I managed to get into a locked bar cabinet; I was going to take the stuff from before the war and hang onto it for a while then sell it."

"Sell it to who? The cities weeded out all of the fences only a matter of months ago."

"Fences?" I asked.

"Yup. People who don't do the stealing themselves, but will buy stolen goods under the table and sell them back to unknowing shop owners for a pretty penny."

"Did you drive them to Avid?"

"Yeah," he answered. "That was my first and only other time driving to Avid."

"So why are you driving me if you're from Eastmeade, and I'm from Rockhallow?" I questioned.

"Most of the drivers to the towns are from Eastmeade. The trucks come from Fallmont, but the drivers often come from Eastmeade. Your town doesn't have any drivers of their own."

"Oh. How far is Eastmeade? And what else is out there, anyways? I've never been outside my city."

"It isn't very far—that's why I got to Rockhallow when I did. And nothing. Not on this side of the country, at least. Just the cities, the exile towns, sand, more sand, and some ruins. I've heard tell of other cities existing in our country still, but we have no communication with them, if they even exist."

"Hasn't anyone tried to travel to those cities?"

"Obviously, but there's so much residual radiation the further out you go from the New Territory that people just… don't."

"They don't even try?"

"I'm sure some have, but not successfully."

I began to try to picture Avid. *Would there be houses? Apartments? Jail cells? Do they have jobs there? What do people do there?* I guess I would find out soon enough—sooner than I cared to.

After a while of sitting in thought, the driver spoke up.

"We're about to pull up to the gates."

I hoisted myself up in my seat to get a look. I saw about a dozen tall buildings, maybe four or five stories high. The buildings were all fairly decrepit, with chunks of concrete chipping off and some glass windows missing, leaving behind flimsy rusted frames. I leaned toward the middle of the backseat to get a better look out the front window, my eyes meeting a monstrous cement wall with a plain grey gate, which was opening slowly in front of us.

Before me was undeniably the most deserted looking place I had ever seen, aside from a few individuals taking obvious pauses to try to stare into the truck to see the newcomer. There was what appeared to be a town circle, with a grey brick well in the center. Lining the center in a large circle were the tall buildings.

The truck came to a stop, and the driver put the vehicle in park.

"This is where I have to ask you to get out," he said neutrally. He opened his door, stepped out, and opened my door.

After he slammed the door shut behind me, he looked me in the eyes, lowering his gaze a bit.

"Name's Aiden," he said, offering a hand.

"Eos," I replied, taken slightly aback. I shook his hand awkwardly.

Aiden got back into the truck and pulled the door shut behind him, rolling down the window as he pulled away.

"Hey, kid," he shouted at me. "You got this."

I nodded, severely doubting what he said.

Once I realized he dropped me off without directing me to the representative, I fully understood that I had no idea what I had gotten myself into.

I looked around at the different buildings, with no noticeable distinctions between them. I swore under my breath. *I'm so screwed.*

The most logical thing to do I suppose would be to try each one and ask around, so I made my way to the building on my far left. I knocked on the door, letting a hollow thud echo. When no one answered, I decided I would try to open the door and just peer inside. I tried to turn the handle, but the door wouldn't budge. *On to the next building, I suppose.*

When I got to the next building over, I saw there wasn't a door.

"Hello?" I called inside.

"Come on in!" replied a cheery feminine voice.

I stepped inside, looking around at a fully grey, concrete room. Obvious dust had collected on the floors. Walking further inside, I saw a couple of worn couches in a makeshift square, with a few people lounging casually.

I stood awkwardly at the door as a short girl stood from the couch, her hair an icy blonde, with countless tight curls. Her skin was pale, her eyes a soft blue. She couldn't have been older than 18. She smiled a charming smile at me as I entered.

"You're new, aren't you?" she asked. Her voice matched the feminine voice that called me in.

"Yeah," I answered. "I need to find the representative."

"He's busy right now, but why don't you come sit

with us?" she said, moving toward the couches.

Figuring I needed to meet people and make connections if I was to be stuck there anyways, I accepted. Walking deeper into the living space, I looked up and saw that the ceiling continued up to the roof of the building, with balcony-like hallways along the walls of every floor, looking down onto the couches. There were large, cracked windows all along the far wall, illuminating the entire room in warm sunlight.

I sat down, dropping my bag on the floor beside the couch.

"So, what's your name?" the blonde girl asked pleasantly.

"Eos."

"That's such a pretty name!" she said, her face lighting up in a smile. "I'm Leanne, but most people just call me 'Lamb.'" She motioned to a boy on my left, sitting on the couch opposite me.

"This is Luka Deston." A slightly heavier guy of about 20 or so with caramel-colored skin, dark hair, and dark eyes gave a half-smile and put a hand up in greeting.

"And this is Zane Hess." She pointed to the other guy, handsome, and visibly a little older than Luka. He smirked, his skin fairly pale. His skin contrasted his nearly black hair, which was in a loosely styled spike, and he had soft brown eyes.

"Hey," I said awkwardly, nodding at the boys.

"Zane, how about you get our guest a drink," she asked lightly. "Is water okay?"

"Yeah, that's perfect."

how hungry I was. *I don't think I've eaten since before I was arrested.*

Then, we were out of the dining hall as quickly as we had come. Jackson crossed the town center and the well, making his way between two different buildings than before.

"Where are we going?" I called after him, trying to keep up.

"I'm going to show you your job."

After clearing the narrow space, we continued walking, following a dirt path surrounded by just as many trash mounds as were near his house. We continued to walk for a while, or rather, Jackson continued to speed-walk, with me occasionally jogging to keep up.

"How far out is this place?" I asked.

"You see those trees?" he stopped and pointed to the distance at some trees that looked no bigger than my thumbnail from where we stood. Once I replied that I did, he continued walking.

"Jackson?" I called.

"Yes, dear?"

"Why are you the representative of Avid?"

"Every few years, the cities check up on the exile towns to make sure they are still livable, and they reassign a representative each time they visit. They just pick from a list of the inhabitants."

"Do you have to accept the position?" I asked.

"No, you don't. They don't want total chaos in the exile towns, so they won't appoint someone who doesn't want to, or that person will purposely get everyone into more trouble. Instead," he continued, "they bribe the person. The representative gets special food rations for just his or herself from the cities. It isn't much, but it is a bit extra, and I quite enjoy the occasional chocolate cake the cities throw in for me for being a good boy." He let out a maddening giggle.

By this point, we had almost reached the trees when he began to describe to me that I would need to water the carrots every day with the water buckets that other people would fill as their job. According to Jackson, many people were assigned different plants to water, weed, or harvest, making the jobs really simple for everyone to keep up with. We got to the trees he had pointed out and continued on the dirt path until we were inside a huge ring of trees, revealing a large field of a wide variety of crops. Jackson motioned to the patch of carrots.

"This is all you are in charge of. Water them a little bit daily. You get the buckets from over there," he pointed to a row of metal buckets. "Make sure you take any empty buckets with you back to the well for the water-runners to fill."

"Do people ever try to escape?" I asked, looking around the tree ring.

"To where? The cities don't want us anymore, and there's nothing more out there. Besides, the wall is too high to climb, even if someone were to be stupid enough to leave," he said, walking back toward the town center.

"Is that it?" I called after him.

"Is what it?"

"Is that all you're going to tell me?"

"That's all you need to know."

CHAPTER SIX

When I got back to the town center, I figured I would make my way to my room. In the common center of my building, Lamb, Luka, and Zane were all sitting on the couches. As soon as Lamb spotted me, she hopped up to come greet me.

"Hi, E!" she said, hugging me as if we were friends. "The boys and I were thinking of helping you get some little decorations for your room to make it a bit more homey!"

"Oh, you guys don't have to do that. Thank you though," I assured her.

"We insist!" She smiled.

I grumbled, sighing a forced "Okay."

She led the way behind the buildings to the trash piles, with the boys and me behind her. Once we had walked past the first few piles, past Jackson's house a little ways, she stopped and turned to me.

"Some of this trash has been here quite a while, and has already been picked through, but some of these are newer. They all come from the cities and the exile towns.

A good bit of the trash in the New Territory eventually gets sent here. The rest goes to some other dump away from here. As the newcomer, you can have the first pick of the piles!" she said, her arms extended outwards.

Oh boy, I thought. *What an honor…*

"Uhmm… I guess I'll start there," I said, pointing to a random hill of garbage.

She smiled happily, nodding her head.

"Good choice! I'll take this one," she said, claiming a pile.

The boys each proceeded to head to their own trash mounds, and the three all began picking through the junk without hesitation. *This is* so *not natural.*

I stood there for a moment, not really sure it was worth digging through trash just to find a few cheap decorations. After a moment, I began picking gingerly at a few things in the pile. I hooked my finger under a decaying cardboard box, flinging it to the side.

"Don't worry about getting a bit dirty," Lamb said upon noticing my obvious disgust. "We have showers, ya' know."

"Yeah," I said, still uncertain, picking at a few empty milk jugs.

"I found a pillow!" called Zane, holding a small throw pillow in the air. "It doesn't look too grungy. Anyone want it?"

Everyone declined and Zane dropped the pillow back into the pile.

As I chucked aside a moldy box, a little glimmer of light caught my eye. Squatting down, I dug around the sparkle until it revealed a tiny mirror about the size of my heel. I pulled on the mirror, lifting up a miniature mirrored box.

"Oooh!" Lamb cooed, trotting over and admiring my find. "Pretty!"

I smiled, slightly satisfied. *With a little scrubbing, I'm sure it'll clean up well.* I pocketed the box in my coat and resumed digging.

About a half hour after picking through what turned out to mostly be boxes and jugs, with a few petite, empty clay pots that I took, Luka called out to get our attention.

"Hey, guys, I found something!" He lifted a thick wooden box above his head.

"Is there anything in it?" Zane asked, walking over to Luka from his spot.

"I don't know; I haven't opened it yet."

"Well, go on! Open it!" chirped Lamb excitedly.

Luka set the heavy box on the ground and unlatched some hinges. He flipped the lid over, revealing a bunch of old papers, still in good shape.

"That's it?" He sighed, aggravated. "A bunch of papers?" He kicked the box and went back to where he left off, digging through garbage.

Lamb shrugged and went back to her place, but I knelt down, thumbing through the papers. Some of them were illegible cursive, with ink blotches smeared across multiple words. I pulled the papers out one by one as I looked at them, setting them on the ground next to the box. Zane stood behind me, peering down over my shoulder curiously at the box's contents. When the box was empty, I spotted a tiny golden knob along the edge of the bottom of the box. Picking at it, I noticed the bottom of the box lifted slightly. I pulled on the little knob until I managed to lift the entire bottom out of the wooden box, revealing a couple additional papers. I picked up the first paper, a small photograph in faded colors. The picture showed some type of silver device with blue, green, and purple stained glass decorating the handle. I picked up the paper beneath it with my other hand and read the words "Skeleton Key" scribbled in messy print, with a page of similar writing beneath it. I pocketed the picture and the papers quickly, figuring maybe I could read through them later at night.

"Hey, what did the paper say?" Zane asked inquisitively upon noticing me shoving the papers in my pocket.

"Nothing much—just some historical looking documents. Figured I could read them before bed tonight, since I don't have a book or anything," I said innocently.

Apparently satisfied, Zane left, going back to his digging. I replaced the removable bottom of the box and stuffed the rest of the papers back on top of it, closing and latching the lid. I decided to bury the box in the pile I had been digging in, for safekeeping. Maybe I could read those other documents sometime.

The sun was beginning to set when everybody began to bring their searches to a close. Just before dark, we all made our way back to our building, chatting excitedly about some of our finds—my mirrored box, a torn poster of an old band none of us had heard of that Lamb dug up, and some other random trinkets.

"What happened to your shirt?" I asked Zane, noticing a grubby black stain on his white t-shirt.

He looked down at the stain, brushing at it with a hand.

"Nothing, just some dirt."

We walked through the doorway to our building, and I said goodnight to my new friends. I unlocked my door and was about to walk back into my room when Zane came running up the stairs, calling after me.

"Yeah?" I asked inquisitively, seeing the look of urgency on his face.

"I wanted to give you something," he said reaching into his jean pockets.

He pulled out a small copper bracelet, with a couple shiny ornaments dangling from it.

"I found it today, I figured it might match that ring of yours, after I cleaned this up a little," he said, dangling the bracelet.

"Is that why your shirt is stained so bad?" I asked. "You used it to clean the bracelet?"

"Yeah, it isn't a big deal though—just some dirt." He reached for my hand and placed the bracelet in it. "Goodnight, E."

Zane wore a half smile on his lips as he turned and retreated down the stairs. I turned back to my door, stopping for a moment to smile to myself before closing the door behind me. I took the mirrored box out of my jacket pocket and placed it on the floor beside my mattress just as I heard a knock at the door.

"Eos!" Lamb called out from behind the door. "I forgot I was supposed to give you something!"

"Come in!" I called back.

She opened the door and came in, a small pile of clothes and a towel in her hands.

"I know it isn't much, but Jackson told me to give these to you," she placed the clothes and towel in my arms and dug a bar of soap out of her pocket. "Make it last, we don't get much to spare. The bathroom is downstairs and to your far left."

I riffled through the clothes—a couple old t-shirts with small stains or tears, a pair of ripped black jeans, some lighter jeans with what looked like a coffee stain on the thigh, a pair of ratty pajamas, and some undergarments.

"I know it isn't much, but we only get what the cities throw out," she said apologetically.

"No, Leanne, it's fine. These will work."

"You can call me Lamb, ya' know," she reminded me.

I smiled sleepily and nodded. "Thanks again."

She said goodnight and closed the door behind her.

I set the clothes on the floor against the wall furthest from my mattress, picked out the pajamas and towel, and undressed, wrapping the towel around myself before heading downstairs to shower.

The bathroom was a little nicer than the rest of the building, with a clean-ish white tile floor, chipping robin's egg blue paint on the walls, and four curtained-off showers. Unfortunately, the bathroom was unisex, but everything in there had some degree of privacy.

I set my towel and new clothes on a bench right outside of the shower, within reach from behind the curtain. When I reached to turn the shower on, I almost stuck my hand on a fuzzy brown spider sitting on the faucet.

"Eughh…" I cringed. I reached for my towel, wrapped myself back up, and migrated myself and my stuff to the next shower over.

After my shower, I shut off the faucet. Wiping the water from my eyes, I reached around the shower curtain for my towel, but my hand was met with an empty bench. I flopped my hand around on the bench, unable to find my towel or my clothes.

You've got to be kidding me.

I stood there for a few minutes, weighing my options. Considering I didn't really have any, I began to call out for Lamb, hoping she was still downstairs and able to hear me. After a few minutes of futile calling, I sucked in a breath, threw the curtain open, and sprinted full speed for my room.

When I ran past the common area, I heard collective laughter coming from the couches as Lamb and Luka rolled with tears streaming down their faces. I didn't stop to confront them, for obvious reasons, so I continued to bolt up the stairs. At the top of the stairs, I all but ran directly into Zane.

"Oh my God," I said, throwing my hands over myself as coverage.

"What are you doing?" Zane asked, a mixture of confusion and amusement on his face.

"Ask the jerks downstairs!" I hissed, blinking back hot tears as I shoved my way past him.

"Full moon tonight!" he hollered after me, his laugh joining the echoing uproar from the two downstairs.

I slammed the door behind me and clicked the lock shut. I slumped over on my knees, sitting on the cold concrete floor, giving in to the tears. After catching my breath and collecting myself, I picked up one of my t-shirts to dry my hair and put on some of my clothes as makeshift pajamas. My bag was still on my bed next to the blanket, so I moved it, along with my dirty clothes, to the corner of the room after digging out the photo of my dad and I. I placed the photo on the mirrored box and lay down on the stained mattress. I had barely become a part of Avid and I already wanted to go home. Wrapping myself up in the blanket to keep warm, I laid there looking at the photo until I fell asleep.

CHAPTER SEVEN

The next morning, I didn't want to get out of bed, and I definitely didn't want to see my "friends". I decided to read through the papers from the wooden box before getting up, so I reached to the side for my coat and pulled them out of the pocket.

I read the words scribbled at the top of the page, reading "Skeleton Key." Squinting at the messy print, I made out some notes about Avid, Bellicose, Clamorite, Delaisse, and Equivox. I think it said something about locks and keys? And a key that could unlock anything? There was a side note about boxes, with a sketch on the back of the paper that closely resembled the box Luka had found. On the sketch, there was an arrow pointing to the back of it, below where the hinges would be. At the other end of the arrow was a drawing of a key. *Weird.* I thought as I threw the papers to the side, knowing I had more important things to do before I could sit and read for the rest of the day.

I sat up slowly, running my hands through my knotted hair. *My room is a mess.* ***I'm*** *a mess,* I thought. I figured the easier of the two to fix would be my disastrous room. Granted, I didn't have many things to use as

45

storage, but I did my best. I organized my clothes against the wall, spread my blanket on my bed, and dumped out the contents of my bag to figure out where to put them. My photo was still on the mirror box beside my bed, the picture of the Key folded inside the mirrored box, the money I decided to hide under my mattress, the papers from the wooden box were under the mirrored box, and the ring was back in my bag. *I guess I should go water the carrots now.*

I moseyed to the gardens, knowing that was the only thing I had to do all day. When I stepped into the ring of tall trees, I grabbed one of the buckets at the entrance. Water sloshed as I made my way to the row of carrots. Starting at one end, I made my way down the row, slowly pouring water from the bucket into the dirt, some of it spattering at my feet. Bored, I sat down next to the rows of crops, drumming idly on the metal pail with my fingers. I sighed. *There's got to be something to do around here.*

I knew one thing for sure—I didn't want to deal with the three from my building, especially not Zane. I carried the empty bucket back with me, dropping it on the ground at the well on my way to my room. In my room, I sat on my bed, pulling out the documents again, thumbing through them. I picked out a paper for a closer read, squinting at the cursive.

After focusing for a while, I was able to gather the gist of the paper I had picked up. According to the writer, there was a key out there somewhere that he or she referred to as the "Skeleton Key." I confirmed what I thought I had read previously, understanding that this key supposedly was able to unlock anything. Skeptical, I read on, uncovering details about five other keys—one in each exile town, all of which had to be used to open the box containing the Skeleton Key. *If these keys are real, that means that one of them is here in Avid,* I thought to myself. Why would anyone even create this key?

There was a knock at my door. When I opened it, Lamb was standing there, looking up at me, her hands clasped together in front of her chest.

"Eos, I am so sorry for what we did last night! We were just trying to have some fun!" she apologized.

"Whatever," I said, staring back at her.

"Look, how about you join us for lunch? We were just about to head that way, and I'm sure the boys would love if you joined us—I know I would!"

"No."

"E, please? I really am sorry. Just… give us another chance. All I'm asking is that you join us for lunch," she pouted.

"Fine," I grumbled.

I'd rather be with poor company than no company.

Once in the cafeteria, I was reminded again of how hungry I was since I got here. I haven't eaten in over a day, and I felt like I could eat the entire storage room of food. The dining hall was fairly crowded, and it was the first time I saw a majority of the members of Avid. There was a table of older men and women, many with greying hair—a man with a hunched back sitting next to a man with visibly white nose hair, a short old woman with sunken eyes, and a few others. Next to their table was a large group of about a dozen more people that looked older than me, but likely younger than my parents. I spotted the food along the far left wall—a long table with trays of fresh vegetables, bread rolls, some kind of brown and chunky soup, and a couple small pies—upon closer look, apple or blueberry seemed to be my choices.

Luka and Zane approached Lamb and me. Luka's eyes scanned me as he chuckled.

"Pig," I growled under my breath.

"Calm down, it was funny and you know it," Zane retorted with a grin, backing Luka up. I rolled my eyes.

Lamb and Luka got in line, with Zane between them and me. I reached toward the dinner rolls, putting one on my tray.

"Just one?" Zane asked. "When was the last time you ate? I remember when I was exiled, I was starved the first day."

I hesitated, not wanting to seem too greedy, but the temptation overcame me, and I shoved a handful of dinner rolls on my plate, followed by a bowl of soup. I followed my lunch party to an empty table, taking my seat next to Lamb and across from Luka, wanting to be as far from Zane as possible.

I caught a whiff of the broth and I pulled my bowl toward me. Ripping off a hunk of the bread, I plunged it into my soup until the bread had soaked up some of the hot liquid. Just as I was about to take a bite, one of the girls from the bigger group looked over and shouted at me.

"Look at the greedy pig!" she squealed, pointing a finger at me. "She took all the rolls!"

I looked down at my plate, trying to ignore the rude comment.

"Hey pig," one of the guys, a tall man with a black soul patch and overly gelled hair crowed. "Save some rolls for the rest of us. You're not supposed to take more than two."

"Oh," I said with a full mouth and muffled voice. "No one told me."

"Well, now you know," he said snippily, walking over and taking two rolls from my tray, tossing one to the woman who pointed at me, a tall, thin woman with frizzy red hair and skin full of freckles. "Next time, don't be so greedy." The group took their trays to a bin and left the dining hall laughing lightheartedly in conversation.

My head sunk, as if I could become invisible to those around me. Zane snorted like a pig, and Luka snickered. I picked up my tray to leave.

"No! E, come on! Please stay!" Lamb pleaded.

"I don't have to put up with this!" I yelled, slamming my tray back on the table as I glared at each of them. Leaving the tray behind, I stormed out of the cafeteria to my room.

I stayed in my room, holed up with the papers, reading strange, incomprehensible riddles about the locations of the five exile keys, imagining what it would be like to unlock anything I wanted with a single key. By the time the sun was down, there was another knock at my door.

"Go away," I called from my mattress.

Another knock.

"I said go away!"

"Open the door, Eos," I heard Jackson say, irritated.

I scrambled from my bed to open the door.

"Oh my gosh, Jackson, I am so, so sorry!"

"I heard you caused a disturbance in the cafeteria today, and that you took more than your share of food, is this true?"

"Yes, but—" I opened.

"There are no excuses. I'll let you off the hook because this was your first offence, but from now on, please just read the sign at the front of the line that tells your food allotment for that meal. It was clearly posted at the start of the food table, stating 'one bowl of soup, two dinner rolls, one scoop of veggies, one slice of pie.' We don't have many rules around here, but the few we do have are very important, and very easy to follow."

I grumbled. "Sorry."

"Yes, well, do better to see it doesn't happen again," the scars on Jackson's face pulled as he furrowed his brow. "There are consequences for those who don't follow the rules, and frankly you are drawing a *lot* of attention to yourself."

Suddenly, I realized the center of Jackson's attention was a very bad place to be.

"It won't happen again," I promised.

"Hello, Jackson!" chirped Lamb as she walked over from the stairs.

"How are you, Leanne?" smiled a sharp-toothed Jackson.

"I'm lovely, thank you! I just came by to invite Eos to join Zane, Luka, and me for a game tonight!"

"Have fun!" Jackson said cheerily, making his way back downstairs.

"No," I said, frowning at Lamb.

"Oh, come on!" she insisted. "You can't stay in your room forever! You'll die of boredom!"

"I'd rather stare at the wall forever than put up with Zane and Luka again. You haven't been exactly pleasant either," I warned, raising my voice slightly.

"I know," she sighed. "And I'm super sorry! Please, just come play a game with us! It'll be fun!"

"I'm not playing some stupid game with you guys. Knowing all of you, the game is going to involve humiliating me for your amusement, and with that in mind, I'm going to have to pass."

"We aren't going to embarrass you or hurt you, Eos! We just want to include you because we know how much this place sucks when you're alone. I was alone when I was first exiled, and I don't want you to be lonely like I was. Come play a game with us later tonight and you'll see!"

"What kind of game?" I questioned.

"Meet me downstairs in about an hour and I'll explain it," she said, skipping to the staircase.

When she left, I contemplated for a moment what to do for the next hour. *I could explore a little*, I thought. *Now is as good a time as any to check out some of the other buildings in Avid.*

I made my way outside. The air was warm, aside from a cooling gentle breeze. The sky was dark but speckled with infinite tiny stars. *It would make the most sense to go in the third building first,* I thought, realizing the first building is just the cafeteria, and the second is my building. I made my way casually to the door, noticing it was left cracked open. Pushing it open just a bit, I awkwardly poked my head through the space. Before my brain could register which building I was at, I heard an unfortunately familiar voice greet me.

"Hey, it's Pig!" The dark-haired man with a soul patch snorted at me.

I pulled my head out of the doorway as quick as I could, speed walking to the next door in hopes he would just leave me alone.

He didn't.

"Where are you going, Pig?" the man called after me as he stepped out from his building.

"I'm just looking around," I said innocently, not making eye contact.

"You searching for scraps, Pig?" He laughed.

I chose not to acknowledge his comment, which provoked him to pick further.

He flicked a pebble and it tapped against my shoulder. Unamused, I glared at him.

"Whatchu' up to, Pig?" He smiled.

"I'm just looking around."

"For what?"

"I'm just looking around," I repeated.

"Are you looking for anything?" he asked, the smile lingered, and I was hesitant but slightly convinced that it actually looked genuine.

"Uh—" I mumbled. "Not really. I just don't know what these other buildings are for, so I was checking them out."

"Well, that one there," he pointed in front of me.

"That's where our middle age members live. On that side," he motioned to the right of it at the next building, "you have a vacant building. A few of these are vacant because we don't have a lot of people here, in case you haven't noticed. The only other building that actually has anyone or anything in it is the one across from your building. That's where our seniors live."

"Thanks," I said hesitantly, walking in the direction of Jackson's house, through the gap between two of the vacant buildings. The man followed me without saying another word.

I continued walking along the path, past Jackson's house and mounds of trash along the way. The man continued to follow, making it obvious he wasn't trying to be secretive, but still he didn't speak.

"Can I help you?" I asked, irritated as I continued to walk, my back to him.

"What, am I not allowed to take a walk?"

"You're following me."

"So?"

"It's creepy. Stop."

"Look, kid, I'm bored. There's nothing interesting that goes on here, and you're something new. Let me take a little interest and see what you're up to."

"I'm not 'up to' anything," I retorted.

"I didn't mean it like that," he admitted, putting his hands up as if declaring his innocence. "I just meant that everyone else around here either goes around stealing crap from others, digging through mounds of trash the cities send our way, or sitting around. It's boring. You're doing something different, and even if you aren't 'up to anything,' it's far more entertaining than anything else I'd be doing tonight."

"Whatever, fine," I submitted. "Just don't be so creepy about it."

"Deal," he agreed, quickening his pace to walk beside me. "So, tell me, Pig—"

"Stop calling me that," I interrupted.

"I was getting to that," he sighed. "So, tell me," he continued, "what's your real name?"

"Eos."

"I'm Nico."

"Pleasure," I said sarcastically.

"What are you hoping to find back here?"

"Something besides trash, preferably," I replied snarkily.

"Hate to disappoint," he said. "You aren't going to find anything else back here. We live in a literal dump. The cities send a bunch of their trash here and take up basically everything but the town center and our garden."

"Oh," I sighed, continuing to walk for a while only to realize Nico was probably right. "I've got plans with some people anyways, I should probably head back," I said.

"See you around, Pi—I mean… Eos," he nodded, taking off toward his building once we reached the town center.

Back in my building, the boys were already lounging on the couch waiting downstairs. Lamb offered me a seat next to the boys as she sat opposite them. I sat beside

Luka reluctantly, returning his smile and greeting with a dramatic eye roll.

"Which game is it gunna' be tonight?" Zane asked Lamb as he clasped his hands in a single clap in front of him, getting her attention.

"I think we should play Quest," chimed Luka. "It'd be a good one for a beginner!"

"Good idea!" Lamb smiled.

"What's Quest?" I asked.

"Quest is when we pick a building, and everybody picks a room in that building. After you pick a room, you search it for whatever specific object we all decide on—basically, we go on a quest for an object. If no one finds the object in their room in round one, we all pick different rooms," Zane explained.

"What kinds of things do you usually search for?" I asked, mildly conflicted. I don't want to steal someone's old family photo or something, but I wouldn't object to stealing simple things they probably wouldn't even notice are missing, especially because the people here collect actual garbage.

"Nothing too crazy. Food related objects, usually. Leftovers from meals that people decide to bring back. Sometimes we go for things like specific types of clothes, like the first person to find a blue shirt wins," Lamb replied.

"I'm in," I said, just thankful to have something to do.

"Great!" Lamb jumped up with a smile, leading the way to the town center. When we were all outside, Lamb spoke.

"E, since this is your first time, I vote that we let you pick which building we go to."

"Uhhh," I said, looking at the identical concrete structures. "That one," I pointed at the building directly across from ours.

"That'll be fun! That's where the elders live! They usually have bigger collections of things in their rooms, since most of them have been in Avid for a long time," Lamb said. "Tonight's quest will be for..." She hummed to herself, thinking. "Chocolate pudding! Find a chocolate pudding cup and you win!"

The boys laughed as the group made their way to the building. I trotted behind them to catch up. The inside of the elder's building looked identical to our building, except there was a larger collection of chairs and sofas in the common area. Zane hurried up the stairs, poking his head down a moment later and giving us a thumbs up. The rest of us climbed the first set of stairs.

"We start on the first floor of rooms," explained Lamb. "Pick any room and stand in front of it."

All the doors looked the same, so I just went for the fourth door over, the identical placement as my room in my building.

"What if it's locked?" I asked. "Or if someone is in it?"

"If you see someone in it, just run and hide for a bit before they see who you are," Lamb said, handing me a couple of paper clips.

Once everyone was standing in front of a door, Lamb gave us a signal to start. I've never been good at lock picking, and this was no exception. I rarely picked locks in Rockhallow, and usually it took a while for me to be successful. I bent the paperclips into a makeshift pick and a tension holder, the two components of lock picking. Then, I fumbled around with the two clips in the keyhole. Nothing. I sighed. I bent the paperclips a different way, moving the pick around in the lock, hoping for the best. At this point, everyone else had already successfully made it into their rooms. A few tries later, the lock clicked, and I made my way into the room, leaving the door cracked behind me.

The room was fairly cluttered, with stacks of dusty books scattered around, small dishes covered in gold and silver necklace chains, and a little statue of a chicken. I dug through the heaps of things on the floor, looking for a pudding cup. While I was looking, my eyes caught sight of a small photograph. I picked up the picture, holding it up so I could see it clearly. The photo was identical to the one I found in the wooden box. *Weird,* I thought.

"Are you lost?" bellowed a deep, croak of a voice from the open doorway, causing my heart to jump.

An old man with short, patchy white hair stood in the doorway. He had a set of reading glasses perched on his nose, his body was a bit heavy, and the skin on his neck saggy. Speechless, I dropped the photo and stood staring back at the man, knowing there was no other way out of the room.

"Are you lost?" he repeated.

"N-no," I stuttered.

"Then what are you doing here?" he asked grouchily.

"I was looking for something. I'm sorry, I'm just going to go," I said, easing toward the blocked door. The man didn't budge.

"What are you looking for?" he asked.

"It's nothing really!" I insisted. "It's stupid. We were just playing a game."

"'We?'" he said questioningly, looking over his room. "Sweetheart, it looks like your friends left you."

"No, they didn't come in here with me, they're somewhere else," I said, not wanting to reveal that they were in other rooms.

"You never answered my question," he nagged. "What were you looking for?"

"A…a pudding cup," I said, feeling stupid.

He laughed heartily. "I can tell you're harmless," he said, walking away from the door and opening a burlap bag that had been shrouded by books. He pulled a chocolate pudding cup out of the bag, holding it out to me with a jittery hand.

"Take it," he nodded to the pudding cup.

"Thanks," I said, confused as I took the pudding.

"Mr. Montgomery," he said, holding out a liver-spotted hand.

"Eos," I said, shaking his hand nervously. *Why is he being nice? I just broke into his room.*

"If you don't mind, I'd like to go to bed now," he started, moving toward his mattress. "Please close the door when you leave."

When I made it back to my building, Lamb, Luka, and Zane were sitting on the couches, noisily in conversation. As soon as they saw me enter the room, their voices died down and they stared at me. I held up the pudding cup in front of me, a frown on my face.

"You ditched me," I stated.

Eos

"We're sorry, E. We heard that man catch you in his room and we all bolted," Lamb apologized.

"Whatever," I snarled, making my way to my room.

That night, no one knocked on my door.

CHAPTER EIGHT

After taking my breakfast portions to my room the next morning, I spread out the Skeleton Key papers and munched on a piece of toast while I studied the notes. I noticed a number scribbled on one of the papers and I squinted, trying to make it out. It was a year. Counting in my head, I did the math, coming to the conclusion that the date on the paper was about 60 years in the past. *I wonder if anyone in Avid knows anything about the Key. Mr. Montgomery had the same picture as the one I found in the box—maybe he knows about it.*

Decidedly angry with Lamb, Luka, and Zane, I came to the conclusion that I was going to spend my day doing some research on the Skeleton Key. If anyone was to know anything about something from 60 years ago, it would be the elders. Unfortunately for me, I was caught stealing from one of them. *He seemed forgiving,* I argued with myself. *And honestly, what have I got to lose?*

I made my way to the elder building. I paused at the door, hesitant. I took a deep breath and made my way to Mr. Montgomery's room, reassuring myself that there was nothing he could do to me even if he wanted to. *If he asks me to leave,* I thought, *I'd leave.* Once at his room, I held my fist to the door, taking a second, then rapping on it a few times. A moment later, I was face to face with Mr. Montgomery.

"Hello again, Miss—" he struggled for a moment.

"Eos," I reminded him.

"What's your last name, if I may ask? I believe it is far more proper to address a lady with her last name."

"Dawn."

"Eos Dawn, a beautiful name for a beautiful young lady. Miss Dawn, would you like to come in?" he welcomed, opening his door for me to enter.

"Sure," I said as Mr. Montgomery closed the door behind me.

"Are you here for more pudding?" he joked, emphasizing the wrinkles at the corners of his eyes. "I'm afraid that was my last cup."

"No, I actually had a couple questions for you," I started. "How old are you?"

Mr. Montgomery burst out laughing. "Miss Dawn, that's no question to ask an old man," he said with a friendly smile, seeing my horrified expression. "But if you must know, I'm 84."

"How long have you been in Avid?"

"Since I was about 22 years old. I've been here 62 years now."

"Oh," I sighed. "I'm sorry to hear that."

"No need to be sorry, dear. I got myself here in the first place. It hasn't been all bad, anyways."

"No? I suppose that's good."

"Do you mind me asking how you got yourself stuck in Avid?"

"Not at all, sir," I said. "I stole some rum. It was valuable—from back before the war. I wanted to keep it for a few years and then sell some of it for good money."

"Were your parents struggling?"

"Pardon?"

"Did you have food on the table? A roof over your head? Mom and Dad happy together?"

"Yes."

"Why'd you want the money?"

"I'm not sure. To buy things I wanted, I suppose."

"Anything in particular?"

"I guess not. I mean, there's just this feeling you get, you know? When you have more money than you need. You don't have to worry, and you know that you can get anything you want. I've never had *that* much money, I guess, but I collected a fair sum."

"Miss Dawn," he started, his voice inquisitive. "What do you want most in life?"

"What everybody else wants, really. Wealth and happiness."

"Are you sure there's nothing else to it?"

"I don't think I see where you're going, sir."

"Wait until you spend 62 years trapped in a dump and you'll understand."

I stared back at Mr. Montgomery, confused and intrigued.

"Freedom," he whispered, leaning in.

"Oh," I said as my eyes wandered the room.

"You'll understand. Give it time. One day, you'll see that freedom is worth more than any rum, more than any cash. I wish I could say you'll not only understand, but will get to experience it, but unfortunately it's a little late for that," he said regretfully.

We sat in silence for a few moments before he spoke up again.

"I know you didn't just come here to spend an afternoon with an old man. What can I help you with?"

"Oh, yeah. So, um, I'm curious, sir, have you ever heard of anything called a 'Skeleton Key?'" I asked.

Mr. Montgomery's face grew serious. "Yes, I have. Why?"

"I came across some papers," I said. "They were in a box I found in the dump. I've been reading them for a few days now, and they talk about something called a Skeleton Key."

"I knew the man who created the Key—"

"It's real?" I interrupted.

"Very real. The man who created it was a member of Avid. His name was Galeno. He was a brilliant man—an inventor. We were friends at the time, until he began to isolate himself more and more. It started after he created the Key out of pieces he collected from the dump. He showed me one day how it worked, testing it on all the doors in our building. I'm sure you saw the pictures, so you know how it is mostly a long, thin piece of metal? The core of the Key is hollow, and somehow Galeno made it so that, with the turn of a tiny dial on the jeweled end of the Key, the metal flexes to fit the interior of the lock in which it is placed. It's remarkable, really. At first he was proud, using the Key to sneak in and out of Avid, but then he grew paranoid, convinced someone was going to steal it from him, and so he designed a box. It was a beautiful little wooden box, and it took five keys just to unlock it. He started off hiding the Key in it, scattering four of the other five keys throughout his house, always keeping one with him. One day, the poor man just snapped entirely. He told me he was going to hide the five keys—one at each exile town so no one individual would ever have the Key again. The keys in each town only help to open the Skeleton Key box—nothing else. He regretted ever creating it because some of the other people in Avid at the time found out about it, and everyone was always on him about it, but he couldn't bring himself to destroy it. Galeno was so afraid of the cities getting ahold of his key—'no one should have this much power,' he told me. So, he hid the keys in five different boxes, and supposedly he was successful in putting one in each exile town. By the time he got back to Avid, however, the city had taken the Skeleton Key in its box, sealing it away somewhere in the cities. I still remember that day, seeing the authorities taking him away. He was screaming when they took him. They were waiting for him in his room," Mr. Montgomery said pensively.

"Has anyone ever tried looking for the keys?" I asked.

"No. The only people that even knew about it were city officials and a handful of people in Avid. The people here that knew about it were all just petty thieves. None of them had a real reason to want to risk getting caught for the Key."

"Speaking of getting caught, what happened to

Galeno anyways? After they took him?" I asked interestedly.

"I imagine they stuck him in prison," he said bluntly.

"I thought the cities completely did away with the prison system ages ago?" I asked.

"They did, in a way—all but one. Don't ask where it is because I have no earthly idea—I may be old, I may know a lot of things, but I'm certainly not old enough to have been around for the development of the system. Over the years, I've just learned that, once in a while, the exile system fails, and the officials take away the defectors, locking them up far away from any other civilization. Certainly, they would lock away a man clever enough to devise a key that could unlock any of their complex locks."

"I guess that makes sense."

"Don't go looking for it—it isn't worth it," Mr. Montgomery warned. "If you leave Avid, there's no coming back unless you want to be sent off to wherever they take people like Galeno. I know Avid is no paradise, but anything would be better than a lifetime in a cell."

"Yeah, but what if he wouldn't have come back?" I pressed.

"I don't know what all is out there. I just know of the cities and the exile towns. Beyond that, I can only imagine there's whatever is left from the war. Unless you want to wander the empty remains of the country, there really is nowhere to go."

"Thank you for your time," I said sincerely. "And I'm really sorry for the other night. Don't worry about me doing anything like that again, I'm done hanging out with those people anyways."

"Don't worry about it, Miss Dawn. If you think the idea of thieves bothers me after 62 years in an exile town full of them, you'd be mistaken. Don't be so quick to give up on your friends—friends are all a person has when everything in life is taken away," he said remorsefully.

I left Mr. Montgomery's room, thanking him again. When I opened the front door to the town center, I noticed a small squabble near the doors to the dining hall. Upon closer look, I noticed Jackson, grabbing at a mousey boy of about 18, who was scrambling to get away from Jackson.

"You're only going to make this worse for yourself," Jackson threatened.

"Let me go!" the boy pleaded, his tennis shoes kicking against the pavement, tossing up dirt as he struggled to get to his feet after having fallen in the struggle.

"You stole from the pantry. If I let you get away with it, I have to let *everyone* get away with it. Do you know what happens when everyone gets away with anything they want?" Jackson said as he grasped the boy's wrist, tugging on him, causing the boy to crash into the asphalt on his hands and knees.

"No?" Jackson continued, jerking on the boy's wrist when he stood again, this time letting go, sending him face first into the ground. At this point, the boy's face was bloody, with bits of gravel stuck to his cheek. The boy grimaced as he tried to stand, only to have his wrist grabbed by Jackson again.

"Anarchy," he answered, dragging the boy after him toward his house.

CHAPTER NINE

Confused and stunned, I wondered what Jackson would do to the boy he caught as I ran back into my building, only to bump into Zane. He gave me his typical half grin.

"Going somewhere?" he asked.

"Yeah. My room," I said, stepping to the side to go around him. He stepped as well, mirroring me. I tried again in the other direction.

"Zane, let me go."

"Nah," he teased, blocking me.

"*Move,*" I warned. He stood motionless, smirking. Irritated, I sent my fist flying into his nose, landing with a crunch.

Zane swore, glaring at me as he clutched his nose, blood trickling from his palm.

I mimicked his signature sly grin as I made my way to my room, leaving Lamb and Luka cackling on the couch.

"Nice hit!" Luka laughed, tears in his eyes as he watched Zane shake blood off of his hand, flicking drops against the concrete floor. Lamb giggled, giving me a little round of applause.

"He had it coming!" she said.

"Some friends you are," Zane spat, running upstairs.

"Sit with us for a bit!" Lamb said, calling to me.

I turned around to see her patting the sofa beside her.

"No, I really shouldn't. I was about to do something. Do any of you guys have a pen I could borrow?" I asked.

"Doing some writing?" Lamb asked, walking toward the underside of the stairs.

"Yeah, sorta'. Taking notes, I guess."

"Notes? Whatever suits your fancy." She shrugged, opening a cabinet hidden under the staircase, revealing stacks of paper and pencils. "Will a pencil do?"

"That's fine. And hey, Lamb?"

"Yeah?"

"Did you see that boy outside with Jackson?"

"Yeah, he's from our building, but he stays holed up in his room most the time. I don't really know him very well."

"Do you know what's going to happen to him?"

"With Jackson? No idea. Jackson doesn't tell anyone what the punishment is for stealing from the pantry, he just tells us we don't want to find out."

I went upstairs, noticing my door was wide open. I looked around the room—nothing seemed out of place, but then I saw it. The chocolate pudding cup from Mr. Montgomery was smeared all over my mattress. Whoever did it was careful to coat as much of the bed as possible in the slimy brown pudding. I growled, knowing it had to have been Zane. I scraped off what I could and flipped the mattress over. Taking a seat on my bed, I pulled out the Skeleton Key papers again, jotting down some quick notes about what I learned from Mr. Montgomery.

"Hey, pig," I heard at the open door. I looked up, seeing Zane, his nose purple with bruises. "Next time you decide to try to punch me, it won't just be a little pudding."

"Is that a *threat?*" I hissed, jumping to my feet, moving toward him.

"What if it is?" he snarled.

I smirked at him for a moment before jerking forward, as if about to punch him. Zane jolted.

"Wimp," I said, glaring at him as he gave me a disgusted look. "Chicken!" I called after him as he walked away. "We've got a pig, a lamb, and a chicken—it's a whole freaking barn!" I laughed, thinking I was clever as I slammed my door behind me.

~

That afternoon, after coming back from lunch, I saw the mousy boy from my building again, making his way inside.

"Hey," I called after him.

He turned around, revealing a black, blue, and red face. One of his eyes was blackened and swollen shut, and his upper lip looked about twice the size it was earlier.

"Oh my gosh," I breathed. "What happened? What did he do to you?"

"I don't wanna' talk about it," he blubbered, his swollen lip hardly moving as he spoke. He turned his head back, his eyes on the ground as he made his way upstairs.

I couldn't believe Jackson had traumatized that boy so severely. Just for stealing from the pantry? *He already gave me one warning*, I thought. Avid was apparently more dangerous than it let on.

In my room, I stripped off my dirty t-shirt and jeans and flopped backward onto my bed. *I want to go home, but I don't even have a home anymore*, I had to remind myself. Homesick, I began to reminisce about when Fabian and I used to play games at my house when we were young. I drew my bag closer to me, digging for my ring. *That's weird.* I shook my bag upside down, growing worried. I frantically dug through my pockets and my belongings looking for the ring from Fabian. *Zane must have taken it again. He knows it's important to me, and he's doing this to get back at me.* The joke was on him, I was going to get my ring back.

Fuming, I threw on the pair of tattered black jeans and an old white blouse, my long coat over it. I slung the strap of my bag across my shoulder and quickly left my room, careful to lock the door behind me. My boots patting against the concrete steps, I hurried downstairs. Not to my surprise, I saw Lamb and Luka lounging on the couches.

"Where's Zane?" I asked with a tone of irritation.

"He's doing his job out by the gardens," Luka answered.

I sighed as I bolted out the door and made my way to the gardens. By the time I was halfway down the dirt path, I spotted Zane's figure walking back toward the town center. I picked the nearest mound of trash and darted behind it, peering out just enough to watch as he passed by, oblivious to my presence. While he was sliding between the two buildings to make his way back to the center, I cautiously sprinted to catch up, my feet bounding quickly and almost noiselessly across the dirt. I made it between the two buildings just as I saw him walk into ours, and I was on his tail within seconds, hiding behind the doorway enough to catch a glimpse of him heading toward the stairs.

Lamb and Luka seemed to be deep in conversation, but I was still careful about making sure my footsteps were soft and steady as I made a beeline for the stairs. Once at the stairwell, I dropped into a squat and made my way up the stairs on all fours, barely keeping Zane in sight. After he hit the top of the stairs and made his way down the hallway, I halted in my crouch, waiting to see which door he opened. When he kept walking past every door, I wondered if he was going to the third floor, which I hadn't seen yet. I crawled down the hall, keeping plenty of distance between Zane and me as I saw him reach another staircase. From behind the final stair on the next staircase, I peered over, watching Zane make his way to the far end of the third floor hallway, fumbling with a door. I made a mental note of which room his was, just as he entered. I sat there for a minute, debating whether I should just wait in the stairwell to the fourth floor and sneak into his room after he leaves, or if I should just wait it out in my room. *He could be in his room for hours*, I thought to myself, just before Zane walked out of his room and shut the door behind him. *Crap.* Zane's pace was quick as he made his way toward me.

I raced down the stairs and across the second floor hallway as quickly as I could. Just as I reached my door, Zane was at the bottom of the stairs. I tried to play casual, taking my key out of my pocket to unlock my door.

"Hey," I said to Zane, trying to seem pleasant.

He stared blankly at me, arms crossed.

"So, I was thinking about earlier—no hard feelings I hope!" I chattered shakily.

Nothing.

"I'm sorry about your nose—it was uncalled for," I apologized in vain.

Still nothing.

"You saw me didn't you?" I asked, defeated.

"Yup."

"Are you mad?"

"Not exactly, but I am curious why you were following me. You aren't as sneaky as you'd like to think."

"I was just curious where your room was," I said. *I'm a terrible liar.*

"Don't lie to me, E," he growled impatiently.

"You took my ring," I started.

"Is that really what this is about?" he glared at me in disbelief. "I gave that back, along with the rest of your stuff! I haven't been in your room since—"

"Seriously? Don't pull that. I know you smeared the pudding on my mattress," I retorted.

"I didn't take anything. I put it in your room and haven't touched it, but Luka has been awful curious of what you had of such value to you, ever since you showed up here."

"So, you mean you don't have my ring?"

"I do," he said, pulling my ring from his pocket.

"Why do you keep lying to me?" I swore at him as I snatched my ring from his hand.

"I didn't lie to you. I put it back."

"Then why did you have it just now?"

"I stole it—"

"I *know!*" I interrupted.

"From *Luka*," he continued.

"Oh," I said awkwardly.

"You're welcome."

"Yeah, *heh*, thanks."

"I'm going on a walk if you want to come, and if you're ready to stop acting like a child," he said. "By the way, you really need to work on your technique. Crouching on the stairs? Really?" His sly, teasing half-smile creeping back on his face.

On our way outside, Zane began to pat at his pockets, a concerning frown on his face.

"I forgot something in my room," he apologized. "Don't wait up—I'll catch up. I was going to walk through the trash, see if I spot anything worth digging at along the way. I'll be there in just a few minutes. Please don't stalk me this time—it's desperate," he joked as he trotted back toward our building.

After waiting, picking through a small trash mound for nearly an hour, I gave up, assuming Zane never really meant to meet with me. On my way back to my building, I spotted Luka and Lamb, arm in arm, chattering away and laughing lightheartedly in the town center.

"Hey, guys, wait—" I stopped them. "Have you seen Zane? He asked me to meet him at the dump, but he never showed up."

Lamb thought for a moment before replying, a residual smile still on her face.

"Yeah, I remember seeing him leave a while ago. He was in some kind of hurry, but he didn't say anything to either of us."

"Oh," I sighed, disappointed, realizing Zane had clearly lied to me. "Thanks."

Luka and Lamb continued their conversation as they made their way toward the garden. I decided to lounge around in our common area until dinner, eventually making my way outside to get some fresh air. I watched for a few hours as people came and went, and I just leaned against the well in the town center, waiting for time to pass.

That evening, I scarfed down a quick dinner, never seeing Zane enter the room with the dinner crowd. I sighed, a bit disappointed, throwing away my trash and moseying to my room. At this point, the sun was almost set, turning the sky a dreamy purple color.

Before even reaching my room, I heard someone running after me, calling my name. A frantic and out of breath Lamb came up behind me.

"Eos!" she puffed. "Luka told me that, when he was picking the weeds from the carrots in the garden, he realized no one watered them today. Aren't you the one who is supposed to do that?"

"Oh, yeah. I forgot about that. I'll head that way in a few minutes," I said calmly.

Eos

"No, you don't understand! Jackson checks the garden *every* sundown to make sure everyone did their jobs. That's one of the few rules here and he's super strict about it. You didn't do your job, E! *Run* and maybe you'll make it!"

I took off sprinting, not wanting to end up like the mousy boy from our building. Just as I was about to reach the gap in the ring of trees surrounding the garden, I spotted Jackson squatting by the crops. As he stood, he kicked a bucket across the garden, splashing water everywhere as he swore, my name making its way into his bouts of cursing. I hesitated for a half second before heading back in the opposite direction without looking back. I scrambled up the stairs and quickly threw my key into the lock and turned. No click. *That's weird.* I turned the doorknob and opened the door without a problem. *I know I locked the door when I left.*

As soon as I stepped foot in my room, I knew there was something wrong. My blanket was thrown in a clump on my floor, my mattress moved, the mirrored box cracked and on its side. I made a mental checklist of my few belongings as I tried to pick up my room. Somebody was clearly looking for something and had trouble finding it. As I sat down on my bed, it hit me.

The Skeleton Key papers were missing.

CHAPTER TEN

It was Zane, I know it. But what would Zane even want with those papers anyways? Is this why he ditched me? He can't possibly know or even believe the Skeleton Key exists.

I stood there for a moment, contemplating if I should really go after him. Maybe it wasn't worth it to go after him, but it might be worth leaving this place—leaving the people who enjoyed harassing me, leaving the representative that would inevitably come after me, and leaving the overall bleak outlook that surrounded the entirety of Avid. With my coat already on, I picked up my bag and made my way to the junkyards, keeping an eye out for Jackson.

As I got closer to the piles of garbage we had dug through when Luka found the box containing the papers, I tried to remember which one was mine, because that's where I hid the box—the one that the sketch that showed where it contained the Key. There's no way Zane would have noticed me hiding the box, so he couldn't have the Avid key already. When I neared the pile, I hid the wooden box in, I realized I was very wrong. There was a large hole in the mound of trash, with the wooden box sitting beside it. I approached the box and crouched down beside it to get a closer look. Zane had clearly seen the sketch about the secret side compartment on the box, because there was a small door hanging open right below the hinges for the top of the box. I sighed in defeat, sitting next to the box. *Was he going to go after the other keys? He had to be—why else would he want the first one?* All I knew was I wanted in on it.

Unsure of what my next step was, I thought back on what little geography I had learned in school. I remember seeing where the exile towns were in comparison to the cities and to each other. Delaisse should be pretty close to Avid, but still far enough that it would probably take a couple days to get there on foot. Before I'd commit to walking that far, especially alone, I needed to pack some things.

I left the junkyard, making my way back to my building as quickly as possible. When I got there, I saw Lamb heading upstairs.

"Wait—" I called after her, quickening my pace.

She turned around, a friendly but questioning look on her pale face.

"Have you seen Zane?" I asked, out of breath.

"Not since he ran out earlier," she answered. "Are you still looking for him? Is everything okay, Eos? Did you manage to water the carrots?"

"I'm fine. I just wanted to know if you've seen him," I lied. "That's all."

"If I see him, I'll let him know you're looking for him," she offered innocently.

"No thank you," I responded quickly. "It's no big deal."

Confused but apparently satisfied, Lamb continued her way up the stairs and down the hall.

"Lamb?" I called after her again.

"Mmm?" she mumbled as she continued to walk.

"Which room is Zane's, anyways?"

"E, honey, you're getting a bit clingy, aren't you?" she said, stopping in her tracks, turning to reveal a slightly uncomfortable face.

"No! No, it isn't like that!" I forced a giggle. "I have something of his, and that's why I'm looking for him, but instead of chasing him around all day, I figured maybe I'd just leave it in his room or something." I almost convinced myself with my lie.

"Oh… Okay…" she said, clearly still concerned. "This way."

I followed her up to the fourth floor, where she motioned to one of the first doors on my left, after which she continued down the hall and unlocked what I assumed was her own room.

I waited until she had closed her door behind her, and then I grabbed at the doorknob. Without a problem, it turned and swung open. Apparently, Zane doesn't feel it's worth the effort to lock his door. That, or maybe he left in a hurry.

Looking around the room, I noticed a few more decorations than my room. Some drawings, photos, and posters taped sloppily to the walls. There was a striped blue and tan comforter covered in holes on the bed, and a few other random things. I looked around, hoping to find some kind of clue to his whereabouts. After rummaging around and finding nothing but a few paperclips, which I pocketed, I sat on his bed for a moment to think. Just as I did, my eyes met a poster of the New Territory, or in other words, the world after the war. I took a closer look, noticing Avid was circled in green marker. Nothing else was marked on the map. Studying the map further, I saw that Avid wasn't too far from my home of Rockhallow, but Avid was reasonably close to Delaisse. Right in between Avid and Delaisse was the smallest of the cities— Nortown. Aside from those, the other cities and towns were fairly far away, making Delaisse my first goal in searching for the keys. I tore down the map, folded it, and put it in one of my coat pockets. Hopefully I'd run into Zane along the way at some point, and I can figure out a way to get the Avid key from him.

Closing Zane's door behind me, I made a quick trip to my room to pack my bag. I stuffed the photo of my dad and me into the bag, along with my money, some clothes, my blanket, the ring from Fabian, and the bracelet from Zane, but I kept my knife in my pocket. Food and water might be a problem. Patting my pockets with my hands, I remembered the paperclips I took from Zane's room and instantly had an idea.

I hid between two of the buildings outside, waiting until the town center had cleared. When I knew I was finally alone, I made my way to the dining hall. I squatted down at the door and fidgeted with a couple paperclips for a minute, making them into simple lock picks before pushing them into the lock of the door, wiggling them around. Nothing. I bent the paperclips a little more and tried again. Still nothing. Growing frustrated, I jammed the paperclips into the lock one more time and shook them impatiently. *Click.*

Proud of myself, I smirked as I hurried into the dining hall and closed the door behind me, running to the locked pantry. I repeated the same motions with the paperclip at the pantry lock, unlocking it significantly faster than I had the main door. When I opened it, my eyes were filled with the glorious sight of the small room full of large wooden shelves stacked to the ceiling with food. I thought back to what Jackson said about breaking into the pantry, and to the mousy boy, hoping I would make it out without crossing Jackson's path. I looked around the room. In a labeled package on the ground were some disposable water bottles from the city's shipment to the exile towns. I shoved a few bottles in my bag, as well as a handful of various vegetables from a shelf, a loaf of bread, and a cup of what looked like chocolate pudding.

The second I closed my bag, it struck me that I had no idea how to even get out of Avid. I remember when Jackson showed me the gardens, he mentioned something about a fence, but he said it was too high to climb. Then again, he didn't say anything about digging.

I sprinted out of the cafeteria and towards the gardens. It was fairly dark at this point, but the combined glow of the lights from the windows of the buildings illuminated the general area. I bolted down the dirt trail, hearing nothing but my own rapid breaths and the grinding of dirt under my feet. From inside the shelter of the circle of trees, I sat to catch my breath, plucking a couple of small tomatoes to munch on and stuffing a few extra vegetables in my bag as well. Now to look for the wall.

Figuring I was bound to hit the wall if I continued in one direction long enough, I wedged my way between a few of the trees at the end of the garden. *Oh.* The wall was literally right behind the trees.

I dropped down into a squat to examine the dirt, and feeling how dense and almost rock-hard it was near the base. At that, I abandoned the plan to dig underneath the wall. I gazed around the area, hoping for inspiration, only to see it nearly surrounding me—the trees. Jackson said a person would be stupid to try to climb the wall. *Who's stupid now,* I thought smugly as I jumped toward the lowest, nearest branch, catching hold of it. Pulling with all of my strength, I tried to hoist myself onto the branch, only to slide off, gaining a few splinters on the way down. I swore under my breath. *Now what?* Deciding it was worth at least another try, I squatted down and pushed up in a jump as hard as I could, arms stretched upward. Again, I managed to hang from the branch with nothing more than a futile attempt at pulling myself up. Clearly, I wasn't as strong as I thought I was.

I stepped backwards a few yards, took a deep breath, and ran at the tree as fast as I could—strength I may not have, but speed is another story. Just as I neared the tree, I leapt at the branch, using the momentum from my sprint to swing my leg over. Straddling the tree branch, I let out an exhausted giggle as I hugged it tight. *I can do this.* I sighed as I looked up to the next branch, which wasn't terribly far from my current one. Placing my feet flat on the branch, I steadied myself as I slowly released my grasp on the branch. I smiled, a sense of newfound independence and freedom beginning to overwhelm me. Trusting myself, I pushed off in a light hop toward the next branch. My bare palms ached as they met the rough bark.

With my arms looped around the branch, I pushed my feet against the trunk, using it to help my feet up to the branch. I continued this method until I had scaled about halfway up the towering tree, where I was finally able to see over the wall. From my perch, I looked out at what appeared to be an endless wasteland. There was a vast scape of sand, only broken up by the scattered blackened frames of buildings and patches of ash.

I pulled myself carefully along the branch as far as it would allow before it began to bend beneath my weight, and even then, the wall was still a few feet away from my grasp. *There's no turning back*, I whispered, collecting every scrap of courage I had. Once again, I steadied my feet on the branch, taking my hands from the tree gently. I stretched my arms out to my sides for balance, orienting my body toward the wall. I inhaled slowly, the world around me silent as I jumped.

CHAPTER ELEVEN

I felt like I was flying—soaring away from the confines of Avid. The freeing moment didn't last long, however, as my chest collided with the tall cement brick wall, forcing the air from my lungs as I moaned in pain.

My legs dangled over the edge of the wall toward the garden as I squirmed my way into a sitting position, straddling the wall—one half of me in Avid, one half of me in an entirely new place. I flung my other leg over the wall and tried to steady myself as I lowered myself backwards down the wall, eventually letting myself fall. There was still a long distance to fall, but the sand was softer on the other side of the wall. As my feet hit the sand, it sank a bit beneath me, causing my ankle to roll, making me stumble and fall on my back. After a moment to catch my breath and calm down, I sighed in relief as I lay there in the warm sand for a minute.

Warmth radiated off of the soft sand, cooled by a gentle breeze that blew away the top layer of sand. I closed my eyes, surrounded by the peace of the moment. *I should probably get going.* I checked myself for injuries, finding none, and then I stood up, brushing the sand from my coat. I remember learning at school that only deserts used to have sand like The New Territory, but over the years, more areas turned to dust, leaving behind the sandy wasteland such as where I found myself at this point.

I pulled Zane's map from my bag, turning it to get a better perspective on my current location. It looked like, from where I had crossed the wall, I was closer to Delaisse than before. I decided to continue in the same direction, starting my trek in the sand.

A couple hours into the journey, seeing nothing but small pockets of ruined towns and cities among the endless sand, I neared what looked like the remnants of a small village. There were small, crumbling brick houses with charred pieces of sofas, kitchen tables, and ovens. Nothing was intact. I stepped over blackened wood and brick, brushing the ash off of a small section of the remnants of some foundation. I sat down, pulling a carrot from my bag for a snack. After I finished the carrot, I sat, running my fingers through a large mound of ash, feeling the small flakes sift through my fingers. I felt something smooth but solid beneath the ashes. I turned, sticking both of my hands into the pile. I cleared away some of the ash and pulled out a human jawbone.

I shrieked, dropping the jawbone immediately, ashes spraying out from where it fell. Then, I heard a distant voice. I jumped, surprised to hear another person in the ruins. Unable to make out what the voice was saying, I decided to keep walking, taking quick, nervous steps, sure to keep away from the source of the voice.

As I walked along the far edge of the ruins, the sound of the burnt remnants crunched under my feet. The sound of cracking wood and stone with every step was interrupted by a loud shout.

"Found one!" a raspy voice yelled.

Eos

Looking to my right, I saw a thin old man in a woolen trench coat. He had a deep scar across his brow, wispy shoulder-length white hair, and his frail body was leaning on a dirty and chipping wooden cane. His dark, sunken eyes locked on mine, almost apologetically before he grinned, revealing a partial set of rotting teeth. He pointed a bony finger at me shakily.

"Catch her!" he commanded an attractive younger man.

Before the words even escaped his mouth, I was running, kicking up sand behind me as I tried to maintain a steady footing. My hair whipped around my head as I flew around the corner of a partial brick wall, I continued to make sharp turns throughout the ruins in hopes of confusing the young man. He was a tall, muscular figure with dark hair, keeping close to me in the chase like a cheetah on a gazelle.

The man turned the same corner, grabbing at the bottom of my long coat, which was trailing out behind me. He tugged at the black fabric and sent my body slamming into the ground, shooting loose sand into the air as I fell. I scrambled to get to my feet, but was shoved down by the man. He proceeded to pin my right arm down with one of his oversized work boots. I stretched my free arm out to claw at him, but he swatted, grabbing it and rendering it motionless as he held it. I flailed in vain, kicking my legs wildly while screaming profanity at the man.

"I got her!" he yelled, struggling to hold me down.

Just then, I pulled one of my knees up swiftly between his legs. He swore, his hands instinctively grabbing at his crotch as he knelt forward, still pinning me down with his weight. I began throwing my arms around, trying to wiggle lose. In the midst of my thrashing, I

85

remembered my grandpa's pocketknife. I pulled it from my coat, flicking out the blade and jamming it into my assailant's shoulder, the easiest target I could hit at the time. He cursed loudly at me, grabbing for his bleeding shoulder. I withdrew the knife quickly as I scrambled away, leaving him reeling in pain.

Breathless, I dropped to the floor against the interior wall of a nearby old building, right into a heap of blackened scraps. I threw the hood of my jacket over the back of my head, tucking all of my blonde and black hair inside it. I curled into a tight ball amid the pieces and pulled what remains I could across my body, camouflaging myself in debris and darkness. I was unable to see anything aside from the ashy pieces of building I threw myself into as I heard quick footsteps turn the corner.

The thudding of his feet across the room slowed as he tried to decide which way to continue. He swore angrily in defeat, kicking something that flew into my back. I bit my lip, holding back a yelp.

"Where's the girl?" The older man growled as he entered the room.

"She stabbed me!"

"Where'd she go?"

"Uncle, doesn't it bother you that I was *stabbed*?" the younger man said breathily in disbelief.

"Of course it bothers me, but you know we need every bit of money we can get from turning in run-aways! This is the only way we can afford to put food on the table, and you let one escape!"

"But we already caught one today! The spikey-haired Avid boy who *bit* me!" the nephew argued. *Zane,* I thought. *He didn't make it to Delaisse, but he has the Avid key.*

Eos

"I was going to use this one to pay my debt to Mr. Courton," the uncle began as the two left, their voices drawing faint. When the two were hardly within earshot, I emerged from my hiding place, shaking and brushing off the ash and soot. *I have to get the Avid key, so I have to find Zane.*

I treaded lightly through the ruins and the soft sand, following the sound of the two men bickering, allowing a safe distance between them and my location so as not to be detected. It continued like this for about an hour, and the sun began to set while I followed them through various ruins until we neared a beautifully intricate gate made of steel, twisted into complexly woven vines, with delicate roses coated in silver. At the center of the gate was the name "Nortown" twisted into the metal—the smallest of the remaining cities. When the men reached the gate, I darted behind a parked truck, squatting and peering out from behind the back tire as the gate swung open. From my spot, I could see two other men, pacing outside of the gate, chatting casually. I waited for a moment as they began to walk past the entrance, their backs toward my path. Once the uncle and nephew were well within the gate, and the guards were far enough past it, I took off sprinting toward the entrance. The gate had almost shut completely just as my body cleared the gap. My right foot, however, got caught on the closing gate, tripping me and sending me face-forward into the sand.

Spitting out sand, I propped myself up so I was on all fours, slumping my head over, sand spilling out of my hood. I groaned, looking backward and realizing that my foot may have made it through the gate, but the same couldn't be said for my right boot. Aggravated, I got up and hobbled to the gate, stretching my arm through the metal vines, pawing for my shoe. I hooked a finger through one of the laces and dragged it to my side of the gate.

Once I stood straight, I got a look at the city for the first time. Similar to Rockhallow, Nortown consisted of small-scale buildings, primarily family houses. The city hall was clearly visible, seated in the middle of the tiny city center, its tan roof a large dome, elevated distinctly higher than the surrounding buildings. *I don't belong here,* I had to remind myself as I made my way cautiously down the streets. *I can't let anybody notice me.* I kept hunched over, my eyes scanning for the uncle and nephew from the ruins. I figured Zane would be somewhere in the city hall, under some degree of supervision, so I was carefully watching for officials as well.

I approached the city hall, the moon and the streetlights illuminating the streets in a dim white glow. When I stopped in front of the large building, I pulled up my hood, tugging it low enough to shade some of my face from the light. I took my knife out and rolled it around in my palm a few times before flicking the blade out. *I can't hurt anyone. I just have to scare them.*

Confident, I marched up to the front doors of the city hall, dropped to my knees, and unlocked the doors with some of the paperclips I stole from Zane's room. Pulling the heavy doors open, I disappeared into the darkened building. After a few wrong turns, I found myself in the basement of the city hall, in a corridor full of locked doors with small windows. Peering through each door's window on my way down the hall, I turned the corner into a similar hallway. I spotted a large man with a thick vest on, sitting on a weak looking metal chair in front of one of the doorways, his back turned slightly away from my direction. I scanned his figure for weapons and didn't notice any. *That has to be where they're keeping Zane*, I thought as my eyes narrowed, locking on the man.

I took long, swift, gentle steps across the charcoal colored tile, the tapping of my feet masked by the buzzing of a single flickering light in the hallway. The dying light sent the hallway into flashes of complete darkness, making my approach even more sudden as I slipped the knife just a hair in front of the man's neck. I dropped to eye-level, my pale green eyes half covered by the top of my hood. I grinned at the man.

"Open the door," I whispered, over annunciating every syllable.

"You aren't supposed to be here," the man warned, his voice deep.

"Pity," I said, tilting my head and glancing at my knife under his chin briefly before locking eyes with him again. I hoped he wasn't going to catch my bluff as I grew shakier, realizing it was too late to run.

The man squinted his eyes, focusing on mine for a moment, testing me, before he slowly raised his empty hands in the air. I withdrew the knife and stepped backwards a safe distance and the man slowly reached for a large key ring attached to his belt, his eyes never looking away from me. *He's scared of me,* I realized. A part of me felt uncomfortable at the thought of making this man fear for his life, after all, he was just doing his job. He unlocked the door and stepped to the side, motioning for me to enter the unlocked room.

"Leave," I hissed.

Without hesitation, the man took off down the hallway and vanished around the corner. I wasn't a fool though; I knew he was going to report me, so I had to act fast. I pushed down on the handle and pulled the door open, and just then I was knocked onto my back and everything went black.

CHAPTER TWELVE

My eyes blinked open slowly, my vision a bit hazy, no thanks to the still flickering light of the hallway. My head was pounding. I groaned, trying to sit up.

"E, I am so sorry!" came a voice.

"Zane?" I called groggily.

"Yeah, it's me. I thought you were the guard, and I had it all planned out to throw myself into him to knock him out the next time he opened my door, but instead I attacked you, and you sorta' fell, and you hit your head on the chair, and I feel terrible… You were trying to bust me out—" he babbled apologetically.

"Don't worry about it," I grunted, running my hand over a bump in the back of my head.

"Take it easy, E, you hit your head pretty bad," he said, lurching forward to steady me with a look of concern in his dark eyes.

"I'm fine," I mumbled, working my way to my feet. As I stumbled, Zane put an arm around my waist, sending a warm, foreign shiver down my spine. I smiled at Zane awkwardly, and he laughed.

"What's so funny?" I frowned.

"Nothing! I'm sorry. It's just... you have a little blood on your teeth, and when you smiled... that and your messy hair, and the fact that you're stumbling... You look a bit psychotic. It's kinda' hot," he smirked.

I felt around in my mouth with my tongue, realizing I must have bit my tongue during my fall. I sighed at him, irritated at first, but then I let out an amused huff.

"You have wonderful manners," I started, "for a thief and a jerk."

"A jerk?" he questioned playfully as he picked through a basket with his name on it near the cell door, pulling out his belongings.

"You lied to me about dinner, broke into my room, stole my stuff, and ran off!" I said, half angry, half laughing at the ridiculousness of the situation as Zane helped me down the long hallway.

Zane rubbed at the back of his neck with his other hand.

"You're not going to try to lie to me again, at least it seems," I said more seriously, looking forward again.

"Eos, I'm sorry. I read the papers over your shoulder when we found them, and I had heard rumors of the Skeleton Key when I was little. I couldn't pass up the opportunity." His voice sounded genuine.

"You're 'sorry?'"

"I didn't realize they meant that much to you. I didn't think you'd actually go looking for the Key!"

"Well I did! That's beside the point! You went through my stuff again and you stole from me!"

"I'm sorry! What else do you want me to say? That I *owe* you for busting me out of here? Because I do. I know! But making me feel like crap for a mistake isn't going to help anyone."

"It certainly makes me feel better."

"Does it really?"

"No," I said, defeated.

"E, I'm sorry. I mean it. I normally wouldn't have gone through your stuff again but I saw what those papers were and I had to see for myself. I didn't know you were going to use them to actually look for the Key."

"It's fine," I said plainly, dismissing the matter.

By the time we made it out, I had regained my balance and Zane no longer had to support me. We made our way out of Nortown, running along the edges of buildings to stay out of the light from the street lamps. When we neared the gate, we listened for the guards, peering through the gate for them. When the coast was clear, Zane scrambled over the gate with me lagging behind, shrouded still by the darkness.

We kept running until we reached a new patch of destroyed land from the war, without looking back. In the ruins, we looked around, inspecting the buildings for a place to stay, and we took shelter in one of the only buildings in the area that was still standing. It was a small brick home, with a crumbling ceiling that revealed patches of the starry night sky. There were a few pieces of furniture, such as an old maroon velvet couch, that were still intact, albeit with singed holes and soot stains.

"I guess this will do," I said as we walked into the house, looking up at the holes in the ceiling. I set my bag on the couch hesitantly, glancing at Zane.

"I'm not going to steal anything," Zane reassured me. "I promise."

I doubted him as I set my bag on the couch, taking out the blanket. I looked to Zane, hands in his pockets as he stood looking up through one of the larger holes in the ceiling at the stars. A cold breeze came gusting in through the shattered windows, chilling the room. I watched as Zane drew his arms in closer to his sides, keeping his hands in his pockets. I opened my bag and withdrew the loaf of bread. Taking out two slices, I walked up to Zane.

"Here," I said softly, holding out a slice. "Eat."

He looked at me, tentative at first. "Are you sure?"

"Yeah, I have enough." He took the bread from me, one of his ice-cold hands brushing against mine as he reached for it. Within seconds the slice was gone.

"Thank you, Eos."

I nodded, moving back toward the couch. I put my bag on the ground and laid on the burnt velvet couch, spreading the blanket over myself. For a while, I just laid there, looking across the room with a weird feeling in the pit of my stomach. Zane tiptoed over, a few feet from the couch, and lay on the ashy floor. After a few moments, I spoke up.

"Goodnight, Zane."

"Goodnight, E," he said, rolling over with his back to me.

I gnawed on the inside of my cheek for a moment, feeling sorry for Zane. I stood up, gathering my blanket in my arms, and I sat behind Zane, throwing the blanket over both of our feet. He turned, startled.

"What are you doing?" he asked in disbelief.

"It's cold in here, and I can't let you freeze to death—" I started.

"I'll manage," he interrupted.

"Let me finish," I said with a grin. "I can't let you freeze to death because if you die, I have to take the Avid key from your dead body. That's gross."

He laughed as he rolled over to face me, propping his head up on his hand.

"How about this," I proposed. "We can get the keys together, and share the Skeleton Key? I mean, I doubt either of us will really need it every day. The papers said it will unlock anything, but how often do either of us really need to unlock things?"

"Really?" he asked, a sparkle in his coffee eyes, the corner of his mouth turned up in a playful smile. "You really trust me after I stole the papers?"

"I mean, I saved you from Nortown, after all," I giggled. "You owe me! You wouldn't turn your back on me!"

Zane laughed. "Alright. Deal."

I lay on my back, looking up at the stars through the holes in the ceiling, and Zane mirrored my movements.

"Zane?"

"Yeah?"

"Why were you exiled?" I asked innocently.

"I was stealing a lot and got sloppy with it," he admitted.

"If you don't mind me asking," I probed. "What did you steal?"

"When I got caught? Jewelry. But I had been a thief for a while before I was arrested. I turned into a criminal a long time ago—I had to. It's okay though, I got used to that life. My family and I lived in Eastmeade, and when I was a boy, my older brother got really sick. My parents worked hard to pay for his medicine, but there was only so much they could afford. Eventually they couldn't afford to keep food on the table, to buy us new clothes when we wore through our old ones—so I stole. I took food—just the basics—bread, milk, eggs, vegetables... Never more than we needed. But over time, I grew to like the rush I got when I took things, and I grew up stealing. Eventually, I did it for fun, pilfering jewelry for my mother, books for my brother... I acted like they were gifts I had worked for, but really they were just the products of my habit," he spoke, dreamily gazing at the stars as he reflected. "When I got caught, I was stealing jewelry from a small shop about a block away from my house. I was reaching for a necklace just as the lights turned on, but I managed to hide a bracelet in my bag."

"Oh," I said, unsure of what else to say.

"Are you going to tell me your story?" he asked, his eyes turning to me.

After I told him how I ended up at Avid, I rolled onto my side with my back to him, trying to get some sleep. Arms behind his head like a pillow, Zane closed his eyes, falling asleep on his back. With the warmth of the sun gone, the cold night wind continued to gush through the broken windows, making the dark house even more frigid. I began to shiver involuntarily, and my teeth chattered, the clicking sounds piercing the silence. Suddenly, I felt Zane's arm slide across my waist, pulling me close.

"For warmth," he said with an airy chuckle.

I smiled to myself as my shivering began to fade. I closed my eyes and allowed myself to drift into darkness.

CHAPTER THIRTEEN

Dawn brought beams of warm sunlight through the gaps in the ceiling. I woke up, squinting in the light as I stretched on the floor. As I rolled onto my back, I realized Zane was gone. Instinctively, I looked for my bag, spotting it immediately, still where I left it. I jumped up, frantically digging through my bag, keeping a mental checklist of my belongings, finding the Skeleton Key papers.

"You okay?" I heard Zane ask, standing in the doorway, squinting at me. "I found something you might like!" He smiled, holding out a small bundle, wrapped loosely in burnt fabric shreds.

I unraveled the blackened cloth, revealing a sharp silver dagger in a worn leather sheath, the hilt simple, with the carving of a serpent coiled around it. The eyes of the serpent were studded with tiny emeralds.

"Oh my gosh, Zane," I gasped. "Where did you find this?"

"I was wandering through the ruins a bit—I woke up early—and I found a couple of skeletons with some supplies on them. I found this one, and one for me. I hope we don't have to use them, but just in case." He pulled out his dagger to show me. It, too, was slipped into a leather case, but the hilt of his was coated in a golden material, with a sapphire-eyed eagle carved into it, wings spread across the length of the handle.

"Thank you, these are incredible," I said in awe, turning my dagger over in my hands. It was light and fit nicely inside one of my hidden jacket pockets.

After a light breakfast, Zane and I cleared out of the house and made our way toward Delaisse. With how soon I had made it to Nortown from my path to Delaisse, I recalculated the length of our trip—if we could resist stopping for breaks, we could make it in only a matter of hours. Along the way, Zane and I joked about our friends back at Avid, pondering what they could be saying about our absences. We came up with a variety of games to play while walking, and we asked each other about our lives before being exiled. When we had finally reached the gates to Delaisse, it felt like we had known each other for years.

"Umm," I hesitated, looking at the vast exile town before us. "Any ideas on how we're supposed to find the Delaisse key?"

"Not a one," he said, looking up at the massive industrial buildings. These buildings were drastically wider than the ones in Avid, and more numerous. Unlike Avid, these buildings were constructed with burgundy bricks, rather than plain grey concrete. I remember learning that Delaisse used to be one of the largest manufacturing sites during the war, and for the most part, the town remained intact, but the factories were no longer functioning.

In front of us was a simple chain link fence that stretched to about three times my height. Beyond that were the immense, seemingly abandoned factories. The only reason we knew we had reached Delaisse was a small, crooked wooden sign near the gate with the word

"Delaisse" painted in neat black paint. The ground here seemed to change, transitioning from the soft sand into hard dirt and areas of asphalt.

"Is this the only security they have?" Zane asked skeptically.

"I guess so," I answered, poking the fence tentatively, half expecting to be shocked.

"Huh," Zane muttered.

"Give me a boost," I asked Zane, situating my bag so it would sit on my back as I grabbed at the fence.

"E, I think we really should come up with a plan first," he said, eyeballing me as I tried to pull myself higher on the fence with no luck.

"Our biggest obstacle right now is getting over this fence," I argued.

"Well, we've never been here before. We don't know the layout—so we can't plan based on that. We don't know where the box is hidden, so it isn't like we can go straight for it. We don't know anyone here, so we can't get help," he rationalized.

I sighed. "Fine."

"Do you see that bridge?" He pointed through one of the gaps in the fence.

"No."

"Look a little more to your right," he said, touching my waist gently to turn me, sending a shiver down my spine.

"What about it?" I asked.

"If you look close enough, it looks like there's an

intersecting road that goes under it. I bet if we got over the fence, we could make it there quickly and hide under there until we figure out our next move. It'll give us a quick glimpse inside the town, without us straight up running around aimlessly."

"Fair enough. Where is everyone though?" I asked. "We've been standing here a little while now and I haven't seen a single person."

"I don't know, and frankly I don't want to find out," he said, bending down a bit and stretching out his hands to help me up.

I stuck my right foot in his hands as he pushed, helping me a couple extra feet off the ground. The fence clanged and rattled as we worked our way over it. Zane seemed to scramble over the fence significantly faster than me, flipping his legs over the top before I was even halfway across.

"How are you doing that so fast?" I asked in disbelief, clinging tight to the thin metal, feeling like I was swaying more the higher I climbed.

"I guess I'm just better at climbing than you." He chuckled as he began to climb down on the inside of the fence.

I looked up at the top of the fence, groaning as I stretched my arm up to pull myself further. I gasped. Zane had climbed right in front of me on the other side of the fence, surprising me in my focus. His white teeth grinned mischievously at me through the chain link fence.

"What?" I hissed a bit impatiently, keeping my voice down so we wouldn't attract attention, should there be anyone nearby.

"Are you ticklish?" His deep eyes narrowed on mine, his smile never fading.

"No! No, no!" I squeaked quietly at him, panicked. "You'll make me fall! Don't!"

He poked a few of his fingers through the fence in a wiggling motion near my side, and I hurriedly pulled myself higher, sending my feet kicking into the fence as I nearly ran to the top, with Zane scuttling to follow me from his side of the fence. Once at the top, I worked my way down the other side, Zane moving sideways, occasionally wiggling his fingers teasingly at me when he got close. I went to put my foot on the next section of fence below me, but was surprised when it met compacted sand.

"Oh," I said, releasing myself from the fence.

"You climb faster than you think——" he started.

"Because you were going to make me fall!"

"Eos, I would never let you fall," he said, his smile fading.

"I wouldn't put it past you—you can be a real jerk sometimes! You were going to tickle me and let me fall!" I argued.

"No, I wasn't. But you *thought* I was going to, which was the point."

"So, you did it to make me go faster?"

"Yup."

"Oh."

"All hail Eos, Climber of Fences," he said as if announcing my entrance, bowing dramatically before me as I rolled my eyes with a grin.

"Dork," I said, shaking my head.

"Nerd," he poked me and smiled.

We began to head through Delaisse, jogging the narrow road, but keeping close to the buildings while we tried to get a feel for the town and where the Delaisse Box might be hidden. The further into the town we went, the more colorful it got, and I mean that in the most literal way. The walls of the decrepit factories and other industrial buildings were covered in bright graffiti. One minute I'd be looking at a complex painting of what looked like a man's face, melting into a puddle of water with fish, the next, I'd be looking at bursts of painted birds taking flight along the brick. The street began to slope down a bit, leading us underground, beneath the asphalt bridge Zane pointed out from the fence. Under the bridge, hidden to my left, I noticed a wide concrete sewage pipe, tall enough to walk through without crouching.

"Maybe it's in there?" I said, motioning to the pipe. "I mean, I don't *want* to go in there, but it looks like a good hiding place. It's our best bet right now. Plus—no one will see us down here."

Zane nodded, leading the way. The ground was covered in a thin layer of muddy water that made wet squelching sounds as we made our way into the tunnel. A few steps into the pipe, Zane stopped dead in his tracks, causing me to bump abruptly into him.

I waited behind him, looking at him confusedly. Gazing toward the opening of an intersecting pipe, without saying a word, he pointed to a piece of graffiti. I squinted in the dim light, making out a beautiful painting of a very human-looking marionette puppet, its eyes glassy and sunken in. The work looked as if a hand was stretching out from the wall, holding strings to force the puppet into a limp salute. Above the hand, the words, "Who holds your strings?" were painted in blockish white text.

I stood there behind Zane for a moment, looking over the graffiti, realizing the entire tube was full of stunning works of art.

"It's kind of beautiful, in a way," he said, dazed.

"Yeah," I said softly, still looking around.

Suddenly, the sound of slow, splashing footsteps echoed from the intersecting tube, interrupting our trances.

"Get *down,*" Zane hissed under his breath to me, pushing me down as he squatted into a wide stance in front of me.

"How goes it, my friends?" said a nasally male voice. "It's too nice out today to be hanging around in the pipes, wouldn't you agree?"

"I could say the same to you," replied Zane defensively.

"Woah, buddy, just making small talk," the voice sniggered. "No need to get defensive. You admiring my work?"

"You did all this?" Zane questioned.

"You bet your over-gelled hair I did."

Zane ran his fingers over his styled hair involuntarily.

"Do you and your friend, hiding back there, want to get something to drink at my place? I'm harmless," he insisted, assuming Zane's decline. "In case you haven't noticed, you're in Delaisse—we aren't exactly violent people," he laughed.

"No, thank you," Zane replied coolly.

"Please, I *insist,*" the man pushed, force in his voice.

Suddenly, I felt a prick in my back. I yelped, turning my head to see a dark figure behind me, flashing both a knife and a snarky grin at me. In response to the noise, Zane looked and saw the man behind us.

"Fine," Zane submitted. "But keep your hands off of her," he threatened.

Zane kept his eyes on the man, who stood with his arms crossed as Zane offered a hesitant hand behind himself to help me up.

When I was on my feet, I was finally able to see the source of the voice. The man was lanky, with an oversized, unbuttoned flannel shirt, dirty jeans, a flashlight illuminating the tunnel, and a green spray paint can in the other. His hair was shaggy and straw-colored, grease matting it to his forehead, a few strands dangling right above his piercing blue eyes. His cheeks and chin were covered in thick stubble. He smiled at me, revealing yellowing, chipped teeth.

"Ma'am," he nodded with a smile before turning on his heels. "This way."

Zane kept between the blue-eyed man and me the entire walk to his house, throwing back frequent paranoid glances to the man with the knife. We approached one of the industrial structures and the man pulled the door open, walking straight in. The large room was no different than the streets outside, with walls covered in flamboyant paints. He continued down the length of the room, which looked like an abandoned manufacturing plant of some sort. He turned into a door on the right, and we followed. Right inside the door was an orange beaded curtain covering the entrance. He pushed aside the beads for us, revealing a small room with dark chocolate colored walls and a deep red carpet. There were five orange chairs situated in the room, a quirky, rusted teal lamp, and a few glass instruments of varying sizes and colors lying around. The room smelled strongly of odorous plants and paint fumes.

"Take a seat and make yourselves at home," the man welcomed, gesturing outwards with his arms, beaming at us.

Zane waited for me to take my seat, his familiar grin missing from his face and replaced with a look of gravity. When I picked a seat at random, he sat in the one nearest me, keeping his eyes on the man, who pulled a seat across from us. The man with the knife stood in the doorway, twiddling his blade, while the other man sat down, holding out two glasses.

"Orange juice," he said as we took the glasses and set them on the floor beside our seats. "So, what are your guys' names?"

Before I could speak, Zane interjected with a "yours first."

"Tanner," the man said, moving a greasy strand of hair from in front of his eye.

"Zeke," Zane lied.

"Elle," I said, taking Zane's hint.

"Lovely name for a lovely lady," Tanner smiled. I nodded in insincere appreciation, skeptical of his intentions. "You aren't from here—I can tell."

"No sh—" Zane started, stopping when I jabbed him with a finger in the thigh.

"Be nice," I mouthed.

Tanner laughed. "It's okay."

"We're cross-city messengers," I responded. "From Nortown."

"Can I talk to my friend for a minute?" Zane asked the man in the doorway, who silently looked back at Tanner.

"No, but I'll let you have the room for a moment. Don't try anything—I'll be right outside the door," Tanner said, stepping through the beaded curtain.

Zane's brow furrowed as he squeezed my forearm, pulling himself close.

"What are you being so weird about?" I glared at his hand, squeezing down on my arm.

"He can report us for being here! You can't give him too much information, even if it's made up—he can find out easily if we are really cross-city messengers," Zane said in an exasperated whisper, his eyes wide. "All he has to do is alert his town official and the authorities will be here faster than we can climb the fence to get back out!"

I smiled, amused.

"What are you smiling about?" he asked, heated. "This isn't funny!"

"What's the worst they could do? Send us back to Avid?" I laughed lightheartedly. "Oh *no*!" I said sarcastically.

"Eos, listen to me! When I was caught and brought into Nortown, before you rescued me, they told me they weren't going to just send me back to Avid. They keep the run-aways in high security prison cells, far away from any of the cities, even the exile towns. They don't give you another chance. If you hadn't gotten there that night when I was in the holding cell, I would have been taken away."

"I thought they did away with the prison system?" I said, my tone suddenly solemn.

"They did, but they need a way to deal with those who the exile system doesn't work on. I guess it isn't a common occurrence, from what my guard told me, so they can manage to keep up with it. They don't need as many people to staff it as they would for a huge prison system, but I don't want us to end up there either way," he warned.

We called Tanner back into the room, and Zane and I apologized to our host.

"Not a problem!" Tanner smiled. "Trouble in paradise?"

"We're peachy keen, thanks," Zane replied simply.

"So, what brings you to Delaisse?" Tanner asked with a tone of simple curiosity.

"It's a long story," I answered. "We were just sent to get something."

"Well," Tanner said. "I hope you got it. Or… get it. Are you still working on getting it?" He eyeballed my bag.

"Yeah," I answered.

"I wish I could be more help, but I don't know what you're here for," he replied, digging into his pocket and pulling out a couple of small, white capsules, which he proceeded to pop into his mouth and swallow. "You haven't touched your juice. Do you want something else to drink?"

Eos

"No, the juice is fine, thank you," I said, grabbing for my glass on the floor.

Zane copied me, taking his glass of juice. We both lifted the glasses to our mouths, pretending to sip on the juice for a while as Tanner sat in silence, his pupils dilating.

After some time had passed, Tanner looked to the beaded curtain, which was unmanned.

"You both better be on your way—seems as if you have important business to tend to." He sighed under his breath, just as I felt a jab in my neck. The room began to blur, and I tried to push myself to my feet, stumbling and crashing to my knees on the carpet as everything went black.

CHAPTER FOURTEEN

I woke up to the feeling of warm fingers on my neck.

I sat up quickly. A pain shot through my wrists as I moved. *Somebody chained me up.* Blinking my eyes until my vision began to clear, I made out Tanner's figure. We weren't in his room anymore, and Zane wasn't with us.

"Oh my God," Tanner breathed a laugh. "Man, I thought you were dead or something!"

"Where am I? Where's…Zeke?" I hesitated for a moment, remembering that Zane and I gave false names.

The room was fairly empty, with brick walls coated in graffiti, spray paint cans littering the cement floor, and a couple of rusty pipes, one of which I was attached to by metal chains wrapped tight around my wrists and held together by a basic metal lock.

"You mean your friend?" He laughed. "He left."

"What do you mean he *left?*"

"Before my friend could inject him with the same stuff we hit you with, he practically surrendered to us and told us everything he knew, so we allowed him to leave peacefully. We figured he would've put up more of a fight than that."

"You're lying," I spat.

"Really?" He grinned toothily. "What makes you think he would stay?"

"We're on a mission together, I know he wouldn't just bail."

"Does he need you for this mission?" Tanner prodded.

"Well, not exactly, but—"

"But? The boy doesn't need you. He can do the job without you," Tanner interrupted. "The question is, what is 'the job' and why would it require you to come to Delaisse? Cross-city messengers don't go to exile towns. Why are you here?"

"I'm telling you, I'm a cross-city messenger. I was just told to pick up a package."

"Who would be sending packages from an exile town? Do you realize how *stupid* you sound?" Tanner snarled, spitting a little on the word 'stupid'.

"Can you let me go now? I have work to do," I said, trying to sound official as I struggled against my restraints.

"Um…" He seemed to think on the notion theatrically. "No?"

"Why do you need me here? How is having me tied up at all beneficial to you?"

"I want to know what it is you're after. Simple as that. Answer the question and I'll let you leave."

"I could report you for this!" I threatened.

"No, you can't. You aren't supposed to be here, and you know it. You aren't a cross-city messenger and I want to know what you're after. I don't even care who you are—I just want to know what of value is in Delaisse."

"What would you do if I told you?"

"You want an honest answer? I'll probably report you to officials either way. I'm not about to lie to you about that." He chuckled.

I looked at him unblinkingly for a moment.

"You're really stupid," I said, dumbfounded. "You know, I'm not going to tell you why I'm here if there's nothing in it for me—not even my freedom. You're an idiot. If you plan to report me, why wouldn't you have reported Zeke if he told you everything? And why bother interrogating me if he supposedly told you why we are here? What's in it for you if you call the officials on me? There are so many flaws in your plan it's almost comical."

"I'm interrogating you because I only need to turn one of you in, and he was much faster to cooperate, so I gave him a free pass. You, on the other hand… If the officials get word of someone here without authorization, they might reward me for my good deed to the community," he said, a tone of mockery in his voice. "And I'm interrogating you to see if your stories match up. That's all. I already know why you're here, so don't bother lying. Just save us both some time and prove whether your little friend told the truth or not. Why are you here?"

I tilted my head slightly, narrowing my eyes and staring at Tanner for a moment before I spoke up.

"I'm looking for a box. The box contains a key that could help me open a different box, which contains a key capable of unlocking anything and everything," I answered coolly.

"You're lying," Tanner accused.

"I'm not."

"I don't believe you."

"You know, I thought it would be fun to try that, but this is wasting my time," I joked. "We were sent to pick up a package of pills for someone in Nortown. That's all. I can't give a name though—I signed a paper stating that the identity of the recipient would remain confidential."

"That's it?" he asked in a sigh, disappointed.

"That's it."

"Alright." He paced the room for a minute.

"Can you let me go now?"

"I'll let you go when I let you go," he glared at me, stopping in his tracks. He paced for another moment before continuing. "God! You know, people used to tell me everything changes, but I've realized—nothing ever changes. You get stuck somewhere in life and that's it. And it isn't just people like me. You people in the cities don't have it any better than us—you just wind up in a job, unchanging until you *rot*," he spat.

"That's not true," I said matter-of-factly.

"You're delusional."

"Funny, coming from someone who pops pills all the time."

"Shut *up*," he snarled, squatting to face level with me on the ground. "You don't know the *half* of it."

"Sure I do. Daddy was mean to you, wasn't he?" I jeered, a smirk growing on my face.

"Don't talk about my fath—"

"Did daddy hurt your feelings?" I interrupted in a false pouty voice, just before Tanner slapped me, stinging my cheek.

I growled and, without a second thought, rammed my boot straight into his chest, forcing the breath out of him and knocking him from his already wobbly squat. Instantly I smashed my feet downwards with all of my strength, aiming for his face. My boots made impact with his jawbone and nose as he rolled over to his hands and knees, reeling in pain. His face drooping to the ground, he clutched his nose as blood began to drip onto the concrete. Before he could lift his head, I pressed my boot against the back of his neck, digging his face into the ground.

"Let," I pressed harder with my boot.

"Me," harder.

"*Go*," I howled, pressing harder still.

"Okay! Just get off!" he shouted, sputtering through the blood oozing from his nose. He swore under his breath, calling me some profane slur as he hesitantly reached into his pocket, squirming under my foot as he handed me a miniscule key.

"See? Now wasn't that easy?" I smiled pleasantly, lifting my foot and unchaining myself. "Where's my bag?"

"By the door, over there," Tanner motioned to his left, a furious look in his bloodshot eyes as he shook drops of blood off his hand.

I hurried out the door, scooping up my bag and

double-checking for all of my belongings. When I was sure they were all there, I decided to make my way to the fence and get out of Delaisse. My hands and legs were shaking as I bolted from the building. *I've never hurt anyone like that before.* I felt a twinge of guilt before rationalizing that I only fought in self-defense. *He deserved* it, I told myself, trying to shake off the jittery feeling. *What about Zane? If Zane really did leave, he probably already found the key. Why would he just ditch me like that?*

I kept watching carefully as I sprinted toward the fence, shoving past a few startled exiles as I ran. I scanned the streets as I ran, hoping for a sign that Zane was for some reason still here, but I found nothing. *What if Tanner actually does have him?* I began to worry. *If he had Zane, he would have interrogated him first, I'm sure. Zane was the one who made it obvious we were worthy of suspicion when he asked to talk to me alone. I bet that's what gave us away. Tanner probably would have questioned Zane first, so it's only logical that Zane is already free, right?*

I continued to reason with myself that Zane was already out of Delaisse and on his way somewhere else. Once over the fence, I pulled out the map from my bag, scanning for my current location. The next closest exile town was Equivox. *Great. An entire town full of people who are sure to be* super *helpful—the liars.*

CHAPTER FIFTEEN

Grrrgglll…

I clutched my growling stomach as if to silence it. *I have no idea where Zane is. I can't stay here though—it's too risky. I hope he got out. I'll figure out a plan to find him after I eat. I just want to get somewhere out of sight before I eat*, I reminded myself, thinking of the loaf of bread in my bag. I made my way into the endless scape of sand, the opposite direction from which we entered Delaisse. The longer I walked, the more distant the chain link fence became, and the more isolated I felt. Once Delaisse was completely out of my sight, I could see nothing but sand, stretching in every direction.

Grrrgglll…

My stomach growled again. *Well, this is as good a place as any,* I thought. *I wanted to be out of sight, and I haven't seen anyone since I left Delaisse.* I sat in the soft sand, feeling some of the warmth through my jeans. Plunging my hand into my bag eagerly, I retrieved the bread, opening the bag and pulling out two slices. Before I allowed myself to take a bite, I resealed the packaging and stuffed the loaf back into my bag. *You have to save some for later,* I told myself, knowing I wouldn't be able to stop eating if I didn't put it away.

I devoured the first slice of bread, but then took it slower on the second, savoring the sweet, doughy taste. While I sipped on some water, I pulled out the map and reviewed the direction I was headed. It didn't seem like I'd have to worry about running into any cities—it was a straight shot to Equivox. If Zane found the Delaisse key, he probably moved onto the next town, which would be Equivox. If he really were free, he probably wouldn't leave Delaisse without the key. *But what if he's still with Tanner? Or what if he moved on to Equivox with no intentions of meeting back up with me? Or what if he's looking for me? Would he know I'd try Equivox next?* Even after I knew it was time to continue on my way, I still sat there, running my fingers through my hair. I didn't know what to do, but I knew I couldn't just sit there and wait. I sighed, sitting for just a moment more. *I know I don't have the best relationship with my parents, especially my mom, but I miss them.* I pulled out the picture I saved from Rockhallow of my grandpa, my dad, and me all laughing together. *Maybe when, or if, I get the Skeleton Key, I'll visit dad, if he even wants to see me. But if I had the key, I could easily get into any place I want. I'd still have to be careful, but I could visit him.*

I sat there for another minute, daydreaming about sneaking into Rockhallow to visit my dad. *I need to get going,* I prompted myself, standing up and brushing the sand from the back of my jeans. I continued this luckily uneventful trek, keeping a pattern of short breaks every couple of hours until it was sundown.

I finally came across the first ruins I had seen since I left Delaisse, spotting them in the distance as the sun was about to dip below sight. I gathered all my remaining energy and sprinted toward the small pocket of black in the vast field of uninterrupted sand, relying on the dim light of the moon and what was left of the setting sun to give me just enough vision to see my destination. Kicking sand up, my feet sank into the smooth ground every step I took, exhausting me further. Minutes later, I reached the beginning edge of the ruins. The building remains were short in stature, likely the relics of some family cottages of a village. I peered inside the remains of some of the houses, partially to see if any would make decent places to spend the night, but mostly I did it to ensure I was alone.

When I was sure I was the only living thing in the area, I backtracked to the most structurally sound building in the area—a small, blackened cottage. Aside from suffering obvious damage from an internal fire that must have burned all of the furniture down to broken wood structures, the petite home was intact.

After sweeping off a patch of ashes and dust from the floor, I laid down, wrapping myself in my blanket and situating my bag as a pillow—a very hard, very lumpy pillow. Lying on my back, I looked up to the ceiling, remembering how Zane and I had fallen asleep under the stars that glimmered through holes in that ruined place before reaching Delaisse. That felt like ages ago, even though it was just the other night. This roof was in an appreciably better state than the one Zane and I had found—there were no holes revealing the stars, but there was still a familiar cold breeze filling the air.

Shivering, I curled up on the firm ground, burying my head under my blanket. I stayed that way until I fell asleep, wondering where Zane was that night.

In the morning, I had a quick breakfast of some of the produce from the Avid garden, the sounds of my chewing filling my head in the nearly maddening silence of the house. The windows were covered in soot, the sun illuminating them in a smudged glow. After I finished my breakfast, I sat for a minute, trying to enjoy the peace of the moment, but instead just finding that I was feeling even more alone. *How could Zane just leave me with Tanner? Was he really as much of a jerk as he first let on?*

I left the house, making my way through the ruined village, back into the scape of sand. I tried to distract myself, focusing on the feeling of my feet pressing into the soft sand with every step I took. *How am I supposed to get the Avid key now? Or the Delaisse key, assuming Zane found it? The best I can hope for is that I will either run into him while looking for the Equivox key, or maybe for one of the other keys... Or maybe he plans to go back to Avid.*

I continued to play through possibilities in my mind along the way, stopping for occasional breaks, until finally my surroundings changed. Slowly, the golden hues of the barren terrain transformed into fertile dirt, which gave way to lush, green life the farther I progressed. When I was fully surrounded by green, I could feel the overgrown blades of grass tickle my calves. It was darker, the ground was shaded by the thick trees, the air was crisp, and the dewdrops on the grass felt cool against my legs as I walked through the foliage.

Deeper in the greenery, I noticed patches of mushrooms with a faint violet color to them. I squatted down, wanting to get a closer look at one, when I noticed the trickling sounds of water in the silence created when I was no longer trudging through the grass. Holding still, I listened closely, trying to detect the location of the water. I still had another full water bottle, but it would be a good opportunity to fill the others if I could find the source of the noise.

I turned to the left, creeping silently, pausing occasionally to listen again for the water. A few yards away, I saw it—a narrow creek in a shallow dip in the land. Crouching next to the water, I held a bottle to it, the icy water rushing through my submerged fingers. The stones in the creek were smooth and rounded from the constant flow of the water, and the rocks just along the water's edge were covered in thick moss. I pulled my boots and socks off, lowering my feet into the frigid water. I was taken aback for a moment by the sudden sensation on my feet, but when it no longer felt so sharp, I pulled out the map, letting my feet soak.

Equivox was labeled on the map in the middle of a region of green ink—presumably the forest area I was currently in. I tucked the map back into my bag, replaced my boots, and decided to continue along, following the flow of the creek. I went on this way for about an hour before I hit a thick wall of trees through the raised roots of which the creek continued. I looked in either direction, noticing that the trees continued in this solid wall as far as I could make out.

Now what?

I searched for a low branch. *I'll just repeat what I did when I left Avid,* I reassured myself, as if I knew what I was doing this time, when I knew I very likely didn't have a clue how to climb a tree again. *Piece of cake.*

Spotting a low-hanging limb well within my reach, I gave myself a running start, swinging my legs around the branch as I clung to it. I shimmied my way upright and eased myself onto my feet, reaching for the next nearest arm. I slowly made my way up the tree until I spotted a lower limb on the other side of the tree that I knew I would be able to reach. *If I can make it to that branch, I can work my way down the tree and continue heading straight.* I clung to the trunk as I stepped across a couple branches until the limb I was hoping to reach was just below me, but still many feet above the ground. The leaves were so thick, I realized, that I couldn't even *see* the ground at that moment. I sighed, half out of exhaustion, half out of nerves as I lowered myself, toeing around for the branch. When my foot had made contact with it, still holding onto the tree, I dropped my weight onto the limb just as it gave out from under my foot with a loud snap.

I let out a startled scream as I hung there, my body pressed to the bark. I could feel splinters pricking my hands as I slid a couple inches. I groaned. Peering down, I couldn't see any visible branches beneath me—only thick leaves and twigs. I pondered for a moment how far of a drop it would be if I just let go. *I can't,* I panicked. *There has to be another way.* I looked to my right, seeing a thick branch just a couple inches below where I was holding on, but too high up for me to reach with my legs.

I counted down from five under my breath. *5... 4... 3... 2... 1*—I let go of my grip on the trunk and rapidly threw my arms towards the branch on my right, narrowly missing it as I began to fall to the ground. Cracking and crunching sounds filled my ears and twigs and leaves around me cut my face as I fell through them. I collided with the grassy floor with a thud, knocking the air out of my lungs as I landed on my hip, crushing my right wrist beneath it. I yelped in pain, my vision searing white for a moment before my eyes welled up with tears. I bit my lip, holding back sobs as I held my hand in front of me. My wrist was already beginning to swell. I sniffled as I carefully inspected the rest of my body for damage. Aside from my wrist, it seemed as though I had only incurred minor cuts and scrapes. My hip was a bit sore from landing on my wrist, but upon inspection, it seemed to be fine aside from a small bruise. I eased myself onto my feet shakily, clutching my right wrist in my left hand as I persisted in the same direction.

A short distance away, I could see that the foliage

abruptly stopped. Making my way to the edge of the green, I noticed that the ground stopped there too. Standing with my toes at the edge of a cliff, I looked down upon the small town of Equivox.

CHAPTER SIXTEEN

At the bottom of the cliff, I could see houses—small cottages with dark thatched roofs and cream-colored walls. The buildings were no more than two stories tall and looked only large enough to house one or two families each. Looking longer at the crater-like valley, I noticed a small lake below me. The water that managed to pass beneath the tree roots proceeded to drip down into the lake below. From my perch at the top of the cliff, the houses seemed as small as my thumb. *That's a long way down...* I observed the edges of the cliff around the entirety of the pit, seeing no feasible way to climb down. *There has to be a way in and out of the pit, otherwise they would have no way of transporting people or supplies.*

I looked around carefully for a route to take but couldn't find anything but cliff sides. *I can figure out how to get out once I've gotten down there—it might be easier close-up to see where the exit is, and it will give me a better chance of waiting it out to see if anyone brings rations or anything—then I can leave the way they come.*

My first obstacle would be to get *into* Equivox at this point. I contemplated trying to climb down the rocky wall of the cliff but realized it would be impossible with my injured wrist. I looked down again at the lake. *No,* I told myself. *Not an option.* I searched desperately for another way down, realizing jumping into the lake might be my best bet. I swore under my breath. *It's too late to turn back now,* I reminded myself.

I took a few steps backwards, still holding my wrist in my other hand as I prepared myself to run and jump. Just as I was about to start, I realized I had papers in my bag—the map, the Key papers, my money, and my family photo. I turned to face the trees behind me. Picking one that the creek did not run beneath, I dug a shallow hole near the roots, folded all of my papers, and tucked them into the hole. I piled some of the dirt back on them and pulled my knife out of my jacket pocket. I turned it over in my hands, letting the light hit the emerald eyes of the silver snakes, the gems glimmering a stunning green. Grasping the handle with my good hand, I stabbed full force at the tree, cutting into the bark. The blade moved slowly as I dragged it across the trunk in the shape of an E.

Once I was satisfied with my hiding place, I turned back to the cliff edge. I pressed my bag tight to my chest with my right arm, holding my right wrist with my left hand for support. I swallowed a deep breath and took off running toward the edge.

I felt the ground disappear beneath my feet as I flew toward the water below. Air rushed past me, whipping my long hair around my face as I began to turn in my fall, my back to the water. I tried to condense myself into a ball as I flew and all I could hear was the whooshing of air in my ears for a few moments until suddenly, my entire body was slammed with the chilly sharpness of the lake. My chest felt tight—my lungs empty as I made impact with the water. I saw black envelop me as my coat billowed around me, a cloud of bubbles rushing to the surface as I sunk. I kicked hard against the water with my boots, struggling to move. In my struggle, a silvery glint of light struck my eye from the bottom of the lake. I kept kicking upwards, eventually surfacing with a gasp. My lungs burned, and my wrist was searing with pain from instinctually using both hands to swim. I brushed my matted hair out of my face as I paddled to the water's edge, toward a patch of small bushes. I pulled myself carefully onto the ground, spread my saturated coat out in the grass nearby, removed my boots, and stuck them and my bag in the coverage of the bushes before dropping back into the water. *What's at the bottom of the lake?*

I took a deep breath and dove straight down as rapidly as I could. The lake wasn't incredibly deep, but I had little experience swimming, and never in deep water— only in a small local pool in Rockhallow. By the time I reached the bottom, I could feel a stinging in my lungs as I searched frantically for the source of the silver light. Suddenly, I saw it. It looked like a mirrored box, slightly larger than the one I had found in the garbage back at Avid, but it was rounded. It was buried partially by mud, which I tried to scoop away. Before I could completely reveal the box, the stinging in my lungs had gotten so severe that my vision was beginning to go dark. Panicked, I propelled myself back toward the surface. Once able to breathe again, I sputtered, choking up water and gulping in oxygen. *One more time,* I persuaded myself. *You don't know what might be in that box. But then again, it might be empty.*

I took in a mouthful of air and weakly pulled myself back down to the box. I pushed aside more of the thick mud, but the water kept pulling it over the box. I buried my fingers into the ground, wrapping them around the box and tugging, but the suction was too great. My lungs burning, I pushed back up to the surface again for air.

Again, I commanded myself, diving down. Unsurprisingly, the mud wouldn't release its grip on the box. *Again*, I pushed, sluggishly dipping down toward the lake bottom. This time, I slipped my fingers into the mud, locking them under the bottom of the box. Instead of pulling directly upwards, I wiggled the box, twisting and turning it through the mud. It finally loosened, and I swam back to the surface and over to the bushes, wanting to get out of the water before opening it. I sat crisscross in the grass with the mirrored box in my lap as I peeked under the lid. It was a tiny silver key. *Is this the Equivox key?* Just as I reached into the box to observe the key, I heard a voice.

"Oooh what'chu' got there?" the voice asked.

I slammed the lid shut.

"Nothing," I hastily replied, turning around and seeing that the source of the voice was a young girl of about 6 or 7.

"What's that in your lap?" she pressed.

"It's—just my old jewelry box," I said, pretending to dust it off. "I was just washing it off because it was really dirty."

"You're lying to me," the girl said with surprising anger. "I can tell."

"No, I'm not. It's just a jewelry box, see?" I held it up innocently.

"Open it."

"I don't want you to see my jewelry—you might want to steal it when I'm not looking," I accused.

"Stealing is for dirty, rotten Avid thieves," she hissed.

"Why are you in Equivox anyways?" I distracted her.

"Aren't you too young?"

"You're making it really obvious you aren't from here. Everybody here knows me, and I know everybody here. I was born here," she said pragmatically.

"I'm new here," I stated plainly.

"Stop lying. You're a terrible liar, and that's why I know you don't belong here. Also, I saw you come from the sky. Did you fall? Were you running from something? Did you find that box here? Why won't you show me what's in it?"

"You ask a lot of questions. None of that matters, I just want to leave and go back home is all."

"You're all wet. Come home with me and my mom can give you a towel and some food, okay? If we give you food and a towel, can you tell me what's really in the box?" She held out a small hand to me.

"Um, okay," I said hesitantly. *If this little girl decided to start screaming at me or something, it could cause a lot more problems than it might if I just humor her,* I rationalized. I grabbed my wet coat and turned to retrieve my bag and boots from the bush, but then realized the little girl's curiosity could get me in more trouble if I brought my bag, so I left it.

The girl grabbed my hand and guided me toward the houses.

"What's your name? Where are you from? Why were you running?" she continued to pry.

"My name is Elle," I lied, using the same name I told Tanner back in Delaisse. "I was just running because I ran away from home and I'm really mad at my parents. I didn't want them to find me, so I jumped. I was hoping to hide here, but now I'm afraid I can't get back out."

"There's a way out," she said.

"Where is it?"

Silent, the corner of her mouth twitched up in an almost smirk as she looked at me.

"How do I get out of here?" I repeated.

"This is my house up here," she changed the subject, pointing at a two-story building with a walnut door. Before we entered, I quickly stuffed the mirrored box into one of my jacket pockets.

The child's house was similar to the other houses in Equivox—cream-colored walls, a deep brown thatched roof, and very few windows. She tugged on my hand, leading me into the house. Tentatively, I stepped into the doorway with her.

"Mom!" she shouted.

No response.

"Mom! I brought a friend home—can she have dinner with us?" she continued to call.

A petite woman with waist-length, wavy russet hair appeared at the top of the stairs.

"Of course," she smiled, the skin around her eyes smooth, lacking the crinkled appearance of someone who is genuinely happy. She descended the stairs, her hand carefully gliding along the banister.

"Renée," she said, offering her hand to me.

"Elle," I said without hesitation, shaking her hand.

"Have you been here long?" she questioned. "I don't think I've seen you before."

"Um—"

"She ran away from home and ended up here," the girl answered for me.

"Oh," Renée sighed worriedly, squinting at me as if concentrating.

"It's a long story," I huffed dramatically. *Don't try so hard,* I reminded myself. *I suck at lying.*

"How long have you been on your own?" Renée asked softly.

"I haven't been away for very long."

"She won't tell me what's in it," the girl whined.

"In what?" her mother questioned.

"Her box! She's hiding a box in her jacket!"

"Eloise, my child, you have yet to learn the art of keeping quiet and minding your own business," Renée laughed airily.

"But mom," she pouted. "She's keeping secrets!"

"Everyone has their fair share of secrets, Eloise," she said calmly.

"Ughhh," Eloise groaned, crossing her arms.

"Why do you want to know what's in the box so badly?" I asked.

"I'm just curious!" she cried defensively.

"I promise, it isn't anything that would be important to you," I said.

"Let me get you a towel," Renée offered, looking down at the puddle forming around my feet. She disappeared behind a door and reappeared a moment later with a thin, stained towel.

"Thanks," I said, drying my hair.

"We're having vegetable soup for dinner if you'd like to join us," she said.

"I don't want to intrude."

"It's not a problem at all. We all get our rations distributed in a couple days anyways—I'm just using up the last of it."

"Are you sure?" I checked.

"Of course! Sit, sit!"

I sat around a lopsided, round family table, feeling my wet clothes squish in my seat. I shifted uncomfortably, and Eloise giggled.

"Go wash your hands before dinner, Eloise," Renée said.

Eloise skipped down a short hallway and turned into one of the doorways.

"She doesn't really have any friends," Renée told me in a hushed voice. "Her situation is rare—not many kids are ever born into exile towns, so the people here closest to her age are still more than *twice* her age. I can tell you are much older than her as well, but it's still nice to see her happy like this. I know tha—"

Eloise made her way back down the hallway, and her mother silenced herself. Renée gave a pot on the stove a few stirs. She smiled without revealing her teeth as she pulled three plastic bowls out of a cabinet and began to spoon the steaming broth into them. She brought the bowls to the table, and her and her daughter began eating instantly. I looked down at the bowl of soup in front of me. The broth was nearly as clear as water, with a thin layer of white rice floating around the lumps of celery and carrot. *These two have so little to spare, but they still shared with me*, I thought, grateful for their generosity. *They almost seem too nice to be in an exile town. But then again, Eloise didn't do anything—she was born into it. Renée may be in a town for pathological liars, but maybe she has changed in her time here, or maybe there's just nothing to lie about to a stranger like me. It isn't like she has told me much anyways.*

I continued to think to myself in silence as I ate until an excited Eloise interrupted my thoughts.

"Oooh, mom! Can Elle spend the night?"

"Uh," she hesitated for a moment, eyeing me as I sat in her chair, still dripping water onto her floor. "Just tonight, okay? After tonight, she has to be on her way." She turned to look at me apologetically. "It isn't anything personal, but I'd prefer not to get caught housing a run-away, and I don't mind sharing my rations for a meal or two, but I'm already having to split my rations between Eloise and myself.".

"What?" I asked, shocked. "What do you mean? They don't give you rations for Eloise?"

"There have only been one or two other cases in history where a pregnant woman has been exiled. They don't have any special clauses or anything when it comes to laws regarding the birth of children into exile towns— the laws just state that all exiles are to be given certain rations. Eloise isn't an exile, persay, so they don't give her rations."

"That's not right!" I bursted. "What do they expect parents to do if they have a child in an exile town?"

"Most people don't decide to start families in exile towns. No parent wishes that for their child. If you ask me, they don't give rations to children because they want to discourage populating exile towns. They don't want *criminals* to *breed*," she said with a dismayed tone.

I looked at Eloise, her russet hair similar to that of her mother's, but rather than hanging loose over her shoulders, hers was tied into a floppy bun. Her olive skin was smooth and unscathed, and her eyes looked a fair grey as she watched us inquisitively. Renée glanced at her daughter and silenced herself for a moment.

"You can have the extra room. There's a room next to Eloise's that is currently vacant. Let me get you a change of clothes," she left for a moment and returned with a small stack of clothes, handing it to me.

"Come on! I'll show you!" Eloise chirped, sprinting up the stairs, her feet thudding against every step.

I followed her, my wet socks sliding against the wooden stairs as I carefully made my way after Eloise. At the top of the stairs, I saw two doorways.

"This is my room," Eloise pointed to the room on the left.

The room was bare—cream colored walls, dark wooden flooring, a simple wooden bed with a thin mattress, and a cracked plywood chest at the foot of the bed. Eloise looked up at me for a moment and squinted.

"What's wrong? Why are you staring?" she asked.

"Nothing. I'm just sleepy."

I turned towards the door on my right. *A child's room should have toys, books, something… anything in it.* The room on the right was equally empty.

"You can stay in here," she said, pressing her back to the door to allow me in the room.

Eos

"Thanks. May I use your shower?"

"Duh! It's downstairs on the right side in the hall. Goodnight, Elle," she said, softly, with a concerned pucker in her brow.

"Goodnight," I forced a smile as I turned to close the door behind me.

I tucked the mirrored box under the bed for the night, covering it with my jacket, and set the change of clothes on the bed—a simple pair of dulled brown jeans and a faded jade green shirt. I peeled off my soaked clothes, laying them out flat on the floor to dry. I shivered, the bitter air stinging my wet skin. Shuddering, I wrapped the towel around myself and made my way downstairs to shower. Their bathroom was small and simple, but clean. It was nice to feel clean again.

Upstairs, I pulled on the jeans and shirt and crawled under the covers. *I'll be on my way first thing in the morning. I can't stay here. The longer I'm here, the better chance I'll get caught—I'll have to get my stuff from the bush and then find a way out of Equivox as soon as possible.*

The next morning, I woke up able to see my own breath in rhythmic puffs in the icy air. I threw my head under the thin covers for a moment, hoping to warm up. Resigning, I decided it was time to leave. *I hate to leave without thanking them, but I can't risk staying any longer than necessary.* My feet hit the frigid wood floor, sending chills across my entire body. Squatting down, I fumbled under the bed with my left hand for my box. Hitting nothing but my cold, wet jacket and the empty floor, I tilted my ear toward the floor as I peered under the bed.

Nothing.

She took my box. Eloise couldn't stand the curiosity and she took it.

I slipped my still-wet coat on with a shudder, grabbing my other outfit before tiptoeing to Eloise's room. The door was cracked open, so I slowly and carefully pushed it open. Her bed was empty, and her covers thrown to the side as if she had just gotten out of bed. I crept toward her bed, checking under it and under her pillow, finding nothing. *Maybe she put it in the chest.*

"*Mom!*" Eloise howled from the doorway. "She's awake!"

Panicked, I retracted my hands from the lid of the wooden chest. Suddenly, I heard multiple heavy sets of footsteps treading up the stairs. Eloise screeched and dove out of the way of two male officials in uniform. The men barreled toward me, and in a moment's thought, I tucked my injured right hand into my hidden pocket, my fingers making contact with the chilled metal hilt of the blade from Zane.

The men grabbed for me from either direction as I skirted backwards, but they followed my every step. As I tried to dart along the far side of the room, the shorter of the two, a man with a younger, round face and buzzed black hair, threw himself at me, slamming my back against the wall. He leaned down, holding a syringe angled at my neck. He jabbed the needle in, pushing down on the plunger. Almost simultaneously, I threw my arm out, plunging the tip of the dagger into his throat. Thick, hot crimson blood poured out on my face as I retracted my dagger. The man's body gave out, crumpling down on me as I scurried out from under him in the warm blood pooled on the floor. My wrist seared with pain, my legs began to tingle and go numb, and then suddenly it was dark.

CHAPTER SEVENTEEN

I woke up in a truck. I tried to make out what we were driving through, but I couldn't see straight. The vehicle rumbled and bounced, making me nauseous. My vision began to clear slowly, and the first thing I noticed was my reflection in the rear-view mirror. My hair was stained with blood, some strands of hair crusted over, others still damp as I touched them. I looked down at my clothes. The brown pants and green top were drenched in reddish brown. Whether from the smell of blood, the bumpy car ride, or pure nerves, I leaned over and got sick on the floor of the truck.

I put my face in my hands, my wrists cuffed and my elbows resting on my knees.

I killed someone.

My eyes started to well up with tears as I sat, biting my lip. *Now they're taking me away and locking me up. I'll be behind bars forever. They found out I ran away from Avid. That, and I'm a murderer.*

I sniffled and let out a whimper, which I cut short by biting on my lip harder.

"We're here. You'll be escorted out of the vehicle,

and your cuffs will be removed from behind an inner layer of security," said the driver, a robust man with a thick red beard. "We need to know your name, and where you were running from so we can notify your city officials and your family of your exile."

"My... my exile?" I asked, lifting my head.

"You have been sentenced to Bellicose for the murder of Officer Renald Harring."

"Wait, what?"

"You're going to Bellicose. You killed an official," the official reiterated impatiently.

"Bellicose?"

"Yes. It's where we send the overly violent. People like you put the rest of society at risk. You'll receive rations and your own living quarters, but you won't have any of the luxuries of living as a *useful* member of society."

They don't know I ran away from an exile town. They have no idea who I am.

"I need your name and your city of birth," he stated plainly.

"Elle Dusk," I lied. "I'm from Eastmeade." Another lie.

He nodded, committing the information to memory.

I looked ahead, through the front window. We were nearing the mouth of a massive cave. As we drove closer, I could see thick iron bars blocking the entrance. The bars began to sink into the floor as we entered. The driver crept forward with the truck until we cleared where the bars had been. Just as we passed over the first set, a second set began to lower and the first set eased back out of the ground. By the time we crossed over a third and final set of bars, the driver put the vehicle in park. He stepped out of the truck, unlocked my door, and opened it.

"Get out."

I wiggled my way out of my seat. Now that I was moving, I could feel the absence of weight in my pockets. *They have my dagger.*

"Where's my knife?" I asked, pausing.

"It was confiscated."

"*Confiscated?* What's that supposed to mean?" I shrieked in anger.

"It was thrown away. It's gone. Move on. Get out of my truck," he said, his voice and face unchanging.

I stared back in disbelief as I stepped out of the vehicle.

"Stay still or I *will* shoot you," he threatened, putting a hand to a gun around his waist. He started the truck back up and the innermost set of bars lowered again. He reversed, backing up just until the front of the truck cleared the sunken bars. As the innermost bars raised again, the middle set lowered. Instead of leaving entirely, he stepped out again.

"Put your hands in front of you and approach me slowly," he instructed.

I did as he said, and he pulled out a key.

"Put your arms through the bars."

I slid my arms through a gap, and he unlocked my handcuffs, taking them from me. Without a word, he stepped back into the truck, and before I knew it, he was gone.

I stood there, confused. *What do I do now? I could get the Bellicose key while I'm here, but I have no idea where the Equivox key is now, and Zane has the keys from Avid and Delaisse.*

A loud cracking, crumbling sound echoed from deep within the cavern, interrupting my thoughts. I turned toward the source of the sound, seeing nothing but the stony throat of the cave leading into pure darkness. I reached for the pocketknife from my grandpa, discovering that luckily the officials must not have found it. I held the blade out in front of me as I crept toward the illusion of oblivion. As I continued, the blackness encased me. I could no longer see the knife in my own hand. I was moving through nothing, toward nothing.

Out of nowhere, a tiny orange light appeared. I changed my path enough to walk directly toward it, but its position began to change. I followed after it—the closer I got, the larger it grew until suddenly, it began to reveal the silhouette of a man. *A lantern. They see with lanterns.*

I crouched to the ground, wielding my small pocketknife. I held my breath as the man turned toward where he must have heard the sound of my feet, still without my boots, against the rock and dirt.

"Hello?" he called in a deep voice.

I breathed softly through my nose, trying to stay as silent as possible.

"Who's there?" He looked down toward me, squinting. He grinned. "I see you." He laughed.

Unsure of what to do next, I stood my ground, unmoving.

"Come on out, darling. I see you, and you see me. I'm not going to hurt you." He raised the grimy lantern, illuminating a handsome face covered in a layer of dirt smudges. His eyes were crystalline blue, and they crinkled as he smiled. His cheeks dimpled as he beamed at me, brushing a filthy hand through his taper-cut, honey blond hair.

"Look," he insisted, squatting down to my level with his lantern. He set the lantern on the ground and held his empty palms out in front of him. "I don't have any weapons. You do, even if it's a bit pathetic." He chuckled sweetly. "Please, stand up." He held out a hand, keeping the other palm open and in sight.

Hesitantly, I placed my left hand in his as he helped me up. He knelt down slowly, keeping eye contact with me as he picked up his lantern. When he was finally able to fully see me, covered in blood and without shoes, his smile faded.

"What happened to you?"

"I ki—" my voice was hoarse. I cleared my throat and continued. "I killed an official."

"I feel like I should be surprised, but look where we are. Nothing surprises me anymore—I know people who have unfortunately done worse than that."

"Does it not bother you that I killed someone?"

"Frankly, darling, it does. But at least half of the people here have killed someone before, so I'm sure you'll fit in."

"You aren't curious why I killed him?" I asked.

"Not particularly. I don't find stories of murder to be of much interest. If you want to tell me, go ahead."

"I don't—" I stammered.

"Then don't tell me."

"But I don't want you to think I'm a monster—"

"I've come to believe in my time here that not all 'monsters' are bad," he interrupted, looking me in the eyes.

"What do you mean?"

"Society deems us exiles as 'monsters.' All of us. In some sense or another, they believe we are all monsters. But everyone has their demons—some are just darker than others. You have people who succumb to them, but you have some people who fight the darkness as best they can. Let me believe that you are one of those people. If you tell me your story, you can't take it back."

"I'm not a bad person," I said, my voice shaking. "I mean... I'm far from perfect. I've stolen, I've lied, and now...But I never meant to hurt anyone."

"I believe you."

"That's it? You just *believe* me?" I stared at him in disbelief, my dry eyes stinging as they began to well up with tears.

"Yes."

"Why?"

"You've given me no reason not to."

I glared at him for a moment.

"What's your name?" he asked.

I hesitated for a moment.

"Is it a hard one?" he teased.

"Eos," I smiled weakly.

"I'm Paren," he smiled infectiously again, bowing his head subtly. "How about I show you around?"

"Um," I glanced at him, genuinely confused.

"What? You'll be able to see soon enough," he laughed heartily. "It isn't all dark like this. Rhyett, one of the guys here, he's kind of a hot head, and he went on a rage spree a few days ago. He broke all the lights around the entrance, but the commons and most the living quarters are still lit. We're hoping someone gets sent from the cities to fix the lights, but I'm personally not too optimistic about it."

"Oh."

"Come on, let me show you around," he smiled, holding a bent arm out to escort me.

I tucked my hand awkwardly through his arm as he escorted me through the rest of the darkness by a lantern.

After Paren led me down a couple turns, I could see the glow of a lit area that gradually grew closer as we continued. Soon, we were in a small passage of the cavern that was fully illuminated by hanging bulbs. There was an aged wire poking out in spots along the ceiling, and the only piece of furniture in the room was a splintering wooden table along one of the sides.

"Through here," he guided, grabbing for my hand to lead the way, but he grabbed for my right wrist with too much force.

I squeaked in pain, retracting my hand and clutching my wrist.

"Oh shoot," he said, looking at me with sincere regret. "Are you okay? I didn't mean to hurt you."

"No, it isn't your fault. I hurt my wrist the other day."

"Are you still able to move it?"

"Yes."

"May I?" he asked, holding his hands out toward mine. "I just want to take a look at it."

"Sure," I said, holding it out for him.

"How did you hurt it?" he asked, gently turning it over in his hands, running his fingers over the skin of my swollen wrist.

"I fell from a tree and landed on it."

"I'd ask why you were in a tree, but I feel like it's a long story," he smiled, looking up at me with his electric blue eyes.

"Heh, yeah. Bit of an understatement."

"Don't worry about it. Maybe you can tell me later. But for now, I'm going to show you around a bit more, and then I'm going to take care of that wrist for you before it gets worse."

I looked at him speechless for a moment.

"Why are you being so nice to me?" I asked.

"Have you given me a reason not to be?"

"But, you're in Bellicose. I mean, doesn't that mean you're violent? I'd be more likely to expect you to punch me than to help me."

"Didn't you listen to me earlier?" he asked. "Some people try to fight the darkness. I don't want to be a bad person."

"Why are you here then? I'm having a hard time believing that someone who was exiled to Bellicose could be *friendly*."

He laughed. "It's a long story why I'm here. How about I tell you over dinner?"

"Are you asking me out?"

"Hah! I don't know if I would call it that. Rations in a cave aren't exactly what I would call romantic, but call it what you want, darling."

I giggled. *I must look completely and utterly mad, sitting here covered in blood, with no shoes, hanging out in a cave and giggling like I'm actually enjoying myself.*

"Is your other hand okay?" he asked, reaching for it tentatively.

"Yeah," I said, taking his hand as he guided me through an opening at the other end of the room. The ceiling was fairly low, but I only had to duck my head slightly to make it through.

The room I saw when we cleared the passage was massive. The atmosphere was filled with a warm amber glow. I looked up, spotting individual soft, auburn light bulbs fixed in the ceiling at various points. Stalactites decorated the ceiling; droplets of water dripped off of some of them and onto the damp stone floor. The water on the ground reflected the amber color of the lights, as well as the radiance of a few lanterns set on rotting wood tables. Half a dozen or so people turned to look at the newcomer as I entered. I stood, angling myself behind Paren as they eyed me.

Paren nodded to the group as he continued escorting me, keeping me close to his side.

"This is the main commons. We eat in here, socialize in here—all that kind of stuff. Occasionally there are organized fights in here... occasionally unorganized, but that's bound to happen if you stick violent people in the same area. If you ask me, exile towns aren't the way to handle crime."

"What do you propose instead of exile towns?"

"Unfortunately, I still believe in the prison system."

"But I'm assuming you know we can't do that, right? There aren't enough stable prisons still standing after the war, and the population is still too low to have enough people to maintain that large of a prison, or that many prisons."

"I know, I know. I'm not saying it's an option in current times, but when conditions are right, I think it would be best if they went back to the old ways. Honestly, I'm not so sure conditions aren't right already—society has recovered quite a bit since the war."

"If they could hypothetically do that now, you'd be in a cell though," I pointed out.

"It's better than a cave of people who struggle with a dangerous problem. Not all of the people in here are truly dangerous, but some of the people are here because they're murderers."

I glared at him.

"Sorry. I meant some of these people take lives for *fun*. And with the old system, people could be released back into society in some cases. If you were arrested for a minor crime, you wouldn't have to spend your life apart from your family and friends."

I looked at him, curious why he was in Bellicose.

"Look here," he pointed. "That room over there is a bathroom. We have showers, but the water doesn't get very warm." He used a thumb to rub a bloodstain from my cheek.

"The room next to that is the representative's room. His name is Cromwell. He's a pretty scary looking guy; I'm not going to lie. Massive, too. He's covered in tribal tattoos, has this weird nose ring, and the typical tough-guy deep voice to match it all. I'd tell you he's a cool guy, but I'm not sure I can really say that. I've never really spoken to the man any more than necessary. Follow me."

He led me into a third small, pocketed room and opened a large crate.

"The city officials know we have a lot of incidents here, seeing the kind of people that are sent here, so we have the largest medical supply of all of the exile towns. It can't even compare to the supply of any of the cities though, of course."

He rummaged through the contents of the crate, pulling out a few things.

"Sit," he motioned to a short crate.

I sat down, and he kneeled in front of me, carefully taking my hand, examining it again. In a matter of a minute, he had fashioned a splint for my wrist.

"How's that?" he asked.

I turned my arm over, admiring his work. I wiggled my fingers.

"It's good."

"I'll show you where you can stay," he led me down another passage, this one longer and taller than the first.

There were shallow pockets along either wall. Each pocket-room had a woven mat on the floor, a thin blanket across the mat, and a single bulb on the ceiling.

"No one is staying in this one," he pointed to one of

the rooms, identical to the rest.

"Thank you, Paren."

"No problem, darling. I'll get you a towel and a change of clothes from the supply room—I'll be right back."

I stood there alone next to the mat and a ratty grey blanket. *I killed an innocent man.* I sat down and brushed my hand along the blanket, poking my fingers through some of the holes. *I don't have my blanket—it's in my bag. I don't have the Key papers—they're under a tree. The only things I have of my own are my jacket and my pocketknife.* I slumped over, sobbing. A few minutes later, Paren came back. Upon seeing me on the floor, he rushed over to me.

"Hey," he said, putting a hand on my shoulder. "You okay?"

I shook my head.

"Eos," he tilted my face up with a finger under my chin. "Darling, you look much prettier with a smile on your face. Cheer up—it isn't as bad as you think. You'll make a couple friends here, and things will get better. If nothing else, look at it this way… I get a chance to get to know a pretty girl now that you're here," he flirted, adding a cheesy wink.

I smiled half-heartedly, sniveling. I wiped the tears from my face, covering my hand in crusty blood.

"When can I meet her?" I joked with a sniffle.

"Smart aleck," he poked me.

"Can I take that shower now?" I giggled stuffily.

I took the towel and change of clothes into the bathroom. There was a grimy shower stall with a moldy shower curtain hanging from a crooked rod. *Better than nothing.*

The crimson and brown of the blood rinsing out of my hair mixed with the amber glow of the lights, making the color appear a burnt umber as it circled around the drain. I watched the blood wash out, feeling numb and exhausted at this point. While in the shower, I figured I'd scrub the blood out of my jacket as well. It was black, so it didn't really stain anything, but I didn't want to leave blood in the fabric.

After my shower, I dried off and put on the new clothes—a simple red tank top, black fitted jeans, clean socks and a pair of shoes made out of a burlap-type material. *Thank you, Paren.* Never have I been so excited to have clean socks and some shoes.

Back in the bedroom corridor, I saw a cup of chocolate pudding and a bent spoon sitting on my mat. I smiled to myself, sitting down. I planned to savor the pudding, but I devoured it and I swear I've never tasted anything so good in my life.

I set the empty cup and the spoon aside as I sat there for a few minutes alone. My stomach growled. *I wonder if they have a scheduled dinnertime.* I figured I'd go look for Paren and ask him how meals work in Bellicose, so I made my way into the common room. There were a few more people that joined the half a dozen from before, sitting at tables. Some played card games and conversed loudly, while others sat alone, staring off at various things in the room. I scanned the faces in the room—there were two other females, and about seven males, but Paren wasn't there. Next, I decided to check where I found him in the first place. I grabbed a lantern from an unoccupied table and retraced the steps we took to reach the common area.

When I neared the area we first met, I could see the shadow of a figure—*Paren*.

"Hey," I called out. "Paren, how does dinner around here work?"

No answer. I approached the shadow, lifting the lantern. It wasn't Paren. Well, one of them was—the one standing, blood on his fist and a crazed look in his eyes was not Paren. The man on the floor, unconscious with a disfigured nose was.

"Paren!" I shouted, running over to him. "What did you do to him?!"

"Put 'im in 'is place," spat the man, towering over me, with jet-black hair in a similar style to Paren's. The man's eyes were almost black in the darkness of the cavern as he glared at me. "He deserved worse—I showed 'im *mercy*."

"What did he do to deserve this?" I shrieked, using the bottom of my tank top to dab at the blood on Paren's face.

"He tried takin' what didn't belong to 'im!"

"He stole from you?"

"Somethin' like that."

"What did he take?"

He grabbed the front of my shirt and threw me on my back across the stone floor. "Stop askin'—ain't yer business." He called me a couple profane names before taking his lantern and my own that had fallen when he threw me, and he left us in total blackness.

I groaned before easing myself up. I reached for the back of my head. There was no blood, but I could already feel a bump forming. I could hear shuffling sounds from over by Paren.

"Paren?" I called out in a half-whisper.

"Eos?"

"Yeah. Are you okay?"

"Yeah, I'm fine. What are you doing here?"

"I was looking for you. I was just going to ask about dinner," I chuckled nervously.

"Heh, yeah I probably should have told you. How long have I been out?"

"Not long, I don't think. I just came over here after eating the pudding cup you left after my shower. Thanks for that, by the way."

"No problem, darling," he thought for a moment before groaning in pain. "I guess that would mean it's probably pretty close to dinner time about now."

"He took my lantern," I complained.

"Don't worry—I think I know the cavern well enough by now. Stick your arm out, I'll find it."

I held out my arm, and I jolted a little when his hand waved around, bumping into mine. He grabbed my hand.

"Grab my waist and stay close—I don't want you hitting your head or tripping on anything." He guided my hand to his waist from behind.

He led the way slowly and carefully, warning me occasionally to duck my head. Before I knew it, we were back in the common area and I could see people dishing up servings of what looked like roast beef with vegetables and bread.

"I'm going to go clean up really quick," Paren said, pointing goofily to his crooked nose.

I nodded.

I went and filled a bowl with some of the stew and took my place at an empty table. Paren returned a few minutes later and filled a bowl for himself, taking the seat across from me.

"So, tell me, why did that guy attack you?" I asked.

"You jump right to the point, don't you?" He laughed heartily. "It's stupid, really. Mikael's a jerk, and when he sees something he wants, he thinks he has every right to it- as if it's his- and when someone else poses a threat to him obtaining it, he feels the need to fight them off."

"What did you take from him?"

"That's the kicker. I didn't take anything."

"Then why does he feel like you did?"

"He told me to stay away from you," Paren's face grew serious. "He said some crude things about you, and he tried to go in the bathroom while you were showering. I told him off and stood in front of the door. He challenged me, saying he would back off if I won. I figured I didn't have much to lose if I tried, so I took him on. I told him I wanted to fight away from the commons, so he grabbed a lantern and we made our way to where you found us. Long story short, a few punches were dodged, a few punches landed. I got him with a couple good ones, but he barely flinched. Of course, you can infer the rest based on how you found me."

"What? He seriously did this to you because you were trying to protect me?"

Eos

"I know you don't believe me, and that's okay."

"I have no reason not to," I repeated his words.

Paren smiled, emphasizing his dimples.

"So, since I'm taking this time to hear you out, and apparently I feel like trusting that you're telling the truth, why don't you tell me why you're in Bellicose?" I asked.

"Alright. Fair enough," he slurped some broth from his spoon. "I used to live in Nortown. I'm 23 now, but when I was 21, I went to the city bar. It wasn't my first time, but I didn't go often—I'm not keen on alcohol—I don't like what it does to people, and I don't care for the taste, even. But I decided to go for social reasons—I have a thing for meeting new people. I sat between these two men. One was significantly older than myself, with grey, thinning hair and bifocals—he was a truly sweet and intelligent man, and the other was about my age, maybe a little older. The younger man was of a slightly bigger build, but he was shorter than me. A gorgeous young woman took an open seat next to him—one of the only seats open at the time. Aside from the fact that he never stopped staring at her chest, he got rather handsy with her. He kept running his hand up her thigh, and occasionally one along the back of her neck as he leaned in as if smelling her hair, and she kept swatting it away, asking him to please stop. Well, he didn't, and she decided to get up and leave, but he just wasn't going to have that. He called her some names, grabbed her wrist, and pulled her back toward him, but she was wearing heels. She lost her balance and fell when he tugged on her. I had enough at that point—I couldn't watch him treat her like that, so I got his attention and punched him square in the face. But I didn't stop at that. I kept wailing on the guy, punching and punching until my fist looked like it was covered in more blood than skin. His face was almost unrecognizable—it swelled almost

151

immediately, his nose was crushed, and his features bathed in his own blood. I think I knocked one of his teeth out. He didn't fight back hard—he mostly squirmed and swore at me. The bartender must have called the officials because they arrived during the incident and pulled me off of him. Needless to say, they took me here almost immediately afterwards."

I looked apologetically at him.

"So, you didn't kill anyone?"

"Nope."

"And you didn't just hurt someone for the fun of it?"

"Nope."

"You were trying to protect that girl, and you were exiled for it?" I clarified.

"Yup."

"I believe you."

He smiled.

"So, darling," he started. "Tell me, why were you exiled?"

"I actually was initially exiled to Avid," I admitted. *I feel like he's harmless. Unlike when I was in Equivox, I don't really have anything to lose at this point anyways.* "I've been stealing things since I was about 15. Nothing major. I'd steal a few dollars here and there—never enough for anyone to notice. I never stole personal items that would be missed."

"What got you exiled in the first place?"

"Well, I stole some rum and got caught. The thought occurred to me when I was delivering a letter to the barkeep. I used to be an in-city messenger in Rockhallow.

When I walked in, he was talking to someone about the 'cost of that rum nowadays,' and I didn't want to interrupt, so I stood and listened until he was done talking. Then I gave him the letter and left, but I kept lingering outside the bar around closing time after that for a while. I did it for a few weeks until I knew his schedule. I knew that he would leave and return later for a while before leaving the bar for good at night. Once I had it down to a science, I decided to make my move. I wanted some of the rum for myself— I've never owned something so expensive and valuable. It was super old rum, really, from well before the war. I was going to steal a bottle for myself, and a bottle to sell after a few years to another city. I wanted to be a cross-city messenger."

"And that's when they caught you?"

"Yes."

"*Phew*," he huffed before he tipped back the remains of his beef stew. "That blows. All of this because you stole some rum... Or *tried*, I suppose."

"It's more than just that," I sighed.

"What do you mean?"

"The reason I escaped Avid, the reason I ended up here instead... everything in-between."

Paren cocked his head to the side questioningly.

"I—" I stammered.

"You don't have to tell me," he said, his face growing serious. "I understand."

"No... You know what? Lying hasn't been working for me. Maybe I'll have better luck with telling someone the truth."

I began to tell him the long story about the Skeleton Key, about how Zane and I had been working together for a while, about how all of my stuff was still near Equivox, and about how the officials who arrested me the second time had no idea who I was or what I had done in the past.

"I don't understand," Paren said innocently. "Why would you be willing to go through all of this for some key?"

"It isn't just a key," I explained. "It's freedom. The ability to go anywhere, to have anything. I wouldn't flaunt it if I had it—I would be strategic about it. Maybe I'd reinvent myself in another city, under another name. I'd have anything I would ever need, but I could go anywhere if I ever needed or wanted. I was already in an exile town, and I hated it there—I wanted out. But I didn't know what it would cost me. I didn't know that all of this was going to happen. And I still need to get the Avid and Delaisse keys from Zane, the Equivox key from the mother and daughter I met, the Bellicose key, and the Clamorite key."

"Well, how does one find these keys?"

"I don't know. Zane technically found the first two. At least, I think. Since he disappeared in Delaisse, I assumed he found it and decided to leave me behind. I know the first one came from the dump in Avid though. And I found the Equivox key in a box at the bottom of the lake."

"From what I can tell, these keys seem to be in places within the exile towns that are symbolic to them. The dumps—people say the thieves of Avid are 'dirty thieves,' right? Dirty… Dump. And the Equivox liars were put near the most pristine lake in the New Territory because it is supposed to be symbolic of clarity, purity, and not having to look far to find the truth—at least, that's what my teachers always told me the lake symbolized. It sounded like bogus to me until you told me about this key thing. Do you follow me?"

"I get what you're saying, but Bellicose is supposed to be in this cavern because the violent people in it are like cavemen, correct? Well, in case you haven't noticed, the entire freaking place is a cave. That doesn't exactly narrow things down."

Paren thought for a moment.

"Well, I don't know. I guess we just have to keep our eyes open, maybe do some exploring sometime," he laughed sweetly.

"They exiled me to Avid. I escaped, and I wound up in Equivox. I met a little girl and her mom, and they said I could stay the night, but when I woke up, there were officials in the house. One came at me with a syringe, and I didn't want to get locked up God-knows-where, and I stabbed him. I wasn't thinking about it; I was just trying to escape."

"Why are you telling me this?"

"I—I don't know," I admitted in an exasperated sigh, allowing my eyes to wander as I thought about everything that had happened, and as they wandered, they caught sight of Mikael, just as he was running at Paren from behind.

CHAPTER EIGHTEEN

"Paren, *move!*" I shouted, giving Paren just enough time to turn around and see Mikael barreling toward him.

Mikael threw himself into Paren, grabbing a fist full of Paren's shirt and throwing him on the ground face first. I stood out of my seat, half in shock, and half trying to contemplate how to react.

"*What'd I tell you?*" Mikael growled.

Paren rolled over on his back, revealing a busted nose and lip.

"That you think I'm pretty," Paren smiled, blood coating his teeth.

Mikael kicked Paren in the side, causing Paren to cough, blood spattering.

"I warned you," Mikael said, as if he had been doing Paren a favor. "You didn't listen."

"I'm sorry I couldn't focus, I just got lost in your eyes," Paren groaned, trying to force a smile and laugh.

Mikael swore, spitting on Paren. He threw his foot

down on Paren's throat, crushing down slowly as
he spoke.

"I don't think I should give ya' another chance. You'll
always be there, goin' aroun' an' takin' what ain't yours. I'd
be doin' everyone a favor if I took you out, right here."

He ground his foot into Paren's throat more, causing
him to squirm and choke.

"Right no—"

I yanked on a handful of Mikael's hair, pulling his
head back and resting the blade of my pocketknife against
his throat. I could feel the blade move against the pulse of
a bulging vein.

"Maybe *I'll* do everyone a favor," I whispered in his
ear, tugging back on his hair more.

Mikael let out a deep, bellowing laugh.

"Princess 'ere thinks she can fight, doesn't she?" he
asked the room.

I held tight to his hair.

"Take your foot off of him and leave him alone."

"Aww, Paren's girlfriend is gunna' fight for 'im. How
cute!" He snickered. "Let's see whatcha' got," he yelled,
grabbing my splint and bending it away from his neck.

I shrieked in pain, grabbing at my wrist. He took his
foot off of an unconscious Paren as he turned to face me
with a wide grin.

"You're almost too pretty to wanna' hurt," he said.
"*Almost.*"

Mikael's fist flew toward my face and I ducked just in

time. I popped back up into a stand and, without hesitation, kneed him in the crotch.

He groaned, grabbing his groin with one hand, but snagging my hair in his other.

He wrenched my hair, making me lose my balance. I fell, but he never released his grasp on my hair as he began dragging me across the room. My scalp was blazing with pain from every hair follicle as he pulled me toward the entrance of the room. I screamed, grappling for his hand without luck.

"Eos!" choked Paren, squinting as he rubbed his neck.

He bolted after Mikael, and once he caught up to us, he threw all of his weight into a punch that landed square on Mikael's nose. A crunching sound echoed in the cave as blood started oozing out. Mikael dropped his grasp on my hair, clutching his nose to stop the blood flow. Paren shot his hand into Mikael's neck, slamming him against the jagged stone wall.

"Don't you *ever* touch her again," he threatened, pulling Mikael's head toward him an inch, just to slam it back against the rock. "If you touch her again, I'll kill you. Don't try me."

Paren stared with a maddened sting in his eyes at Mikael, and he slammed his head once more into the rock. Mikael's body went limp as he fell to the floor.

"Is he dead?" I asked, undeniably a little hopeful.

"No. He'll be back on his feet in a matter of time."

I looked down at Mikael, slumped over on the ground.

"You don't want to be here when he wakes up, come on."

We went back into the common room. Paren cleaned the blood from his face once again and tended to his broken nose after repairing my splint. For the remainder of the evening, he and I sat in my pocket "bedroom" just talking and sharing stories.

"So, how do you know what time of day it is if you can't see the sun?" I asked.

"You get used to it. Your body will tell you when it's time for things like dinner and sleep."

"I think my body's doing that 'telling me it's time for sleep' thing," I laughed drowsily.

"You should probably listen to it—you look exhausted. If you need anything, my room is just over there," he pointed diagonally from mine.

"Thank you, Paren."

"My pleasure, darling. Sweet dreams." He walked out toward the common room, leaving me to curl up under the ratted blanket on top of my dull green bed mat.

I shifted around, trying to get comfortable, but I could feel every groove in the rock floor beneath me. I groaned in discomfort, frustrated as I rolled over on my other side. The process continued until I finally fell asleep.

I woke up with a calloused, rough hand tightly covering my mouth. My eyes shot open, meeting Mikael's. He stroked my cheek with the back of a finger on his other hand.

"Mornin'," he whispered with a sly grin.

I tried to move to punch him but realized my wrists

had been tied together by sharp wire.

"Rhmmmphhhrmmuh!!" I mumbled from under his hand.

He kept smiling at me, as his finger began to trace down my neck.

"RHHUGHH!!" I tried to scream, my eyes wide.

I moved my legs from under my blanket as quickly as I could, scrambling to move. My lips slipped from under his hand for a half second before he cupped my mouth shut again, but it left me just enough time to let out a sharp, piercing scream to echo through the bedrooms. Mikael forced me in place, straddling me to keep me still, keeping my mouth covered. I kicked my legs wildly, my knees occasionally making impact with his back, but he seemed unphased. He ran his hand down my chest as I growled, thrashing around under him.

Suddenly, Mikael was ripped off of me, and I heard a loud boom. Paren was on top of Mikael, pummeling his face. He repeatedly brought back his fist, sending it soaring into Mikael, like a scorpion stinging its prey.

Mikael barely had time to respond before Paren had beat him unconscious yet again. I watched in horror as he picked Mikael's head up, lobbing it into the ground repeatedly until blood pooled around it.

He sat there for a moment, breathing heavy, his head hung low as he looked at his blood-stained hands.

"Eos?" he called to me, without looking up. "Are you okay?"

"I-I'm fine," I said in a half whisper.

"Did he—"

"No," I interrupted. "I think that was his intention though."

He nodded, his head still drooping toward the ground and Mikael's body.

"I didn't know what else to do," he breathed.

Paren stood up and stormed out, angrily snatching a lantern from a table.

"Paren," I called, getting up clumsily, with my wrists still bound.

I trotted after him. When I got to the common room, he wasn't there.

"Paren?" I continued out toward the path leading to the entrance of Bellicose.

It was dark, and I didn't have a lantern. I figured I could follow Paren, but I couldn't see him. I walked carefully, calling out his name. Glass crunched under my feet as I tripped over the remains of a lantern. I swore as I smashed into the ground, unable to catch myself because of my tied wrists. I felt tiny glass shards prick my palms as I tried to steady myself into a stand. I searched blindly for a few more minutes before resigning, making my way into the commons.

I was too shook up to go back to sleep, so I picked a seat in the nearly empty room and sat down, laying my head on the table. I sighed in exhaustion. *I'd be lying to myself if I said I could ever leave this place. There's no wall or fence to climb, there's no lock to pick... this is it. I'm stuck here until I die. I'm rooming with murderers, so even that might not be too long.*

Sitting up, my eyes were met with a man now sitting across from me. His arms were almost thicker than my waist, his head was shaved smooth, his veiny arms and shaved head were decorated in tribal tattoos, and he had a thick black ring dangling from the middle of the cartilage of his nose. He squinted at me and bowed his head in a subtle nod.

I nervously nodded back, my lips pursed tight.

The man flicked a knife open and motioned to my wrists with his head. I glanced down, seeing the thin wire cutting into my pale and dusty skin.

"Please," I asked quietly, holding my wrists out.

He snapped the wire in one swift motion with the knife, closing it back up and tucking it into a pocket.

"Thank you."

He nodded subtly again.

"Are you Cromwell? The representative?" I asked, remembering Paren's description.

Another nod.

"I'm Eos."

Cromwell stood, walking toward his room.

"*Nice to meet you, too,*" I whispered sarcastically.

When Cromwell reached his door, he turned to face me and motioned me to him.

Crap, he heard me.

My heart was racing as I got up and approached his room. He stood to the side, hinting for me to enter. When I stepped into his room, I saw a few lanterns hanging from hooks on the walls, illuminating the room the same amber glow as the rest of Bellicose, only slightly brighter. There was a thin mattress on the floor, with springs jutting out from the fabric in a few places. The walls were smoother than the rest of the cavern, almost as if they had been sanded and chiseled down. Upon closer observation, I saw that almost every inch of the walls was covered in intricate white chalk sketches of trees, waterfalls, and mountains.

"These are beautiful," I said, staring at the walls in awe.

"14 years I've been here," he said in a deep, rumbling voice. "I was chosen as the representative after 3 years and have been ever since. I started these 11 years ago. I used to love nature."

"How did you ever get to see things like this? The cities don't allow people to just wander outside wherever."

"I was a hunter. Once every month, my city would transport myself and a few others to hunt in the woods for about a week straight—we supplied a lot of the meat for the city."

"I thought that's what the cattle fields were for?"

"You didn't honestly think those petty stocks of cows were enough to feed everyone, did you? Those are mostly all dairy cows anyways."

"Oh."

"I'm just going to cut to the chase here," he started. "I know you're from Avid."

"What?" I asked, my heart sinking.

"I heard you speaking to that blond boy. I know you're from Avid, I know the officials didn't know who you were, and I know what you were looking for when you got caught."

I stood in silence, stunned.

"I don't know what you're talking about," I lied coolly, crossing my arms and cocking an eyebrow.

"I'm not going to report you. I don't care who you are," he said plainly. "I actually might be able to help."

"What do you mean, 'help'?"

"I might know where the Bellicose key is."

"What? How would you know? And why would you want to help me? What's in it for you?" I asked skeptically.

"One question at a time."

"How would you know that you found it?"

"Years ago, I found a box hidden in the caves with a small key in it, and nothing here really needs a key to unlock it. One can assume what it's for, knowing about this Skeleton Key now."

"Where is it?" I asked anxiously.

"I'm not going to tell you that." His laugh bellowed in the room.

"I thought you were going to give it to me?"

"I never said that."

"Yes, you did! You told me you knew where it was and that you might be able to help!"

"*Might.*"

"Well, what do I have to do for it?"

"Fight me."

"Pardon?"

"*Fight me,*" he repeated.

"You can't be serious," I laughed nervously.

"I am. If you want that key, beat me in a fight."

"I don't know how to fight though!" I protested. "And in case you haven't noticed, you're a bit bigger than me."

"You have to fight for things sometimes if you think you're worthy of them. But yes, you do know how to fight—I saw you with that knife and Mikael. You know how to fight dirty, but if you kill me, I obviously can't tell you where the key is. Provides me with a little protection, you see? I want you to learn how to properly fight. Without the knife. You have as much time as you need— I'm certainly not going anywhere."

"Why do you care if I know how to fight?"

"Part of me just wants the challenge. Part of me sees a lot of potential in you, and it'd be a waste if I didn't push you to see what you can do with it."

I rolled my eyes and he chuckled.

"If you don't, now you know it'll be your loss."

"I wouldn't even begin to know how to leave Bellicose even if I won," I whined.

"You'll figure something out," he said in a mumble, opening his door and motioning me out. I stepped outside his room, turning back to say something to him but instead he just nodded silently and closed himself in his room.

CHAPTER NINETEEN

I didn't see Paren for three days. When I finally saw him again, he was sitting alone in his pocket room. His eyes looked sunken in, his face was pale, and his jaw covered in blond stubble.

"Where have you been?" I asked, stunned when I walked into the bedroom corridor.

"Thinking," he replied softly, without making eye contact.

"What happened to you?"

"I've just been thinking."

"About?"

"Eos, I killed someone!" he let out in a bellowing yell, turning and looking at me with wild red eyes.

"I know…" I said in a sigh, unsure of how to react.

"I'm a monster," he said, his eyes welling up as he looked at me with shame.

"No, you aren't. You were protecting me!" I raised my voice, my eyes wide as I looked back at him with sympathy.

"I could've handled it differently. What did they do with his body?" he asked, his voice weak and full of guilt.

"I saw Cromwell carry it off somewhere—I think he brought it to the front gates. And I don't believe that you could've handled it any differently. Do you really think he would've stopped any other way?"

Paren thought for a moment. "I guess not. It still doesn't feel right."

"I don't think killing is *supposed* to feel right," I said, placing a hand on his back. "Have you had anything to eat since you disappeared?"

"No."

"Here," I said, moving to my room and digging under my blanket, retrieving a cup of chocolate pudding. "I was saving it for later, but you missed dinnertime, so I'm going to guess you need this more than I do."

I tossed him the pudding and he smiled sweetly.

"Thanks."

That night, I lay awake on my mat, unable to fall asleep. Hours had passed, but all I could do was toss and turn. When I was finally nearing sleep, I heard a familiar voice whisper my name.

"Eos! Wake up!"

"Is she still sleeping?" another voice asked in a raspy whisper.

"She's moving. Eos! Get up!"

I rolled over, rubbing my eyes as I tried to make out the dark, blurry figures.

"*Lamb? Zane?*"

"Hey, girl!" Lamb whispered excitedly. "We're here to bust you out!"

"How did you guys get here?" I asked in disbelief.

"Through the bars!" Lamb said.

There's no way you fit through those bars," I said credulously.

"If you time it just right when vehicles enter or exit, you can pass them, section by section," Zane clarified.

"And no one caught you?"

"It's nighttime, even the mouth of the cavern is dark right now. We're wearing all black—they didn't see a thing!"

"If we're going to leave, we have to leave *now*," Zane urged. "There's a truck dropping off weekly rations, and they'll probably be leaving soon."

Lamb tugged on my arm, trying to help me to my feet.

"Guys, wait, stop," I said. "I can't."

"What do you mean you 'can't'?" Zane asked.

"I mean I can't leave right now. I might have a way to get the Belli—" I started, biting my tongue.

"It's okay, E, she knows about the Key."

"I might have a way to get the Bellicose key," I finished.

"How?" he asked.

"Cromwell, the representative here. He said he has it—"

"You *told* him about it?" Zane interrupted, trying not to yell.

"No! I sorta' told someone else though—a friend of mine. And Cromwell overheard. But he says he knows where it is, but he won't give it to me—"

"Why not? What use does he have for it?"

"Zane, please. Stop interrupting," Lamb said daintily. "Go ahead, E."

I paused for a moment, eyeing Zane.

"Anyways, he won't give it to me unless I beat him in a fight. No knives—a clean fight."

"You're joking, right?" Zane stifled a laugh.

I stared at him blankly.

"Aw, crap, you're not joking. Look, why don't you just steal the key from the stupid brute and we can move on?"

"It isn't that simple," I said. "He's always in his room. I never see him outside his room unless he's calling me over to talk to him. I'm not about to try stealing from someone like him."

"So, you're going to fight him?"

"I don't really have another choice. But I have no idea how to fight."

"Easy!" Lamb chirped, a bit too excitedly as the sound of her voice echoed sharply. She cupped her hands over her mouth. "*Sorry!*" she whispered.

"How is it easy?" I asked.

"I didn't mean fighting is easy, but I mean all we have

to do is help prepare you! We can train you. We can stay here and just leave when another shipment of rations comes."

"How do you expect to stay here and not get caught?"

"We could just hide away in one of the darker parts, near the entrance of the cavern. We have a little bit of food left—it'll suffice," Zane answered.

"I could share some of my rations with you guys. I'll save what I can manage. But what if someone sees you?"

"We'll cross that bridge when and if we come to it."

"Eos?" I heard Paren call out sleepily. "Eos, are you okay?"

"Yeah, I'm fine. Go back to sleep," I said hurriedly, not wanting him to see my visitors.

Too late.

Paren grabbed Zane's shirt from behind, pulling him away from me and pushing him up against a wall by his shoulders.

"Woah, hey, *watch it!*" Zane snarled.

"Who are you?" Paren demanded.

"I'm a friend of Eos's," he answered calmly.

Someone across from us began shiftily turning in his sleep and groaning from the disturbance.

"Why are you here?" Paren asked in a hushed hiss.

"I'm here to help Eos out."

Paren looked over his shoulder at me.

"That's Zane," I said. "This is Leanne."

"You can call me Lamb." She turned her lips up in a forced smile.

Paren released Zane, who was now rubbing his shoulders bitterly.

"How did they—" he started.

I filled him in. After a little convincing, Paren agreed to help keep Zane and Lamb hidden from the rest of Bellicose. However, he didn't seem so keen on the idea of me training to fight Cromwell.

"You don't stand a chance," he protested.

"Way to have faith in me," I sneered.

He gave me an unamused look.

"Fine! I don't stand a chance *now*," I emphasized. "But you can train me. All three of you."

"Those two are *thieves*, what do they know about fighting?" Paren spat.

"Hey, don't forget I'm a thief too, and I may not be great at fighting, but I can defend myself well enough."

"We just have to train you to go on the offensive, and not just the defensive," Lamb suggested.

"Those two are thieves—they won't be any good about teaching you how to fight!" Paren insisted.

"They're my *friends*—stop referring to them as 'thieves'," I growled through gritted teeth.

"They *are* thieves—" Paren retorted, flinging little droplets of spit as he spoke.

"So am I," I replied quickly, clenching my fists at my sides. "What are you not understanding?"

"Fine. But let me help."

"Of course—"

"But—" Zane cut in.

"I could use all the help I can get," I said, glaring at Zane.

"I have somewhere we can go," Paren said. "No one really knows about it. Just a separate room in the caverns."

"That'd be perfect," Lamb said.

"Grab a couple lanterns and follow me," Paren said, swiftly making his way toward the common area.

There was no one in the common room except one of the few women in Bellicose. Her face was covered in skin tags and scars, with patches of missing hair on her scalp. She sat slumped over in a chair, unconscious and snoring.

"Quickly," Paren said as we hurried our paces to keep up.

He darted under the low ceiling of the other entrance into the common room and out into the dark part of the cave. Holding his lantern steady ahead of him, he danced gracefully over jutting rocks as if this was a rehearsed routine. As for Lamb, Zane, and myself, we stumbled clumsily, occasionally tripping over loose rocks. Paren took a sharp left, and a couple of turns later, we found ourselves in a room with a high ceiling like the common area, but without the hanging bulbs. There were a couple tables, but these were significantly more rotted than any of the others in Bellicose. We set all of the lanterns down on tables, illuminating the space.

"This is *perfect*," Lamb squeaked, clapping. "We can

start right away! The sooner you're ready, E, the sooner we can get out."

"Speaking of getting out," I started. "I know how you guys got in here in the first place, but how did you know I was here?"

Zane smiled, reaching into a burlap backpack and pulling out my dagger.

"Oh my gosh, Zane! Where did you find it?"

"It's a long story."

"I wanna' hear it."

"Alright," Zane laughed, looking at Lamb and Paren for objections. When he realized they had none, he proceeded.

"So, at Delaisse, Tanner told me that he had already talked to you and told you I went home. He didn't know where we were from, and I assumed you didn't tell him. At first, I was skeptical that you would just go back to Avid, but I knew you weren't going back to your city. I decided to look for you around Delaisse when I got away from Tanner. He wasn't too eager to let me go, but I escaped and then I searched—with no luck… Though I did find the Delaisse key—it was in the sewers where we were, in a little spray-painted box. I found a bunch of other things in the box with the key. Apparently, the people of Delaisse didn't care what the key could be for, they just thought the box was a good place to hide drugs." Zane chuckled. "Eventually, I figured maybe you really did go back to Avid, so I began the trek back. When I got there, I had to wait by the gate carefully for a couple of days before a truck finally came with rations. I snuck into Avid by jogging alongside the truck as it came through the gate. Back in Avid, I searched your room and I knew you hadn't been there, so I asked Lamb about it. She said she hadn't seen you, but I had to explain to her why the two of us had been missing so long."

"That's when we decided to pack up some supplies and head out in search of you," Lamb added. "He thought maybe you went to a different exile town to look for another key. When it was dark that night, we went to the dump to look for things that might be useful to bring. We didn't find a whole lot—these bags Zane and I have now, some rope... random stuff like that. But then, there was something shiny that caught my eye, so I picked it up, and it was this blade, but it was covered in dried blood."

"Why would they send my dagger off to an exile town?" I asked.

"I don't know if they meant to—they just combine garbage from the cities and some gets sent to Avid. If they have a big load of garbage, they bring it somewhere else because Avid can't fit all of it. I don't think they really cared about the dagger itself—they just needed to confiscate it from you," Lamb answered.

"She showed me the dagger and I told her I gave it to you. The only reason I could think of that it could end up there is either if you went all the way to Avid just to throw it away—which didn't seem logical—or you had gotten caught with it and had it confiscated. The dried blood is what led me to believe you got caught doing something a bit... messy. I had a hard time believing it, but nonetheless, I thought that maybe you were here, so we decided to make this our first guess. A couple days later of hiding in Lamb's room, a truck came one night to Avid to deliver rations. Just as it was about to leave, we threw ourselves into the back and hitched a ride. They stopped at Delaisse before Bellicose, so we just hopped out and hid until they were done, then we continued until we got here," Zane said. "And you know the rest."

Zane held the dagger's hilt out for me.

"I cleaned it for you," he said.

"Thanks," I smiled, turning it over in my hands, admiring the way the lantern light made it glimmer.

"You ready to fight, darling?" Paren smiled, teasingly putting up his fists and bouncing in place.

"*Darling'?*" Zane snickered in a whisper to Lamb.

Lamb elbowed Zane in the side without her pleasant expression changing or ever even looking at him. Zane hunched over and grabbed at his side, glaring at Lamb. She looked down at him, crouched over to eye-level, and shrugged with a full smile.

"Yeah," I said. "I'm ready."

"I want you to fight me. Pretend I'm Cromwell. I won't actually hurt you, but you just do you. I'm just going to try to block."

"Alright."

I awkwardly stuck my fists up. I crept closer to Paren slowly and threw my left fist weakly toward his chest. Without even trying to block me, he put his hands down and just looked down at his chest.

"What was *that*?" he asked.

"A punch," I answered plainly.

"Is that what you call it?" His laugh echoed in the room.

"I'm right-handed, but my wrist is still hurt," I said,

pointing out my splint. "You should know—you put the splint on."

"Give it," he said, holding his hands out.

I looked at him confused.

"Just give me your wrist. I want to look at it."

He looked it over for a few moments, gently pressing on a few points on my skin.

"It isn't broken," he said surely.

"How do you know?" I asked.

"Look," he said, turning my wrist over. "It isn't swollen or anything anymore. It isn't even bruised. Has it even hurt in a while?"

"Not for a few days, really, but I've been worried to take the splint off."

"You're fine. It'll probably be a bit stiff, and I think it *is* a good idea to avoid punching with it, at least for now. You know what? Let's focus on other things besides punching right now," he said, chucking my splint to the floor.

"Like what?" I asked, rolling my freed wrist around and wiggling my fingers.

"You're significantly smaller than Cromwell—"

"No, you don't say?" I rolled my eyes. Zane laughed.

"You just have to use it to your advantage," Paren said, ignoring my snarky comment.

"How?"

"When he goes to punch you, since you're shorter, it'll be easier to reach his abdomen—his arm will be up and he will leave it unprotected. That's when you jab him with your best hit. We don't have to practice hitting with any force today. Just use your good arm and pretend to punch me. Practice your timing."

Paren put his fists back up, readying himself in a fight stance. He eyed me seriously for a moment, and without blinking, shot his fist toward my face. I ducked reflexively, my heart racing and my eyes wide.

"I wasn't *actually* going to punch you!" he hollered in incredulity. "I can't believe you don't trust me at this point!"

"It certainly *looked* like you were going to! Your fist was going straight for my nose!" I protested.

Paren sighed.

Try it again."

Again, I failed to react the way he hoped.

"Again!" he barked.

We kept trying until I successfully tapped the bottom of his ribcage with a careful fist.

"Again!"

"But I did it!"

"Do it again."

We continued drilling this move until my shoulders burned so much I couldn't continue.

"We'll work on another skill tomorrow," Paren said.

"I can teach you something tomorrow!" Lamb offered.

"Sounds like a plan," Paren smiled. "We can take

turns with who teaches Eos what. I'm going to head back—it's probably close to breakfast time. I'll save a little of my food for you guys, too."

Paren made his way out, and just as I was about to follow, Zane yanked me back.

"What?" I asked, startled.

"Why did you tell him about the Skeleton Key?" Zane hissed.

"You told Lamb! How is that any different?"

"I couldn't just come back after being missing without an explanation—she's my friend. I had to tell her why I was gone, why you were gone, and why we can't stay there."

"Paren is my friend, too!"

"How long did you wait until you told him?"

"Not—not very. But that's beside the point! You have no *idea* what I've been through since you disappeared!"

"Don't get all defensive. I'm not mad at you—I'm just not sure we can trust this guy. He's in Bellicose—he's a murderer."

"No, he isn't! He's never—" I stopped myself, thinking of Mikael.

Zane cocked an eyebrow at me.

"I mean... that isn't why he's here. They aren't all murderers. He was defending someone. Paren is a good guy. You can trust him."

"He isn't coming with us," Zane warned.

"He hasn't expressed any interest in doing so," I said snippily.

"Well, he's certainly hanging around you an awful lot, isn't he? If nothing else, he seems to be really into you."

"Are you *jealous*?" I squinted in disbelief at Zane, turning to Lamb to back me up, but she just shrugged.

"No! I just don't trust him!"

"Why not? He's been nothing but helpful this whole time! We'd be better off if he *did* come along!"

"He may not be a huge guy, but he's bigger than me, and definitely bigger than you and Lamb. If we are out there searching for the Key, and he decides to take the exile town keys just before we get the Skeleton Key, or if we get the Skeleton Key and he takes *that*—there's no way we could get it back!"

"Paren isn't going to *take* anything! He's not a thief— that kind of stuff doesn't interest him anyways. The only reason he would want to leave with us is to be free from this place."

"I just don't trust him."

"*You* don't have to," I said, storming off after Paren.

CHAPTER TWENTY

The week was spent sneaking portions of Paren's rations and mine to Lamb and Zane, training in Paren's secret room, and discussing tactics with him in the common room. As initially planned, my friends took turns leading the training. Paren focused on teaching me how use my size to my advantage, Zane had me practice methods of speedy attacks, and Lamb taught me how to dodge and defend.

"Not quite," Lamb said, as I moved sideways to avoid one of her punches. "See, if he tries to punch you this way, and you move to the side, he can throw his other fist at you and you might not be able to react as fast to the second one. If you duck and then use the techniques Paren taught you, you can dodge the punch and get a hit in all in one motion! Here, go like you're going to punch me and I'll show you."

I drew my fist back and flung it toward her as she dropped to an almost squat, throwing a punch that stopped only a hair short of my stomach.

"Is my input allowed on a day that's not my turn to train her?" Paren asked with a dimpled smile.

"Of course!" Lamb chirped, moving over to give her place up to Paren.

"No—no stay there, I'm going to show you," he said, stepping behind her.

Paren put a palm just below her ribcage, looking at me as he spoke.

"Right there is where you'd want to punch. It's a weaker spot and you're more likely to knock the breath out of Cromwell if you position it right."

Lamb's pale face burned a bright crimson as she nervously smiled at Paren, his hand still resting at the bottom of her ribcage.

He stepped in front of Lamb and nodded as if signaling her to continue her lesson.

"Are you okay, Lamb?" he asked, seeing her red face.

"Yeah!" she sputtered a bit too quickly. "I just— yeah!" She smiled, her eyes shifting from Paren to me with a twinge of panic.

Paren stared at her with concern for a moment before taking up his place next to Zane along the wall again. He nodded his head for us to commence.

When training was done for the afternoon, Paren and I made our way to the common area for lunch. Cromwell stood by his open door, staring me down. He motioned subtly for me to come to him.

"Uh," I mumbled to Paren. "I'll—I'll be back in a few minutes. Go ahead and get your food; I'll join you in a minute."

"Everything okay?" he asked, an inquisitive look on his face.

I didn't answer. Instead, I jogged off to Cromwell, slipping into the room and disappearing behind the door.

"Have you given any more thought to my offer?" Cromwell asked, as if doing business.

"I have. I'm going to do it. I'm just trying to get ready."

"Do you think you have a chance?" he laughed.

"Uhm… Not particularly, if I'm being quite honest."

His chuckle echoed in the small cave room.

"Why do you even want me to fight you?" I asked. "Especially if I don't have a chance?"

"I know you've been training. I know who you've been training with—"

"Wait, what?" I interrupted. "What do you mean?"

"I know you've been training with Paren and those two who thought they were clever for sneaking in here about a week ago."

"How do you know?" I asked, dumbfounded.

"Paren isn't the only one who uses that little room your friends are staying in. I saw your friends in there the other day. They were sleeping, so they had no idea I saw them."

"Why do you need that room? You have your own bedroom."

"Next time you are in that room, take a closer look at the walls," Cromwell advised plainly. "Anyways, I know you've been training."

"I'm sorry—I just needed some help preparing,

otherwise I may as well not even try to fight. This is the only way I remotely stand a chance."

"I'm not angry—this is what I wanted you to do—albeit I didn't anticipate people coming to Bellicose to help, but I have no intentions on reporting them. I wanted you to train; I wanted you to dedicate yourself to this. You are."

"Why are you letting them stay? Why aren't you reporting them?"

"Do you *want* me to report them?"

"No! That's not what I meant. I just meant, like… why are you being nice?"

This comment elicited an even more booming chuckle from Cromwell.

"You have an interesting definition of 'nice'. I'm not reporting your little team because, like I said, I see potential in you, and it'd be a waste to not let you develop it. Plus, if you plan on going in search of that key, you'll probably need to know some skills. How do you plan on going through the city to get the Skeleton Key, once you have the exile keys? Do you plan on going through, sprinkling flowers and sunshine as you walk? If that's what you think, you have another thing coming. *Why do I want you to succeed?* Go ahead, ask. I know that's what you want to ask next! The reason I want you to succeed is because I'm sick of this system. I didn't kill people for fun, and I wasn't some mass murderer or serial killer. Yes, I killed a couple people. It wasn't my goal, I didn't enjoy it, and I don't plan to do it again. For the situation I was in, if this were before the war, I would have been sentenced to jail for some years and then I would be released. Because of this system, I'm stuck in here until I rot. For once, I'd like to see someone defy the city officials—even if it's just some thief finding some hidden key they're hanging onto and using it to have some personal freedom. It's the closest we can get to spitting in their faces, and I *love* it."

"Then why don't you just *give* me the Bellicose key?" I asked impatiently.

"Because, like I said, you aren't ready to go into the city. If you screw this up, it just gives the city more of a reason to keep us trapped in these towns. They'll destroy you if you even make it that far. I don't want you to give them the satisfaction."

"But I have a knife—I can use it against them, but you won't give me the key unless I beat you in a fight without a knife."

"You're surprisingly good with a knife, from what I've seen, at least. You don't need work on that, but you might not always have a weapon available. I don't expect you to knock me out or anything—I'll determine if you've 'won' based on whether I think you can properly fight. I'm a far bigger opponent than you'll likely come across in the cities anyways. Show me you can fight and can protect yourself, and I'll give you the key."

"Fair enough," I said.

"How about tomorrow?" Cromwell asked. "You can give it a shot if you think you're ready."

I looked at him in disbelief and shock as I let out a forced laugh.

"You don't think you're ready?" he taunted.

"No!"

"What have you got to lose? If you don't succeed tomorrow, it isn't like I'm not going to give you another chance whenever you want. You already know I want you to succeed."

I stood there for a moment, simply contemplating the idea of trying to fight Cromwell tomorrow.

"So?" he pushed.

"Alright," I said. "Alright. Tomorrow before lunch."

I left Cromwell's room and rejoined Paren, grabbing a plate of rice and beans with chunks of mystery meat. I sat across from Paren at a table with just the two of us.

"It must be time to get a shipment of rations," I said, poking at the mystery meat with my fork.

"No kidding," Paren smiled. "Usually you can at least *guess* what kind of meat it is in our food. So, I have to ask... what did Cromwell want?"

"He just wanted to see if I was almost ready to fight or not."

"You told him no, right?" Paren asked casually, munching on his rice.

"Not exactly," I sighed.

"What do you mean?"

"We're fighting tomorrow morning."

"What?" Paren's jaw dropped as he stared in disbelief at me.

"He wants me to succeed, Paren. He thinks it'll be some big insult to the cities if I manage to get the Skeleton Key."

"Then why doesn't he just give you the key so you can move on?"

"I asked him that same question. He thinks I'm not prepared to go into the city, and he wants to be sure I am."

"That makes sense," Paren thought for a moment. "So, how are you supposed to 'win' the fight?"

"I don't know. He just said he will tell me if I win based on whether he feels I am ready to leave or not," I said. I summarized the rest of what Cromwell told me, and Paren seemed at ease.

"So, he's probably going to go pretty easy on you, if he thinks he would be harder than any opponent you would have in the cities. We will just do a review of all of the things we've practiced, and then just get some sleep tonight," Paren advised.

That night, sleep didn't happen. I spent the entire night, tossing and turning on my mat. *What do I do after Cromwell gives me the key, even if I win? Do I invite Paren? Do I leave Paren here? No matter what, Equivox is our next stop—I need my stuff back. After that, we need to get the key from Renée and Eloise. Then what? Clamorite? What will that be like? And what about after that? What city is the Skeleton Key even in?*

The questions didn't stop flooding my mind, even after Paren crouched by my side the next morning to get me up.

"Mornin', darling," he said softly. "How'd you sleep?"

"I didn't," I replied bitterly, sitting up.

"You can do this, Eos," he said, putting his arms around me and hugging me close.

He's hugging me—what do I do?

"Is this your way of saying goodbye?" I joked

awkwardly. "You think he's going to kill me, don't you? Thought you'd hug me goodbye?"

"No!" he retorted with a sweet smile as he released me. "I was just trying to be encouraging!"

"Kay?" I eyed him as though I found him suspicious. "Thanks?" I laughed.

"Let's get a quick breakfast in you before it's time."

When we entered the common area, I could see plates of stale muffins on a table.

"They restocked the rations last night?" I asked.

"Must have."

Even if I win this fight, I'll be stuck here for another week until the next shipment.

I sighed as I grabbed what looked like a cranberry muffin and I dropped back into a seat with a sleepy moan. The door to Cromwell's room swung open as he lumbered out. He made his way toward Paren and me.

"I don't want to make a public spectacle of this," he said just above a whisper. "I don't need people badgering me about 'why' and all that. Let's meet in that room you've been training in. One hour."

I nodded.

Cromwell picked up a muffin and locked himself away in his room again. I sighed dramatically, dropping my face into my arms on the table's surface.

"What am I going to do?" I asked in a muffled whine.

"You got this! He doesn't expect you to beat him bloody or anything. Just prove to him you can fight and defend yourself—piece of cake! You can do this," Paren encouraged me.

"I hope you're right," I grumbled, peeking up at him from under my arms.

We spent the next hour merely sitting and talking, as Paren tried to calm my nerves and boost my confidence without much luck. *I'm hopeless without a weapon. I'm not even that great* with *a weapon.* When the hour was about up, Paren and I snuck out to the hidden room. Zane and Lamb were anxiously conversing about plans for leaving Bellicose. Paren and I informed them of the fight that was about to happen, and Zane and Lamb both hopped to their feet and hurried toward me.

"Are you sure she's ready?" Lamb asked nervously.

"I think she is," Zane answered quickly. "She's fast, and she's gotten a lot better at dodging punches. She might not have a lot of strength, but I think she has a chance."

"I agree," Paren added.

Lamb hugged me as I stood there, awkwardly stiff.

"Why do I feel like you guys think I'm going to die today or something?" I said shakily.

No response. Zane and Lamb stood, staring with horrified expressions at the entrance to the room. There stood Cromwell, his muscles covered in bulging veins as he hulked over.

"Ready?" he asked, as if asking me if I was ready to go on a leisurely stroll.

"Ready as I'll ever be," I answered flatly.

"They can't interfere," he added.

"I know. They won't," upon my words, my friends all

backed up to a wall, standing apprehensively in wait.

"No weapons, either—I know we already discussed this," he said.

I took off my coat, tossing it to Zane. I reached into the pockets of my pants and turned them outwards, showing that they were empty.

"I'll countdown to start, and I will let you know if I think you fight well enough to stop. I will say when we're done."

I nodded.

"3," he started.

I saw Lamb reach for both Paren and Zane's hands.

"2."

She bit her lip.

"1," he said, his fist sailing toward my eyes.

"Duck!" Lamb squeaked.

I ducked, cutting it so close that I could feel the rush of air from his punch above my head. Remembering what my friends had taught me, as I ducked, I threw my fist right below Cromwell's ribcage. The muscles in his abdomen took me by surprise, as there was no give when I punched.

He reached down for me, but I scampered to the side on all fours. While still on the ground, I swung my leg toward the back of his knee with all of my strength. Cromwell fell clumsily, catching himself promptly. Before he had a chance to push himself up again, I kicked again, this time aiming for his shoulder while his balance was off. This caught him by surprise as he toppled over on his side.

He rolled out of his fall, however, and got back into a powerful stance.

Cromwell grinned slyly as he did a deceptively graceful maneuver for such a bulky man, diving down and grabbing my legs from under me, forcing me on my back and knocking the breath out of me.

"*Get up!*" Paren growled at me from the wall.

Stunned for a moment, I tried to catch my breath. Cromwell hurried toward me and his fist sailed into my cheek with a searing pain. My vision flashed white for a moment as I fell, but as soon as it cleared, I scuttled like a crab across the ground to gain some distance between Cromwell and me as he stomped toward me. I pushed myself to my feet just as Cromwell began to tower over me, and in one swift motion I grabbed my right fist and slammed my right elbow into his nose. Sticky warmth began to cover my arm as I looked at a bloody Cromwell, clutching his disfigured nose.

"Oh my gosh, I'm so sorry! I know this wasn't an actual fight for my life but I—" I stammered.

Cromwell's laugh boomed in the small room.

I watched in both horror and confusion, glancing nervously at Lamb, Zane, and Paren, who all looked equally perplexed. He let his laugh dwindle to a chuckle before speaking.

"Eos…" Cromwell started, looking at me puzzled for a second.

"Dawn," I answered, curing his confusion.

"Eos Dawn," he said. "You win. That was quite impressive for someone as small as yourself."

"*What?*" I asked breathily, still processing what had happened.

"I don't mean that as an insult—" he began to coolly defend himself.

"No—no not that! I just meant—I'm just… I didn't figure I stood a chance."

"You proved to me that you can recover quickly, that you know weak points on even your stronger opponents, and that you can think fairly fast—that's more than I can say I expected."

"Eos! I can't believe you did it! You *actually* did it!" Lamb cheered, skipping toward me.

"You sound like you had so much faith in me," I joked.

"I mean, well, you know! Oh! Stop that!" She laughed and poked me.

"Here," Zane said to Cromwell, handing him a tattered cloth from his backpack.

"Thank you," Cromwell nodded, pressing the cloth to his dripping nose. "Eos, I'll give you the key, and Paren can load up on supplies from my room for your group. I want to give you the best chance possible at sticking it to the officials. Don't make this all a waste."

"I won't."

Cromwell led the way through the empty common room and to his room, ushering Paren and me inside. Paren was carrying Zane's backpack to fill with supplies, leaving Zane and Lamb in the other room so as not to draw attention to them. Cromwell lifted his mattress, revealing a small hole in the cave floor, in the middle of which was a small wooden box. He handed me the box.

"I believe this is what you're looking for."

I opened the box. Inside it was a simple, small iron key. I pocketed the key as Cromwell began digging through a crate.

"This should do. I can't give you too much, or people will suspect something," he said, shoving a few bandages, a tube of some kind of ointment, a couple full bottles of water, and a generous assortment of food inside the backpack and into mine and Paren's arms.

"I don't know what to say," I said, looking down at what felt like a bounty.

"Again—just... make them pay for this."

"I don't know if getting this key is going to really be revenge enough for the entire exile system..."

"It isn't. Not in itself. But if you cause enough chaos, word will spread. Eventually, it will hopefully reach the towns themselves. Do you really think a bunch of criminals are going to sit still if they hear that a few others escaped the system—*multiple times*— and infiltrated a city but still lived to tell the tale? Hah! They'll cause so much chaos of their own that the officials won't be able to control it. It has the potential to unite us against them, if you play your cards right."

"You really think it will do all of that?" I asked, letting out a quiet scoff.

"It can, but you have to be careful. That's why I wanted to make sure you were prepared. I want you to make it out of all of this alive—give us hope. Hope alone is enough to give us freedom, Eos. So many of us have lost everything—you might be our last chance at something more."

"I still don't understand how I can do all of that."

"Because no one else besides your little trio is stupid enough to actually attempt something so reckless, and I mean that in the best way." He laughed.

"Wait," I said, thinking for a moment. "Rations came in last night. There won't be another shipment for a week."

"Don't worry about that, just be ready by the gates in about fifteen minutes, and stay hidden," he smirked.

Confused but grateful, I thanked Cromwell again before Paren and I made our way back to Lamb and Zane. We filled Lamb's bag and our pockets with supplies until our arms were once again empty.

"So, how are we supposed to get out of here?" Zane asked.

"I'm not sure. Cromwell just said to be ready by the gate, and to stay hidden. I guess he knows something we don't, but at this point, I'm not really going to question him."

"Fair enough."

Zane, Lamb, and I began to make our way toward the gate, but then I noticed that Paren was standing stationary in the room.

"Paren, what are you doing? Come on! We have to hurry," I urged.

"I'm not coming with."

"What?"

"I'm not coming," he repeated.

"Why not?" I asked, my heart sinking. I had started to hope that he would.

"Darling, this isn't my mission. This is yours. Plus, I'm not a thief. I don't mean that in a negative way toward any of you—you've all proven to me that thieves aren't the scum that people say they are. I just mean that I'm not cut out for this, and I don't need a Skeleton Key. You're clever, Eos. You're clever, and you're strong, and you're fast, and you have a really good chance at succeeding. I don't want to mess that up. Plus, I'm not a part of this anyways."

"Yes, you are! You've *become* a part of this! We can't leave without you."

"You have to—I'm not going."

"Eos, I'm sorry, but we *have* to hurry!" Lamb pressed.

"Paren, *please*," I begged.

"I'm sorry, darling," he said, squeezing my hand and looking at me with apologetic eyes before he turned, walking toward the common room.

I bit my lip for a moment, blinking back tears. *I don't have time to stand here.* I took a deep, shaky breath, and rushed to the gate with Zane and Lamb, feeling the walls along the way as guidance.

When we made it to the gate, a city truck was already crossing the outermost layer of bars.

"*Get down,*" Zane hissed at Lamb and me.

We squatted in the shadows, pressed to the wall. As the truck began to cross over the innermost layer of bars, we crawled rapidly over the sunken metal and crouched in wait.

"What are they even here for? How long until they leave?" Zane whispered.

"I don't know," I said, just as Cromwell appeared in front of the truck.

"Where are the intruders?" the driver asked, stepping out of his vehicle in full body armor and a helmet, a few syringes and a couple sets of handcuffs in his hands.

Suddenly, my veins felt like ice.

Cromwell betrayed us.

CHAPTER TWENTY-ONE

I can't believe it. After all of the speeches about hope and "spitting in the faces of the officials" ... he reported us.

"This way!" Cromwell said, with a tone of sincere urgency in his voice as he beckoned the truck driver to follow him as he led the way toward the common area.

It's a cover, I realized. *He called an official here under false alarm to open the gates for us. He made it so an official himself would be the one to free us.* I smiled to myself.

In the middle of all of my thoughts, I lost track of Zane and Lamb.

"Get over here, E!" Zane hissed in a whisper from inside the truck.

"What are you doing in there? You're going to get us caught!"

"Not if you hurry up! Let's go!"

I rushed into the back seat of the truck, slamming the door behind me.

"Step on it!" Lamb commanded Zane. "I think he heard the truck doors! I hear him yelling!"

Zane turned the key in the ignition and the truck rumbled to life. Lamb screamed as the truck lurched forward.

"Sorry!" Zane said. "I don't know how to drive!"

Since cars aren't commonly used in the cities anymore, I don't know what I expected when Zane decided that driving was a good idea.

Suddenly, the truck was pulled backwards again. Lamb began to frantically push buttons all over the dashboard.

"I don't know how to make the bars lower!" she squeaked.

"Keep trying!" Zane yelled.

A moment later, Lamb must have hit the right button, and the middle set of bars began to lower, allowing Zane to back the truck up further. Just as we cleared the middle set, the official appeared, running toward the rising inner set of bars.

"Go, go, *go!*" I panicked, leaning forward between the front seats.

Zane continued backing up as the inner set reached the cave ceiling once more.

The official, who had narrowly missed his chance to catch the truck, was screaming something inaudible, banging on the bars of Bellicose as we cleared the middle and outer layers of bars. Zane switched the gear back, and we were moving forward again, but this time, he steered us away from the Bellicose caverns.

Zane rolled down the windows as we cruised along the compacted sand road, the caverns growing more and more miniscule behind us.

"This is amazing!" Lamb shouted over the air whipping through the vehicle.

"Do we have any idea where we're going?" I asked Zane.

"Uhh," he thought for a moment. "We're going to Equivox. Lamb, can you get your map out?"

"Mhm!" She rummaged through her bag, unfolding a map. She turned the map a few times, trying to get her bearings. "That way!" She pointed.

"Speaking of maps," I started. "My stuff is still at Equivox. My bag, my boots, the Skeleton Key papers…"

"We'll get it back," Zane said confidently.

I smiled half-heartedly, even though I knew he couldn't see it with his focus ahead of him. His knuckles were white as he death-gripped the pleather steering wheel. Lamb's face was still one of pure ecstasy, her eyes closed as her fuzzy, curly blonde hair blew wildly, occasionally flapping into her mouth, causing her to sputter to detach it from her lips.

"How long did it take you to get from Equivox to Bellicose, E?" Zane asked.

"I'm not really sure," I answered. "I mean, they got me with one of those tranq syringes back in Equivox, and I woke up in the truck. I have no recollection of even being put in the truck."

"Dang."

I scoffed.

We drove in silence for a while, watching the endless scape of sand, the shallow dunes appearing to undulate as we passed. I stared out the window, mesmerized, until Zane slammed on the breaks.

"What is it?" Lamb asked, her eyes opening with panic.

"I can't drive anymore. My hands are killing me! I don't know how the drivers do this!" He shook his hands loosely, a frustrated and confused look on his face.

"Can I?" Lamb offered excitedly.

"Be my guest."

The two stepped out of the truck and switched places. Lamb rubbed her hands together for a moment, looking down at the pedals eagerly.

"The right one is gas," Zane explained.

"Ah."

The truck blasted off from its position, zooming down the road significantly faster than when Zane had been behind the wheel.

"THIS IS AMAZING!" she shouted over the wind, laughing maniacally.

Zane held his arms stiff in front of him, his hands pressed against the dashboard. His face turned a sickly yellow-green. I reached in his bag, which had been tossed into the seat beside me, and pulled out one of the bottles of water, handing it to him.

"*Thank you,*" he mouthed, sipping on the water.

Lamb drove at the same ridiculous speed for about an hour before eventually braking, slamming violently on the brakes.

"Can we have something to eat? I'm starving," she proposed.

We left the engine running as we dug out some of the food from Zane and Lamb's bags and sat outside the truck in the warm sand eating. Zane and Lamb began conversing about things they would want to use the Skeleton Key for, when in the distance, I spotted a blurry figure.

"Guys," I said softly, trying to get their attention. When they kept talking over me, I said it a little louder.

"What?" Lamb asked, looking a little irritated that I had interrupted her.

I pointed at the figure.

"Oh! Um. Do you think they see us?" she asked, seemingly unworried.

"I'm not sure. It looks like they're coming toward us a little."

Sure enough, the figure was growing in size. Whoever it was, they were running directly for us.

"Get in the truck and get down! Roll up the windows. Lock the doors and keep yourselves covered," I commanded, rushing into the truck.

When we were all in the truck, squished down on the floor between the seats, I clicked the locks of each of the doors. All I could hear was our combined breathing, and all I could see was the dark floor of the truck.

A few minutes into the silence, Zane spoke up.

"How long are we going to stay like this?" he asked.

"Until we can be sure whoever that was is gone."

"But, if they saw us before, wouldn't they have seen us get into the truck?"

"Yes, but I couldn't make out anything about that person from that distance, so at least this way, they don't know who we are."

"But, isn't it suspicious to have an 'abandoned' truck just sitting here, even if they didn't notice us? Or wouldn't they suspect something if someone were to duck down in here?"

"Well, yes, but what were our other options? We don't know who they are! We don't know what they want!"

"Can we go back a little ways and hope they go a different direction before reaching us?" Lamb asked.

"Too risky," Zane answered. "They could see the plate number by now if we turn around, and they could report it—then everyone will be looking for this truck."

"They were coming from directly in front of the truck, meaning they are blocking the road in front of us. So we don't have anywhere to go," I said.

"Can we assume whoever it is, they probably aren't someone we would want to tangle with? Because if they are, then we can just keep driving in that direction! It's a scare tactic. They'll move out of the way eventually! Unless Lamb is driving, in which case they don't have time to move." Zane snickered.

"I mean, we can try that, but then we risk them seeing who we are."

"What difference does it make?"

"It'd be easier to spot us in the future, especially if they give our description to the cities. It'll be impossible to stay hidden when we go looking for the Key in the cities if everyone recognizes us! We may not blend in that well, but we could lose every chance of that if we le—"

"*OPEN THE DOOR!*" an angry female voice roared at us, accompanied by an aggressive thumping on one of the windows. "Don't play stupid! I know you're in there! I have a gun! Show yourself or I'll unload this freaking clip into the side of your truck!"

I turned to throw Zane and Lamb a panicked look, and Zane popped his head up from his hiding position, his hands out in surrender.

"Don't shoot!" he said hurriedly. "Don't shoot."

"You're not an official," the voice said in surprised observation. *It sounds like a girl about our age.*

"No, I'm not," he admitted calmly.

"How did you get this truck?" she lowered her voice.

"I…" Zane sighed. "I took it."

"You *took* it?" The voice let out a quick, high-pitched laugh.

"I didn't kill the official. He's fine. It's a long story. How'd you get the gun?"

"I took it. Long story."

"Fair enough."

"Who are you?" she asked with a calmed voice.

"Who wants to know?" Zane retorted smugly.

"My name is Skylar," she answered. "I'm from Delaisse."

"Zane. Avid."

Lamb poked up to see the source of the voice and smiled.

"Hi! I'm Leanne. You can call me Lamb! Eos," she called down to me on the floor. "I don't think she's going to cause us any trouble. You can come out now."

"What are you doing?" I hissed under my breath.

"She's like us, E."

I hesitantly eased myself upright, nodding in an unwilling greeting to Skylar. She was unnaturally pretty, with unblemished skin, sharp eyebrows, and a subtle cleft chin. Her chestnut hair was slightly bumped up on her head, with narrow braids like a crown from her temples. Her stance was comfortable, yet defensive as she held a handgun in her right hand toward the floor. The moment she made eye contact with me, she squinted, and her petite nose wrinkled as if she had smelled something foul. Her olive green, cat-like eyes flew from mine to Zane's, and her mood seemed to lighten again.

"Do you guys know where Fortitude is?" she asked.

"Where what is?" I interjected.

"Fortitude," she repeated, not breaking her eye contact with Zane.

"What's that?" Zane asked.

"It's a refuge. For exiles who manage to escape. There aren't many, but when they do escape, I heard they tend to head toward Fortitude. It's essentially like a city for those who want to escape exile towns but can't go back into the cities."

"Where did you hear about this?" Zane asked.

"My great-uncle. He's still in Delaisse. I guess he

knew people who made it there or something like that, and he told me about it. He didn't want to come with because he figured he was too old to make the trip, but he wasn't super specific about where to go. I thought I understood his directions, but apparently not."

"What were his directions like?" Zane urged her to continue.

"He said to head past Bellicose, toward the sea. He said I would see a purple light," she spread her arms out, motioning dramatically around her. "I don't see the sea, let alone a freaking *purple light!* I don't have a clue where I am anymore!"

"We've never heard of Fortitude, sorry. I wish I could help. We have a map though, so I could probably point you in the right direction," Zane offered.

"Hey, can I just hitch a ride with you guys? We can head there together! I mean, where were you guys going? I'm assuming you recently escaped?"

"Something like that," I mumbled.

"Where are you guys headed?"

"Uhh…" Zane struggled.

"We aren't headed in that direction," I answered for him.

Skylar sucked her teeth and rolled her eyes. "Doesn't answer my question."

"Here, I'll show you where you are on the map," Zane offered again, climbing into the front seat with Lamb's map, scanning it for an estimate on our coordinates.

Tap tap.

Skylar rapped her gun lightly on the window beside Zane.

"Better idea!" she said. "Leave the map in the truck and get out."

"How about no?" I said snarkily, drawing her attention from Zane.

"I'm not really giving you much of a choice," she threatened, pointing the gun toward me. "I've been out here for days, and I'm running low on supplies. I'm sick of wandering around in this crap-hole looking for something that I don't even know if it exists, let alone if—"

Her words were cut short as Zane slammed on the gas pedal, the truck kicking up sand behind it as we raced away. I looked in the rear window, seeing a fuming and very sandy Skylar screaming in rage.

"You're lucky she didn't shoot Eos, Zane!" Lamb shot Zane a dirty look. "She had her gun pointed right at her!"

"That's why I drove away!"

"But what if she would have reacted fast enough and shot Eos?"

"She wouldn't have been aiming at Eos at the rate we got out of there. The most she would have hit would have been the very back of the truck. Just a scratch."

Lamb looked at Zane with both disbelief and slight admiration.

"I sorta' feel bad for that girl. She's wandering around all by herself. What if she runs out of food or water and there's no one to help her?"

"Not our problem," I said plainly.

Lamb looked uneasy for a moment before we adjusted ourselves in the back seats. Suddenly, there was a dinging sound from the front seat.

"What was that?" Lamb asked, poking her head between the front seats.

"I think it's the gas."

Zane stopped the truck and cut the engine.

"Check the trunk, see if we have any extra gas," he asked us.

"There are a bunch of red jugs," Lamb answered, leaning to peer into the trunk.

"They probably have gas in them. I'll handle it," Zane said, stepping out of the truck.

He opened the trunk, pulling out some of the containers. After a few minutes of fumbling around outside, he began to pour the gas. When he was done, some of the jugs were empty and he threw them back into the trunk, causing them to make hollow rattling noises.

"It's getting late. Would anyone object to just calling it quits for today?" he asked.

Lamb and I shook our heads.

"So, how is the sleeping situation supposed to work?" Lamb asked uncomfortably. "There isn't a lot of room to lie down in here."

"Shouldn't someone take watch?" Zane asked.

"Yeah, good idea," she agreed.

"Well," I started. "Whoever takes watch can sprawl out a little in the back seats if they want—that way they have some leg room at least. The other two can probably fit in the trunk—it's a decent size, and we can crack the trunk door and all so it isn't too claustrophobic."

"Good idea. Who goes where though? I guess you and I can take the trunk?" Lamb proposed.

"Uhh, yeah. Yeah, sure, that works," I responded, noticing a soft look on Zane's face as his eyes met mine.

Lamb sat in silence for a moment, then furrowed her brow, her eyes bouncing between my face and Zane's.

"Ohhh!" she said. "I get it! Not a problem. I'll take first watch."

Lamb smirked, throwing me a subtle wink.

"No! Not like that!"

She laughed. "I'm just messing with you. Go ahead with your cuddle buddy and I'll just get nice and cozy with all my friends in the backseat."

Lamb sighed in a woe-is-me fashion as she smiled, stretching out in the backseat before I had a chance to move. She kicked her feet up leisurely on my lap.

"Ehem! Do you mind? I'm trying to get comfortable," she joked with a lighthearted laugh.

Zane stepped out and made his way around to the trunk.

"Thanks, Leanne. Zane and I will both take next watch so you can have the trunk to yourself to get comfortable," I whispered with a genuine smile, climbing over the backseat and flopping into the trunk.

Why am I thanking her? Why am I even so eager to be back here with him? I still don't know if I can even trust Zane. I mean, I trust him, as far as Skeleton Key stuff goes, but I don't know if I trust him as anything more than a friend. Doubts about Zane kept running through my mind as memories flashed back from my time in Avid, when he was involved in so many of the things that pushed me to leave in the first place. *But then again… he got my ring back from Luka, and even when he was involved in the things that happened to me, usually he wasn't the ringleader. I couldn't have gotten this far without him, and he's become a good friend since we left.*

Zane climbed into the trunk beside me. I reached to pull the door shut, but he threw his hand in front of mine.

"Don't," he said. "Leave it open."

"I'm sorry I don't have a blanket to give you," he apologized.

"It's okay. Mine is in my bag back in Equivox, so hopefully I will have it back soon enough."

"We'll get your stuff back, I promise," he said, lowering himself onto his back with an exhausted groan. He let out a sigh as he stretched on the floor of the trunk.

I lay down on my side, facing Zane.

"What are we going to do when we find the Skeleton Key?" I asked.

"I don't know. I mean, we can do anything we want—we just have to stick together."

"We can't go back to Avid, not permanently anyways."

"Why would you want to? I thought that was part of why we all left? So we never have to go back."

"We can't go back to the cities either. I mean, technically speaking we can, but we'd have to be careful, and there wouldn't be much use in it."

"Geez. Someone is negative. Fine then, dream-crusher, what would you like to do with it?"

"I'd like to use it to sneak into any of the cities whenever I needed for supplies or anything I want, and I'd like to find somewhere away from all of this to set up and call 'home.' I want to just rest for a while, and then I'll see what I want to do next. I've thought about using the Key to break people out of the exile towns, but they would have nowhere to go either."

"That doesn't sound too bad," he thought for a moment. "What about Fortitude? That place Skylar was talking about?"

"Zane," I said. "We don't even know if that place exists, or what to expect."

"Neither does Skylar, but she's trying anyways. I mean, why not? If we have the Key, we can always fall back on your plan of just settling somewhere if it doesn't work out with Fortitude."

"Okay, but why do you want to go there anyways?"

"Why not? I mean, it could be cool. A bunch of people who managed to evade the system and start their own little society. We could find it, mark it on our maps, and then go lead other exiles there. It would be worth a shot, if nothing else, just to see if it exists."

"I like that idea!" Lamb said, peeking her head over the tops of the seats and looking down at us. "We've already met some sweet people along the way, like your friend Paren! We could totally free people like that and bring them to Fortitude!"

I sighed in disagreement and Lamb lay back down.

"I just don't know what to expect if we find Fortitude," I said.

"If it exists, we will find it, and then it doesn't matter what you *expect*."

"Alright, fine. If we get the K—"

"*When*," Zane corrected.

"We don't even know what city it's in, Zane. We are going to do the best we can, but I'm just being realistic—"

"Fallmont."

"What?"

"It's in Fallmont."

"How do you know that?"

"I talked to Mr. Montgomery about the Key, and he told me the officials that arrested Galeno were from Fallmont. He said if he had to take a guess, that's where the Key is now."

"The Key is in Fallmont? We know where it is? Zane, this is incredible!" I started babbling excitedly. "We actually have a chance at this!"

"Yeah, the only problem is that Fallmont is the biggest of the cities, and the most heavily guarded."

"Who's being a pessimist now?" I teased, resting my head on Zane's chest. His heartbeat was quick, and he felt warm compared to the chill of the fresh air outside.

My attention drifted from the conversation and from Zane to the sky, which was now full of thin but fluffy magenta clouds against a crimson sky.

Zane let out a quiet, puffy sigh as he noticed the sunset as well, beginning to speak softly.

Eos

"If freedom means I get to see this every night, I'd be content with having nothing more in life."

CHAPTER TWENTY-TWO

We left early the next morning and arrived at the forest surrounding Equivox after only about an hour's drive.

"This is it!" I said, pointing to the thick trees.

"It's in the woods?" Lamb asked.

"Sorta'. You'll see—just follow me."

We left the truck and I led the way, following the creek until I found the wall of trees I had climbed before.

"The only way I know of through these is by climbing over them," I said, picking a tree. "But be careful because this is how I hurt my wrist."

"Wait, E, how about we go around them?" Lamb suggested.

"I already checked—I have no idea how far you'd have to walk to just *potentially* walk around them. From past these trees, I remember it didn't look like there was any other way. Plus—the papers are right under this tree, on the other side."

"I guess we better get moving then," Zane said,

squatting and cupping his hands near the ground. "Here, I'll give you girls a boost."

I put my foot in Zane's hands and he eased me up a few extra feet, helping me onto a branch. I moved along the other branches as Lamb joined me in the tree from the first branch, and Zane shortly after her. When I successfully made it to the other side of the tree, I began easing myself down, much more cautiously than my first time. I hugged the trunk of the tree when I neared the bottom. *If I'm careful, I can just jump from here—it's only a few feet to the ground if I hang from this branch.* I let go of the trunk, instead putting my arms around the branch below me.

I took a deep breath, lowering my body from the branch while still hanging onto it with my arms looped around. Splinters from the bark pricked my bare hands and wrists. I stared down at the ground, and then released my grip, dropping into the dirt, grass, and leaves below me. I almost landed on my feet this time, but lost my balance as my feet hit the ground, and I stumbled clumsily for a moment before flopping awkwardly into a sitting position. I heard laughter from the tree as Lamb and Zane looked down at me from the tree.

"Let's see you try!" I taunted, smirking at them as I moved out of the way, brushing myself off.

"Hmph!" Lamb huffed confidently as she mimicked my motions for getting down from the tree.

Flump.

Her landing was almost identical to mine, but she wasn't even close to landing sturdy on her feet. She fell backwards into the leaves giggling before she joined at my side.

"I'll show you ladies how it's done!" Zane said, puffing his chest out as he dropped from the branch.

When he landed, rather than falling backwards like Lamb and I did, he stumbled forwards, looking like a baby bird trying and failing to run and take off in flight as he flapped and tripped over his own feet, catching himself with his arms out in front of him.

"Points for display!" I called jokingly.

Zane grinned at me.

"So, where are the papers?" Lamb asked, having never read them herself.

"Under this tree," I said, tracing my fingers over a carved letter E in the bark. I dug at the dirt by the roots of the tree, revealing the papers, my money, and my family photo, covered in soil. The corner of my lip twitched upwards in a smile upon seeing the photo, which I quickly pulled from the dirt and wiped clean.

"What's that?" Lamb asked.

"Just… an old picture. It's mine and I didn't want it to get ruined, so I put it here."

"May I see it?" she asked innocently, holding out a hand.

"I guess," I said, hesitantly handing it over.

She smiled.

"Who's this?" She pointed to my dad carrying me.

"That's my dad. I was pretty little at the time. That's my grandpa," I pointed to the man in the photo eating a hamburger.

"This is a really sweet picture, E. Is this one of the five things you brought from home?"

"Yeah."

She smiled at me again before reaching for the Skeleton Key papers.

"So, these are what were in that wooden box from the dump? The one Luka found?"

"Yup. I took them because I was curious, but long story short, you can see where they took us."

"Huh," she said, her eyes eagerly scanning over the words and pictures of the Key. "This is… wow."

As she looked over the papers, Zane looked over the edge of the cliff, down at Equivox.

"Equivox?" he assumed.

I nodded.

"How do we get down?"

"Jump."

He pointed to the lake below us, raising his eyebrows at me.

I nodded again.

He ran his fingers through his hair, his cheeks puffing out in an exasperated sigh.

"Alright," he clapped his hands together. "What about the papers? And how do we get out?"

"I don't know, and I… don't know," I admitted.

"Well, they get their rations somehow," Zane noted. "And they bring in new exiles somehow. So, there's got to be another way in and out."

"I have an idea! We can put the papers back in the truck, and we can camp out near the road—maybe we will see how they bring rations in. We can just take watches, that way one of us is always awake," Lamb suggested.

"That could work," I said, looking to Zane for confirmation.

We made our way up a different tree with the papers and worked back toward the truck. When we got in the truck, we pulled it off the road just enough to shelter it in trees. I stood in the road to see if the truck was visible from there, and though it was, it was hard to spot in the thick of the trees, but we were still able to watch the road from it.

"This could take up to a week," I warned Lamb and Zane.

"We know. Bellicose just got their rations a couple days ago, so either it'll be very soon, or it'll be in a little less than a week. Or anytime in-between that. Your guess is as good as mine."

~

It was about two days later, in the dark of the night during Zane's watch, that the rations finally came.

"Guys," he called, shaking me awake in the backseat. "Guys! They're here!"

Lamb looked drowsy as she peeked from the trunk at us.

"What? Where?"

Zane pointed at a set of lights. Sure enough, there was a similar truck to ours, creeping slowly toward the edge of the road. Suddenly, it stopped, and I could see the lights sinking lower into the ground until they disappeared.

"What just happened?" I asked, scurrying into the front seat to get a better look.

"I can't tell. They were right there! I swear!"

"I know—I saw it too! But they just disappeared."

"Um," Lamb hummed. "I think they went underground."

"How?" Zane asked.

"Wait," I said. "She might be right. Think about it! There was a button to activate the bars at Bellicose, maybe there's some kind of secret door or something we can get to with the truck that will let us in there."

"That's a good point," Zane thought for a moment. "Let's wait until they leave and we know they are far enough away, then we can go to the edge of the road over there and just start trying buttons."

Sometime later, the lights of the truck rose out of the ground again. They backed up slowly, turning the vehicle around before driving off along the road again.

"Let's go," Lamb said.

"Not yet," Zane sat still behind the wheel. "We want to give them some time to get far enough away where they won't see the lights from our truck."

When he was convinced the officials were far away, he pulled the truck carefully from our hiding place and back onto the road. He slowly brought it to the edge of the road and stopped the truck. He looked over the buttons on a small control panel. He paused for a moment and picked a random blue button, pushing it in and holding it for a split second before releasing it.

Nothing.

"Try the orange one!" Lamb guessed, looking over at the buttons.

Nothing.

"What's your guess?" Zane asked me lightly.

"Uhh… I guess the yellow one. Not the one on the left—the one on the right."

Nothing.

"Psshh, I meant the one on the left," I joked.

He pushed the yellow button on the left, and there was a sudden rumbling from beneath the truck. Our eyes were wide as we watched ourselves sink into the ground slowly. Once below ground level, I could see a spiraling road ahead of us, with both sides lined with glowing white strips of light. The platform beneath us suddenly jolted and stopped. I looked at Zane.

"I guess we just keep moving," he said, driving onto the lit road slowly.

As he pulled off the platform, there was a grinding sound of machinery as the platform began to rise again. The ceiling was fairly low, and the walls were narrow. We drove along the road, spiraling down deeper into the ground. Just when I was beginning to wonder where the road might lead, we reached the end, revealing the interior of a building. The end of the spiral road led directly into an empty house, pressed against the edge of the cliff. Boxes full of rations sat pushed against a wall, and the rest of the house was barren. Zane eased the truck off of the end of the road and into the wide, open room. He took the keys to the truck as we all stepped out. I began to make my way toward the door when Zane spoke up.

"What are you doing?" he asked.

"Going to get my bag," I answered, confused as to why he was even asking.

"Aren't we going to make some kind of plan first?"

"Yeah—the first step is to get my bag back."

"But we don't have a meeting place—what if we get in trouble?"

"Back at the truck."

"Fine. What if one of us can't run to the truck and we get caught by someone—what do we do then?"

"Run anyways. Run and hide. If that isn't an option, fight."

"We can't just go fighting people, E. That's how you wind up back in Bellicose, or worse."

"What do you propose?"

"I don't know, but fighting isn't the answer to that!"

"Well, running and hiding will almost always be options unless you are being held against your will, in which case it is self-defense, if you ask me."

"Officials won't see it like that. You were lucky they didn't recognize you the last time you were here and send you off somewhere worse than Bellicose!"

I shrugged.

"Eos! You can't be reckless this time! Please just listen to me," he begged desperately.

"I *am* listening!" I whined.

"No, you aren't! You aren't hearing me. Don't fight—no matter what! I don't want them taking you."

"I won't fight."

"Promise me," he pleaded.

"No."

"Eos!"

"Fine. I *promise* not to fight," I said, defeated.

Zane nodded.

"Unless it's my only choice," I continued in a hushed voice.

Zane's eyes turned back to me wildly.

"I won't!"

"We need a plan. I know we are going to get your bag. We will go together and watch your back. After that?"

"After that, we need to somehow get the key from Renée and Eloise—they're the ones who stole it from me. I know where they live, so we can just lock pick the door and see if we can find it tonight, before the sun comes up. If not, we go at it again tomorrow, and take the truck back above ground until the next night. Once one of us finds the key, let the other two know, and then we will leave as fast as we can so no one spots us."

"Sounds like a plan."

"That *is* what you wanted?" I teased.

Zane smiled as he rolled his eyes.

I led the way from the storage house to the lake, clinging to walls, bushes, anything that could shield us even more from view than the night itself. Once the lake was within sight, I took off sprinting full speed toward the bush I hid my bag in.

It's still there.

I snatched up my bag, throwing my boots into it and situating the bag over my shoulder. I peeked down into it, rifling through my belongings out of curiosity until I could account for all of them. Nothing was missing.

I led the way toward Renée and Eloise's house from the lake. Once we reached the door, I described the two to Lamb and Zane, so they would know who to be extra careful of.

"I don't know if anyone new has moved into Equivox, so I don't know if it's still just those two, but even if it is, you have to be careful."

"You be careful too, E," Lamb said, putting a hand on my shoulder. "These two know you, and if they see you and word gets out to the officials that you're running around—everyone in the New Territory will be on watch—there'll be a pretty bounty out for Eos Dawn. Don't let them see you."

"I won't," I promised.

As we talked, Zane knelt down at the door, fumbling with the lock until we heard a faint *click*. He cautiously turned the knob, easing the door open silently. Then, he went in first, looked around briefly, and motioned us in. He closed the door softly behind us. Zane pointed at me, then himself, then the stairs. I nodded in understanding. He pointed next at Lamb and then the kitchen. She saluted with a smile, turning on her heel and making her way to the kitchen to search for the key.

Zane began walking up the stairs, placing his feet lightly on each step. I started to follow him, but he held up a hand behind him to signal for me to stop. Confused, I stopped and waited until he got to the top of the stairs. He looked left and right, and waved me to join him. At the top of the stairs, I saw that both the left and the right door were closed.

"Eloise," I mouthed to Zane, pointing to the door on the left.

Zane pointed to the door on the right, raising an eyebrow.

"Empty?" I shrugged.

Zane pointed to himself and then to Eloise's door, then he paired me to the other door.

I nodded subtly.

We both reached for our respective doorknobs at the same time, turning them little by little until we could get the doors open. I gave Zane a final look before peeking my head into the room on the right—the room I had stayed in. It was still vacant. I let out a quiet sigh of relief as I began searching. I peered under the bed, dug through the trunk at the foot of the bed, and even checked under the mattress. *The key isn't in this room*, I realized. *Why would it be? I guess it didn't hurt to check.*

Before I left the room, I heard a bloodcurdling shriek.

Eloise.

My body went numb as I cupped my hands over my mouth, panicking. *If I go try to help Zane, she'll see me and that'll be it. But if I don't help him, he'll get taken away instead.*

Unable to bear the thought of them locking Zane away who-knows-where, I tiptoed out of the room, poking my head out from behind the door only to see Zane clumsily thundering down the stairs as fast as he could. Eloise stood in her doorway, her eyes wide and afraid, her chest heaving. I pulled my head back into the room rapidly, but not fast enough. I could hear Eloise whimper as she tentatively pushed the door open with a finger. Her eyes met mine and I saw her take a deep breath.

"*MOM!*" she screeched.

What do I do? I patted my jacket pockets and felt the dagger. I just have to scare her and she will move away from the doorway. We have to make a run for it.

I pulled the dagger out of my jacket, flashing it menacingly at Eloise. Her eyes welled up immediately with tears as she wailed, trailing down the stairs as fast as her legs could move. Keeping the dagger in hand, I rushed downstairs after Eloise to look for Zane. In the kitchen I could see Zane on his knees, his hands empty in the air in surrender. His legs were bound in a thin rope around the ankles to prevent him from running. Across the kitchen was Renée, Eloise cowering behind her, peeking out from behind her mother. Renée had her fingers laced in Lamb's hair, keeping her head pulled backward against her. In her other hand was a simple kitchen knife, held against Lamb's throat.

"*Please,*" Zane begged. "Don't hurt her. I'll take her place—just please don't hurt her."

"I think you've given up every right to ask me for *favors* after you not only broke into my house, but terrorized my daughter!" Renée fumed.

"I know! I know and I'm sorry! It's just, you have something of ours, and we just wanted to get it back. That's it—I promise! We didn't mean to cause any trouble!" Zane said desperately.

Just then, Renée caught sight of me at the bottom of the stairs.

"I should have known it was you!" she howled at me.

"I should slit your friend's throat just like you killed that official! Give me one good reason why I shouldn't!"

"Because she didn't do anything to you. If anyone is guilty of anything, it's me," I said, fiddling with my dagger.

"I see you got your knife back," she said with a frown. I smirked at her.

"Take me instead," I offered.

She laughed. "I'm not that stupid."

"What do you mean?"

She nodded her head down toward my dagger.

"Oh this?" I said casually, setting it on a table.

"Eos, what are you doing?" Lamb whimpered.

"Eos? I thought your name was Elle?" Eloise asked innocently from her hiding place.

"I lied," I admitted. "But you should be used to it here."

Renée groaned and rolled her eyes.

"So, like I was saying. Take me. You've got more against me than her—she's not here of her own accord. I didn't give her a choice. It wouldn't be right to hurt her. Me?" I snuffed. "That would make more sense."

"Again, I'm not that stupid. Clearly you are though, for thinking I'd just let her go." Her tone changed as she began speaking to her daughter. "Eloise? Honey? Go tell Mr. Nolan to call the officials. Please hurry, Elly!"

Eloise scampered across the room and out the front door.

"What's the key for?" Renée asked.

"*I'm not that stupid,*" I said, mocking her words. "I'm not telling you. Not like you'd have much use for it anyways."

"Tell me what it's for!" she commanded, tugging back on Lamb's hair, forcing her to squeak in pain.

"It's a long story," I started, creeping forward almost unnoticeably toward Lamb and Renée. "We need that key, and one from somewhere else. We collect these keys. They're to unlock a special box with something in it for us."

"Just shut up with the stalling and tell me what the key is for."

"The box is like a huge treasure chest, in a way. It has money, jewelry, diamonds… Rumor has it that the box contains a very valuable and very old classic painting that was saved from the war."

"Why would you want useless stuff like that when you're an exile? There's nothing you can do with it. You're lying."

"No. We may know some people… Those things can be worth more than the average share of rations. We could feast daily. I think I'd fancy keeping the painting for my room, though. Adds a bit of class, wouldn't you agree?" At this point, I was within arm's reach of Lamb.

"I'd have to be careful though, other people might want to take—" I stopped speaking as I spontaneously threw a punch at Renée's nose.

She ducked reflexively, releasing her grasp on Lamb, and my hit missed. Lamb stumbled over to Zane, trying to help him to his feet, forgetting the rope around his ankles. I grabbed Renée's wrist, trying to wrestle the knife out of her hand. She was pushing with all of her strength against me, and the knife began to move toward my waist. I kept turning her wrist back on itself, but she was stronger. In the struggle, her knife grazed my side, slicing open my shirt and leaving behind a clean cut. I yelped, grabbing at my bleeding side with both hands. I saw Renée, lunging toward me with her knife again. I saw Lamb dart in front of her. I saw the look of terror on Lamb's face. I also saw the knife sink into Lamb's stomach.

CHAPTER TWENTY-THREE

"No!" Zane shouted, writhing against the floor as he tried to break free of the rope around his ankles. "No, no, no, no, no!"

I gaped in shock at Lamb, crumpled over on the floor. Glaring back up at Renée, who was also in apparent shock as she held her bloody kitchen knife, I pounced forward, clawing at her. I felt her nose crunch as I punched it in the middle of my furious flurry of attacks. She gasped, blood trickling down her face. She dropped the knife and immediately clutched at the blood flow, and I took the knife. I broke the ropes binding Zane, and without hesitation, he stumbled to Lamb in a panicked run. His eyes were full of tears, his face void of any color, and his hands visibly shaking.

"I got you," he whispered to Lamb, who was breathing laboriously on the ground. He scooped her up gently in his arms and hurried to the door, his steps careful. "Eos! Let's go!"

I dropped the kitchen knife, grabbed my dagger, and rushed out of the house. A couple of armed officials appeared from around a nearby house, so Zane and I crouched down behind a bush along the side of Renée's home. I looked over at Lamb in Zane's arms. She was in obvious pain but held her silence in the moment.

"On the floor!" one of the officials yelled, bursting in through the front door with a loud crash.

"No! You don't understand! People broke into my house! They were trying to steal from me, and they threatened my daughter! This was self-defense!" Renée plead honestly.

"You're covered in blood that clearly isn't your own, it looks like there was an altercation, and there's a kitchen knife on the floor. Your daughter isn't here and is scared speechless. Get on your knees!" I could hear the other officer demand.

"I didn't do anything! It's a misunderst—" her voice cut out. *They must have used a tranq shot.*

We waited in the bushes for another few minutes as the two officials walked out of the house, one of them carrying Renée, handcuffed and unconscious in their arms as they groaned about Equivoxes always trying to lie to get out of situations.

When we were sure the officials were gone, we almost stood to our feet, but stopped short when we heard the timid voice of Eloise as she approached the front door of her home.

"Mom? *Mom?* Mom, where are you?" her voice cracked, and she began to sniffle.

I motioned to Zane for him to stay put as I emerged from the bush. I entered the house and saw Eloise, crumpled up in a ball on the floor. Her face buried in her hands, she was sobbing uncontrollably.

"Eloise?" I called softly.

She scurried into a stand, her eyes red, teary, and full of terror.

"Please don't hurt me!" she begged.

"I won't. I promise! I just wanted to make sure you were okay."

"You killed my mom!" she accused, letting out a horrific wail before bursting into tears again.

"Eloise!" I said, trying to get her attention again. "I didn't kill your mom! She's alive and she isn't hurt or anything."

"But… there's blood over there. And a knife!"

"There was an accident, and my friend got very badly hurt. Your mom is okay though."

"But… But where is she?"

"The officials came, and they saw your mom covered in my friend's blood. I think they took her somewhere— probably just to ask her some questions and help clean her up!" I lied, seeing the panic in her wide eyes.

"When will they bring her back?" she asked.

"I'm not sure. It might take a while, but only because her shirt was stained really bad and they probably will have to work really hard to clean it is all."

"Where did they take her?"

"Probably back to one of the cities. They have special rooms for things like this. It's a long, long trip, but she will come back! You just have to be super patient. You have to be brave and take care of yourself while she's gone though."

"Why are you being nice to me?" she asked, squinting at me.

"Because I know how important family is, and I know how scared you must be. I didn't want to leave you all alone without explaining that everything will be okay."

"But you came here to hurt us!" she accused.

"No! No, Eloise. I don't like hurting people. I'm just missing that box I had when I was here last time, and I really, really need it."

"Why do you need it? It just has some stupid little key in it. It isn't even anything fun!"

"It's to open an even more important box I have at home. I can't open it without my key, and so I've been really sad about that! Do you know where your mom put the key?" I asked.

"My mommy didn't take it. My mommy never steals."

"Did *you* take my key, Eloise?"

"Yes," she admitted.

"Eloise, where is my key now?"

"I lost it," she said, reaching her hand into her pocket and holding it still.

I raised an eyebrow.

"I don't believe you, Eloise. I think you're lying."

"I'm not lying! I lost it!"

"You know you don't have to lie like your mommy did. That's why you're at this place—because lying is bad."

"This place is nice," she said. "And I'm not lying! I promise!"

"The cities are even *nicer*. There is more food than you can imagine, and a lot more kids. Lots of toys and other cool things, too. You'd have all of that, but your mom must have told some really, really bad lies before you were born, so that's why you were born here instead."

"Because she lied?"

"Yup. And you don't have to follow in her footsteps, Eloise. You can be a better person. Lying hurts people, that's why liars get sent away to live here—because no one likes how liars hurt them."

She paused for a moment of contemplation.

"I'm sorry I lied to you," she apologized innocently, pulling the key from her pocket and holding it out to me in her tiny palm.

"I forgive you, Eloise."

I rushed back out of the house and over to Zane and Lamb. We went back to the storage house, with Zane carrying Lamb, who had grown alarmingly weak.

"Stay with us, Lamb," Zane urged as we slipped into the house.

"Put her down over here," I said, opening the back door of the truck. "Just lay her across the backseat."

I pulled the blanket out of my bag and balled it up like a pillow to lay beneath Lamb's head as Zane and I helped set her down. Her face scrunched as she winced in pain, biting her lip.

I looked down at her, getting a close look at the wound for the first time. It was deep, and Lamb had lost a lot of blood. Her shirt was soaked through, and her hands were glistening red as she attempted to hold back all of the blood.

"It's bad isn't it?" She mustered a nervous giggle, which quickly turned into sobs.

"I don't know what to do!" Zane whispered as he turned away from Lamb. "We have to do something! Look at her!"

"I know! But I don't know what to do either," I said under my breath, my throat feeling tight. "I have bandages, and some ointment. But I don't know what it does, and I think this is beyond bandages…"

"We have to try something. We have to stop the bleeding. Please, Eos! Just try something—*anything*!" he begged angrily and desperately, struggling to stay quiet enough to spare Lamb of our dismal conversation.

"Alright. The bandages and ointment should be in your bag, can you bring them here?" I turned back to Lamb. "We're going to fix this, okay? You're going to be okay."

I don't believe the words myself, how do I expect her to believe them?

"E, look!" Zane called to me, holding up a small bottle of a clear liquid. "I forgot! I stole some alcohol from back in Avid—it was in the pantry! I think it's just some medical alcohol—it might help."

"Perfect—bring that, too."

Zane handed me a wad of cloth bandages, the bottle of alcohol, and the ointment. I paused for a moment, taking a deep breath. *I can do this.*

"Lamb, I need to see it," I said lightly, reaching for her hands.

"O-Okay," she blubbered, nodding her head repeatedly as she mustered up the courage to move her hands.

I slid the bottom of her shirt up gently, revealing a deep incision in her pasty skin. Lamb shivered violently as she sobbed.

"This is going to hurt a bit, I'm not going to lie. But you can do this—you're tough!" I encouraged her, and then turned to whisper to Zane. "Zane, sit by her head, hold her shoulders down and try to keep her calm, okay?"

He nodded, sitting by Lamb's head and pressing his hands firmly on her shoulders, a solemn look on his face as he looked down at her.

I took a deep, shaky breath, unscrewing the lid of the alcohol. I blinked back tears, trying to clear my vision as I steadied the bottle over the wound. I slowly turned the bottle over, letting the clear liquid pour out and splash against the cut. Lamb let out a piercing scream as she writhed. I stepped away from the truck, my hands over my mouth as I tried to catch my breath. The screams continued for a few more moments as I sat on a crate, plugging my ears and closing my eyes. *I can't, I can't, I can't.*

There was a hurried shaking on my shoulders. I opened my eyes and unplugged my ears.

"Eos, are you okay?" Zane asked, his eyes bloodshot, his hair ruffled, and his hands twitching.

"No," I breathed, answering honestly. "I can't handle this. I don't know what to do."

"I bandaged her up. She's resting now. She's lost a lot of blood, E."

"She'll make it," I said, looking to my feet.

"Yeah," Zane sighed.

There were still a couple hours of darkness left, so Zane went on a walk around the lake while I went back to the truck to sit with Lamb. I sat by her head—her eyes closed, her hands folded over her bandage, and her chest rising and falling slowly.

"E?" she whispered, her eyes fluttering open.

"Hey, Lamb," I responded, gently stroking her soft, fuzzy blonde hair.

She smiled weakly at me.

"Just relax," I said. "You need rest so you can get better."

"Eos," she contested. "I'm not going to get better."

"Don't say that. You're fine. We patched you up and cleaned it and everything. It'll just take time—that's all."

"No, E. I'm sorry. I know. I can tell what's going to happen, but it's okay. I've got you and Zane… Where's Zane?"

"He's taking a walk. He'll be back soon."

"Do you ever miss your family?" she asked.

"Yeah, sometimes," I admitted. "My parents didn't even say goodbye when I was arrested. I went to see them before I was exiled, but they locked the door and wouldn't let me in. I didn't get to say goodbye…"

"I'm sorry, E. That's rough," she apologized genuinely.

"Don't. You shouldn't be apologizing to me about anything. I should be apologizing to you. It's because of me that you're even in this mess."

"It isn't your fault. Don't blame yourself."

"So… do *you* miss your family sometimes?" I asked, reverting the subject.

"I do," she said sweetly. "I used to live in Eastmeade, like Zane. We went to school together. He was friends with my big sister."

"I didn't know you had a sister," I said.

"Two. I actually have two sisters—one older, one younger. The older one, Daniella, is four years older than me. Tessa, my little sister, is about nine years old now."

"Daniella, Leanne, and Tessa," I repeated their names, smiling. "Why do people call you Lamb?"

She smiled at me. "When Tessy was a baby first learning how to talk, she couldn't pronounce her own name right, let alone mine or Daniella's names. Daniella became Della, Tessa became Tessy, and Leanne became something that we thought sounded like Lamb. The names just kinda' stuck. She still calls me that. At least, she did the last time I saw her."

I wish I could tell her she's going to see her sisters again.

"It's so cold," Lamb shuttered.

Just then, Zane returned, his eyes even more puffy than before. He ran his sleeve under his nose with a sniff before getting into the driver's seat.

"Let's get out of here," he said, easing the truck back onto the spiraled road.

Zane lowered the platform at the end of the road and

pulled onto it, raising us back to the ground. Above ground, Zane kept driving, his eyes rarely blinking as he stared at the road. Lamb's eyes closed weakly, but her chest was still rising and falling gently as she rested.

"Zane," I hissed in a whisper over the seat. "Where are we going?"

"Eastmeade."

CHAPTER TWENTY-FOUR

"Eastmeade?" I echoed. "Why?"

"So she can be with family."

"I don't know if she's going to make it, Zane," I whispered.

"Yes, she will. Don't say that. It isn't that far of a drive anyways."

Zane accelerated, kicking up sand behind the truck as he raced along, making a couple fast decisions whenever we came to a fork in the road. Every time Zane hit a slight bump, Lamb's face contorted, and she moaned in pain.

"What are you trying to do, Zane? Kill us?" She forced a labored chuckle.

It was about an hour into the drive when someone finally spoke again.

"We're almost there," Zane said.

I could finally see the sun peak over the horizon, gradually illuminating the sky in pastel pinks and blues.

"Lamb," I called, nudging her. "Wake up—we're

almost at Eastmeade. We're going to sneak you in so you can see Della and Tessy."

Nothing.

"Lamb? Lamb, wake up," I said, more urgency in my voice as I shook her gently.

Zane stopped the truck, turning back with a look of fear on his face.

"Lamb, please wake up," I said, my voice cracking with a squeak as I began to sob uncontrollably. "Zane, she won't wake up! Help! She won't wake up—Lamb!"

Zane's lip began to quiver until he bit down on it, turning away from me. In the middle of me shaking her, one of her arms slid limp from her abdomen, revealing her blood-soaked bandage.

The bandages didn't stop the bleeding—it just slowed it. She's gone.

"She's gone," I breathed in disbelief.

No response.

"Zane," I called, my voice trembling.

Zane ignored me, accelerating again.

"Zane, what are you doing? I said she's gone!" I yowled. It didn't really sink in until I said it the second time. *Lamb's gone. She's never coming back.* The tears began to roll out of my eyes, one after another without stopping.

"I'm going to Eastmeade," he said, clearing his throat.

"Why? She's gone," I sniffed, wiping the tears from my cheeks, but they just kept coming.

"She needs to be with her family!" he protested aggressively.

"Just let them believe she's alive and well!"

"I can't do that to Lamb. You didn't grow up knowing her and her family. Family was everything to her and the only time she wasn't with at least one of her family members was once she was exiled. She'd want to be reunited with them, even if she is…" his voice trailed off.

A few minutes later, I could see the gate to Eastmeade, the second largest of the cities. Significantly larger than Rockhallow, Eastmeade had a thicker gate and walls with superior metal reinforcements. The buildings began to tower over us, the nearer we got to the city gates, and before I knew it, my entire peripheral vision was filled with skyscrapers.

"Zane, I think you should stop. Someone is going to see us!"

"We're in a truck."

"So? Even worse! We're criminals who stole a truck from a city official!"

"Most drivers are from Eastmeade—it's not an uncommon job here. They won't question a truck," he began mumbling

The opening in the gate widened, and Zane confidently continued forward.

"Keep your head down," he said. "I can get away with being in the driver's seat, but there are rarely people in the backseat unless they are criminals. I don't want to draw attention. They'll let me in because they'll think I'm just a driver."

I ducked my head below the window as I waited.

"Her house is about two blocks away from the gate, but I have to drive slow. There are already quite a few of people on the streets."

Suddenly, I heard a faint beeping sound.

"What was that? How's it going up there?" I called out.

"Fine. I think it's our gas. Otherwise, we're fine. A couple of people gave me some suspiciously prolonged looks, but I think we're fine," he grumbled. "Here we are. I pulled the truck over where the door on your side isn't visible from the street. I'm going to go get Lamb's mom. Stay hidden for now. You can get out of the truck, just don't let anyone see you."

"I won't," I said, stepping out of the truck and behind a tree.

Zane jogged over to the back door of a ranch style house with a neatly tended garden encircling it. While I waited for him to return, I tilted my head back, searching for the tops of some of the city's skyscrapers, unable to find them. The city itself was massive—I've never been anywhere with so many buildings. Out of nowhere, I heard a wail, followed by the appearance of a frantic, petite blonde woman running toward the truck. I jumped out of the way as the woman fell over the backseat, howling Lamb's name. Following the woman was a girl, slightly older than me, who looked like a taller version of Lamb with golden blonde hair instead of the familiar white-blonde of Lamb's hair. *That must be Della, Lamb's older sister.* The girl stumbled toward the truck as well, tears in her eyes. When she caught sight of Lamb's lifeless body, she pulled her hands over her mouth in shock.

"Don't let Tessy see," the petite woman commanded Della.

"Someone needs to tell her though!" Della protested, tears spilling out of her eyes.

"But she doesn't need to see this!"

"I don't need to see what, mom?" a little girl asked, poking her head out from the side of the house. Her hair was long, with ringlet curls of fair, fuzzy hair. Her skin was pale, and she had pale blue eyes.

"Nothing, Tessy, go finish your chores!" her mother said, her voice shaking.

"Mama? What's wrong?" Tessy asked curiously, approaching her mom.

"Go back inside!"

"Is that Lamb?" Tessy shrieked upon seeing her sister's body in the backseat.

"Just go back inside the house!"

"Mama, no! That's Lamb! What's wrong with her?" she asked, stumbling as she ran over.

"She's gone, Tessy," Della said, crouching down to eye level with Tessy.

"What do you mean?"

"Lamb is gone. She's sleeping, and she isn't going to wake up," she explained.

"Just pour water on her like she used to do to you before I was born. Remember? You told me about it! Try it!"

"Tessy, it doesn't work like that. She passed away. She's not alive anymore," Della whimpered, trying to stay strong as she explained death to her sister.

"What? What happened to her?"

"An accident happened," I spoke up.

"I want her to come back," Tessy sniveled.

"We all want her to come back," Della said, hugging her sister.

"Zane, honey, may I talk to you in private? And your friend, too, if she was there when it happened," Lamb's mother requested.

"Of course. And yes, she was there."

The two of us joined her, away from her daughters for a moment.

"So, tell me what really happened. Don't spare me any details. I need to know."

"Ma'am," Zane began to protest.

"She was stabbed," I interjected, my throat tightening. "She was trying to protect me, and she got hurt when it should have been me."

Lamb's mother smiled through her tears.

"I don't know how you two got here, and I don't know what you three were doing when it happened, but whatever you do, please don't let her death be in vain. I need to know that whatever the reason, it's a just one."

I hesitated for a moment, feeling guilty. *All of this was for the Skeleton Key. At first, I just wanted it so I could do whatever I wanted, have whatever I wanted, be wherever I wanted. The longer I search for it and the more I go through, the more I'm beginning to agree with Cromwell—I want this to taint the system. I want this to be the chink in the armor. The exile system isn't right. Some people deserve to be locked up longer than others, and some deserve to be locked up in higher security places. But some deserve a chance. Lamb didn't deserve to be there like she was. Maybe she wouldn't have left*

Avid if she didn't have a life sentence there. I wouldn't have left either, I'm sure. None of this would have happened. And people like Paren don't deserve to spend their lives in caves or other prisons. Not all criminals are monsters, but the cities don't understand that. This is about more than just a key.

"It is," I replied. "I promise."

"Is there anything you two need? Food? Water? More medical supplies?"

"Is there any way we could get more bandages and alcohol—for medical purposes," I asked.

"Of course! Anything else? Would you two like to spend the night?"

"That would be fant—" Zane started.

"We can't," I interrupted. "We don't want to risk getting any of you in trouble. The longer we are here, the more likely we are to be noticed. It's best for all of us if Zane and I leave as soon as possible."

"Understandable. Let me get you the supplies," she said, rushing into the house.

She returned shortly after, her arms full of bandages and bottles.

"Here, take this," she said, dumping the supplies into our bags. "Are you sure there's nothing else I can do for you?"

"We could use more gas for the truck," I said. "We used up almost all of the extra gas."

"Done. Della's boyfriend was a good friend of Lamb's, and he's actually training to be a driver. He has access to gas."

She called Della over, asking her the favor. Della

nodded her head and took off down the road. A short while later, she returned, dragging a child's wagon behind her with a blanket thrown over it. She threw the blanket off, revealing a few red jugs.

"Thank you," I said as she began to fill the truck's tank, placing the extra jugs in the trunk.

"Of course!" she said sweetly, a look of care in her eyes mingled with redness as a single tear ran down her face.

"Is there anything else we can do for you both?" her mother asked, her face solemn.

"You've done plenty, thank you," Zane said.

"We will take her now. We can take care of it all," she said, looking sorrowfully at Lamb. "I guess you should be on your way."

She approached the truck, commanding Tessy, who was sobbing dreadfully, to go back in the house. Della and her mother gently scooped Lamb up between the two of them and carried her in through the back door, bidding Zane and me farewell.

For careful measure, even though I was in the front passenger seat on the way out of Eastmeade, I kept my head ducked low as Zane drove us carefully out of the city limits.

"To Clamorite?" I asked, pulling myself up.

"I guess so," answered Zane, looking at Lamb's map for a second before picking a direction and driving off.

The next couple days were silent. Zane always was the one to drive—for hours on end, and every day, he would stare out at the ruins and the endless sand ahead of us without saying a word. He rarely stopped for meals, always saying he "wasn't hungry," except for the food he would pick at before going to sleep and after waking up. During the nights, we both slept in the trunk, neither of us able to bear the thought of sleeping in the backseat, and he knew I didn't want to be completely alone. Instead of talking like we used to, once we laid down for bed, Zane would turn his back to me and not say a word. This continued until we finally reached Clamorite.

"Are you sure this is it?" Zane finally spoke, staring up at an intimidating mountain range ahead of us.

"I think so. But where's the waterfall? I thought Clamorite was by a waterfall?"

"I don't know."

"Maybe it's on the other side?"

"Let's check it out," he said, cruising along a surrounding road.

We continued for a while until I spotted the entrance to a lit tunnel in the mountain.

"There!" I pointed.

The closer Zane pulled to the tunnel, the better I could make out the fact that a rusty gate barricaded it.

"Try one of the buttons," I said, pointing at the small control panel.

Zane pressed a few buttons until the gate creaked slowly open.

The tunnel through the mountain was short, with dim lights along the edges of the walls to guide us. We reached the end, and there it was—the waterfall.

I could see the waterfall in the distance through the trees, and a fair hike up the mountain. There were trees all along the sides and base of the mountains. The waterfall looked small from our position, but when we tried to follow the road, the truck sputtered for a moment and stopped altogether.

"Why'd you stop?" I asked.

"I didn't. It isn't working," Zane said, frustrated as he continuously pressed and released the gas pedal.

"Is it out of gas?"

"I don't know!"

Zane slammed the door behind him as he went around to the trunk.

"We're out of extra gas," he growled, spouting some profanity as he chucked a jug from the trunk.

"Let's just take our stuff and walk, I guess," I suggested.

"What are we supposed to do after here though? How are we supposed to get to Fallmont?"

"We'll have to walk."

"Do you have any idea how long that could take?" Zane yelled.

"We've walked farther before!" I retorted, flashing him the map. "It'll take a couple days is all, as long as we keep a steady pace. But one thing at a time! We have to figure out how to get up *there*," I pointed toward the waterfall.

Zane groaned, grabbing his pack and Lamb's before tromping off through the trees without waiting for me. I gathered any stray items strewn throughout the backseat and jammed them in my bag before taking off sprinting after Zane.

"Wait… up!" I huffed from behind him. "Where are you going? The road goes *that* way."

"We've got a lot of distance to cover before we make it up there. If we go that way by foot, we won't make it by dark. This is a more direct path."

"What do you expect to do when we do make it up there?"

"What do you mean? We have to look for the key."

"Yeah, duh. But I mean, we've technically had places to stay in the other towns, or we were out before anyone would see us. We won't be out of here that fast—it's a long walk, and we don't know what to look for. What do you expect to do when we get up there? We have to be careful."

"We will just camp out in the woods nearby tonight and observe the place in the morning. Then we can make a decision."

"We have to be careful. What if they can see us coming from up there?"

"Do you see anyone up there?" Zane shot.

"Well, no… But it doesn't mean that no one can see us!" I whined.

"If you're so worried about them noticing you, put your hood up. Your hair stands out when we're out here. You blend better with it up."

Without a response, I pulled my hood over my head, tucking back my hair.

The leaves rustled as we walked. A twittering whistle interrupted the rustling. I swore under my breath as I stopped in my tracks.

"What the hell was that?" Zane exclaimed, wielding his dagger.

"I don't know," I breathed, trying to stay silent.

"It sounded like—"

"I know what it *sounded* like," I said. "But that's impossible."

"Maybe it's not," Zane pondered.

"No way."

"But think about it! Does this place look like it's been rebuilt? I think this place wasn't affected by the war."

"But Equivox looked similar to this, with all the trees."

"These trees are much bigger, and there are all these other plants, isn't it a possibility?"

"Zane, that's crazy. There's no way that was a bird— they aren't around anymore. Not in the New Territory, at least."

"Well, it was either that, or a person. I'd like to believe it was a bird!"

Suddenly, there was a rapid and melodic chirping.

"That one was different! E, there are *birds* here!" Zane laughed excitedly.

Then, a tiny, brown-feathered bird fluttered down from the tree, landing in the leaves a few feet away from us. Zane and I froze, mesmerized by the little creature as he kicked up leaves and pecked at the dirt, pulling up a fat earthworm. Clearly satisfied by his find, the bird flapped its wings and carried itself and its lunch up into a tree.

I turned to Zane, mirroring his excitement. *We were*

taught that birds were killed off through a mixture of the explosions during war, the radiation in some of the areas farther away from the cities and exile towns, and the loss of trees for them to live in and find food around. I never thought I would see one.

I looked closer at the leaves and spotted a delicate looking tan feather with white speckles. I picked it up and tucked it carefully in my bag. *I want to remember this.*

"Let's keep going," Zane reminded me, motioning to the waterfall far ahead.

I nodded, trotting to catch up.

"How do you think birds survived?" I asked as we walked.

"These trees must have made it through the war untouched, so the birds still had places to build nests and find food and all that."

"I wonder if there are other places like this," I pondered aloud.

"Maybe."

We continued toward the base of the mountain, taking only a couple short breaks for snacks and rest. After time, the ground started sloping upwards, making the hike progressively more difficult. The waterfall, luckily, was only about a third of the way up the side of the mountain.

"I think we should stop here," Zane said past the base of the mountain as the sun began to set.

"Good plan," I said, dropping my bag, exhausted.

"We should take watches."

"Probably not a bad idea," I agreed. "I'll take first watch."

That evening, Zane curled up across from me, his back pressed to the exposed roots of a tree. His lips were turned downwards into a loose frown as he slept. While he slept, I sat there, casually twisting my dagger in my hands. A couple hours went by of me poking my palm gently with the tip of the dagger, just to stay awake, before I heard a rustling in the leaves. My eyes jolted open wide as I clambered to my feet, staying in a crouch in the darkness.

It was a few minutes before I heard the noise again— this time sounding like it was nearing Zane.

"I know you're there," I said, warning the mystery presence.

Silence, and then more rustling, growing closer. I wielded my dagger, ready to fight. A few more scuffling sounds, and suddenly a furry white animal, barely larger than my palm, with long, floppy ears appeared from behind Zane's tree. *Is that a rabbit? I thought those were gone too—I've only ever seen them in children's books and in books for my old classes. It's so cute!* The bunny scampered off, clearly terrified of me as I stood cooing over it.

"Come back!" I whispered after the baby rabbit, sneaking after it. "Where'd you go?"

I gasped, my eyes wide in horror as they met the sight of the bunny, his little white body stained red under the talons of a ruffled-looking owl. The bird's eyes glowed yellow in the darkness of the forest as he glared back at me, tightening his grip on the white rabbit as it twitched beneath his feet. *The poor thing!* I sighed, disappointed as I rounded the tree again to return to my spot.

As I turned, my eyes met Zane's, wild and panicked as he held his golden dagger out to me.

"Oh my God, Eos," he exhaled. "I woke up and you weren't there, and I heard leaves and—don't do that!"

"Sorry!" I apologized. "I heard noises, and there was this bunny, and an owl, and—I'm so sorry I didn't mean to scare you!"

"I thought someone got you or something," he said.

"No—I was only gone for a minute. I wasn't going to leave you there unconscious in the woods either. I just wanted a closer look at the bunny."

"It's alright. I'm just glad you're okay. It's my turn for watch anyways—go ahead and get some sleep."

I nodded sleepily, digging my blanket out of my pack and making myself comfortable in the leaves. It didn't take long before I was asleep.

~

When I woke up, I could hear crackling sounds, and the air was full of the smell of fire. I scrambled up, blinking back sunlight as I tried to see what was happening.

"Good morning, E," Zane said sweetly.

"What's going on?" I asked, rubbing my eyes.

"I found some eggs in a nest nearby and figured I'd make us some breakfast!"

"You… wait… what?" I said, my vision clearing. Zane had started a tiny fire with twigs, dried leaves, and some matches from his bag.

"They aren't chicken eggs," he laughed lightly. "But I figured it'd be something different for once."

"What are you cooking them on?"

"While it was just Lamb and I, we actually snagged a small pan back in Avid. She kept it in her bag. We made a couple fires out of scraps in the ruins while we were out on our own so we could at least have hot meals sometimes, even if we were just heating up vegetables and bread some days."

He pulled out a miniature pan and I let out a breathy laugh of disbelief. Then, he revealed four small eggs in the leaves near his feet where he sat. While I waited on breakfast, I dug through my bag for a change of clothes—a simple green shirt and black jeans.

"Eos, don't look!" Zane said, his voice uneasy.

"Don't look at wha—" I turned to him. "Zane! What is that?"

"I said don't look!" he said, shooing me away with a hand frantically.

"Is that a dead baby bird?" I shrieked, staring heartbroken at the contents of the egg spilled out on the pan.

"I—Eos, please! Stop looking at it!" he said, dumping the carcass on the ground and smoothing leaves over it.

"You can't just throw it on the ground!"

"What else do you want me to do with it?!"

"Bury it, or something! Put the other eggs back!"

Zane scooped up the other three eggs and hurried off into the trees, returning a moment later.

"I didn't know there were baby birds in those eggs," he apologized.

"Let's just bury this poor little guy," I sighed, gingerly picking up the limp shape from the leaves.

Eos

Zane went over to a tree and scratched a shallow hole in the ground near the trunk. I placed the little bird in the hole and we covered it with dirt and leaves.

"Better?" Zane asked.

"No! You just killed a baby!"

"Don't say it like that! It was a bird!"

"A baby bird! Until yesterday, we didn't even know things like this still existed, and now here you are! Tromping through the woods, slaughtering their babies!" I accused.

"Now you're just exaggerating! I was just trying to make us a nice breakfast!"

"I know… I'm sorry. Thank you for trying. Let's just stay away from eggs," I suggested.

"Fine."

After we got ready to set out for the day, we began to make our way up part of the base of the mountain. My legs felt like lead after just an hour, and it didn't look like we were any closer than we started that morning.

"I still don't see any people, Zane."

"I don't either. Let's just keep moving."

The crashing sounds of the rushing water grew so loud that it became difficult to hear each other. Time passed with few words said, and eventually, we dragged ourselves to the flat level of the waterfall. I fell to my knees, panting for a moment before I realized.

There's nobody up here.

CHAPTER TWENTY-FIVE

"Where is everyone?" I asked Zane, shouting over the sounds of the waterfall.

"I don't know," he answered, donning a clueless expression.

"Should we just look around? I mean, we don't need people here to find the key, as long as we have the right place."

"Do we know this is even the right place?"

"No."

We pulled out our daggers, cautiously drawing closer to the waterfall. It was incredible. The water poured from a source that towered over us and down into a shimmering body of crystalline water. The body of water drained itself into a stream that bent along the far side of the mountain, away from us. Ferns and other greenery filled the open area, with colorful flowers speckled against the green. I took off toward the water after tucking my blade back into my jacket.

"E! What are you doing?" Zane shouted over the

crashing water after me, putting away his blade and chasing me.

"I knew it!" I hollered, turning to him with a wide grin. "Fish!"

Underneath the surface of the water were dozens of golden-orange, black, and cream colored fish slicing through the water as they swam. I searched through my bag until I found a slice of bread. Ripping off a chunk, I crumbled it up in my palms and tossed it into the water. The water began splashing and frothing as the fish frantically fought their ways to the surface, eagerly gulping up the bread. I smiled and laughed, looking back at Zane, who returned my smile.

"Look at that one!" He pointed, grabbing my shoulders to orient me more toward the waterfall.

He pointed at the water and my eyes followed his finger, spotting a bright red fish. The fish began to swim toward the waterfall, so out of sheer curiosity, I followed the fish from the edge of the land. Zane followed me as I neared the waterfall.

"E," he said, too quiet to hear over the crashing water. "E—look. Come here!"

Zane began to change direction, moving toward the back edge of the rock wall of the mountain—behind the waterfall.

"Eos, there's something *behind* the waterfall!"

"What? What do you mean?"

"I think we found it!" he exclaimed enthusiastically when he turned to face me.

"Clamorite?"

When I caught up with him, I saw it. Behind the waterfall, there was a narrow passage into a sort of grotto in the mountainside. We carefully made our way across the walkway, our feet mushing into the wet ground as the waterfall fell to our right, creating a sort of thick wall. We peeked around the corner, and inside the mountain was a circle of several dozen people who were sitting on the ground, singing and clapping their hands rhythmically. A few others stood outside the circle and stomped their feet every few claps that the others gave, and everyone looked peaceful and content.

I looked at Zane, confused and slightly uneasy about the abnormally cheerful prisoners. He returned my confusion with a shrug. We stood there for a moment watching the people. *I'm just going to go for it.*

I left my hiding place and walked confidently toward the circle without looking back at Zane. One of the group members facing my direction met my eyes with a warm smile and enthusiastically waved his arm, scooting over and patting the new empty seat in the circle. The boy must have been about 20 years old, with smooth ginger hair, pale skin, freckles, and caring eyes. When others noticed my entrance, a tan woman, young looking but noticeably older than me, with thick blonde hair in a messy bun and a nose piercing shaped like a star, sitting on the other side of the ginger-haired boy, called out to me.

"Come on in! Welcome to Clamorite!" she shouted over the singing, re-crossing her long legs.

The rest of the circle turned around to look at me, and my heart began racing even faster as I wondered what might happen if I didn't turn around and run. Instead of running, I kept walking toward them, taking the seat next to the ginger-haired boy as the group members called out their welcome to me. I nodded, almost too shyly.

"It's not too bad here! You'll learn to love it!" the blonde woman said, leaning over the ginger boy and patting my knee. "I'm Lisette."

"One of us!" the ginger-haired boy said, giving me a friendly side hug.

"This is Flynn," the girl said with a cheery laugh.

They think I was arrested and brought here. They don't even suspect me.

"Welcome," said a deep voice from across the circle.

The source of a voice was a tall, muscular, dark man, with stunningly white teeth as he smiled sincerely at me.

"I'm Morgan," he said. "I'm the representative. Do you play any instruments or sing?"

I shook my head.

"That's okay! Not everyone here does. You can just join in with those clapping, or stomping if you'd prefer. Whatever you're comfortable with!" Morgan said.

My eyes scanned the wide room, looking for places where the key could be hidden, but there were no passages to other places—not even any nooks or crannies within the walls to check. *Hopefully Zane keeps an eye out for it from the outside.*

Just then, there began a melodious sound as Morgan started singing a new song. His voice was rich, and I caught myself staring as he sang. Shortly into the song, Flynn began to pat on his legs to the beat.

Right, right, left. Right, right, right, left.

Lisette joined in with Flynn, and a few others began patting at their legs, while others hummed at different pitches along with the vocals. I nervously watched the circle, quietly joining in by drumming on my thighs along with the others. Once I got the hang of the beat, I grew more comfortable and lowered my guard. *These people are some of the nicest I think I've ever met.*

After a few more songs with the group, people began to disperse, making their way out of the grotto and out toward the waterfall. I wondered if Zane was still out there, but figured he had already taken cover somewhere. At least, that's what I thought until a scrawny, sandy-haired man ran back into the grotto toward the rest of us, yelling something about another new member. Right behind this man was Zane, crowded by some of the Clamorites. Morgan introduced himself and apologized that we were done with songs for the afternoon. When people were done greeting Zane, he approached me, pulling me to the side.

"Any sign of where it might be?" he asked.

"Not a clue. It's empty in here. I don't even see their rations."

"The rations are outside. While you were in here, I poked around some more outside and found what looks like a little campsite along the mountain. I think that's where they stay."

"Can I help you two with anything?" interrupted Morgan, ambling over.

"No. Thank you, we're—"

"Actually," I cut in. "We are looking for something and we were wondering if you might know where it is."

Zane shot me a furious glare.

"*What?*" I mouthed at him.

"Don't pay her any mind. We both came from the

same city—she was known for being a liar. They almost
took her to Equivox for it, but she was more loud and
disruptive in the city than anything. Her lies weren't usually
too harmful, so the officials took her here instead," Zane
lied, looking genuine.

"That's not true!" I said, grabbing his shoulder,
pulling his ear close to my mouth as I continued. "Zane, I
really think these people can help us! Please trust me
on this!"

Zane shook his head.

"*Please.*"

Zane let out a deep grumble and a sigh.

"Morgan," I started. "We are looking for a small key.
It might be in a box. Maybe wooden or mirrored or
something of the sort."

"I don't think I know of it," he smiled brightly at me.
He turned to Zane and his smile transformed into an
angered grimace. "Even if I knew where the key was, I
wouldn't give it to you if you were with him. I respect your
honesty and openness. I'm not going to reward lying."

"He's a good person, deep down! He just wasn't
ready to trust you is all. We've been through a lot,
including a lot of situations with some truly terrible people,
and he was just trying to protect us."

Morgan raised an eyebrow.

"We're from Avid," I admitted.

"Oh," Morgan processed. "I see. What are you doing
in Clamorite?"

"This key we're looking for is in Clamorite
somewhere."

"You're sure?"

"Yes."

"I'll keep an eye out. Meanwhile, keep a low profile. You're safe here—these are good people. But you can never be too safe. I don't know why you want this key so bad, but I probably don't want to ask more questions," Morgan said, looking at me with suspicion. "And you aren't one of us, so you don't have rations. We don't have enough for you—I'm sorry."

"Thank you," I said. "And as for the rations—we have food to last us a while, so we should be fine."

Morgan nodded, turning to leave.

"Oh!" he said, looking back for a moment. "There's another gathering tonight at sundown. Try to be there," he smiled.

"Now what?" asked Zane.

"Now, we search."

That afternoon, Zane and I searched the woods around the campsite. Whenever someone would ask us what we were doing, we would both casually respond with a "just looking around". We continued until the sun started to set, with no luck finding the key.

Back in the grotto, Zane and I joined the exiles around a circle. Group members were excitedly chatting with one another while we waited. When Morgan arrived, a saxophone in his hands, the circle began cheering and whooping. He greeted them with a smile and took a seat at the far end of the circle, opposite Zane and I. In contrast to the circle earlier in the day, multiple people held instruments this time. Flynn began lazily strumming a guitar that he kept situated on his lap. A couple others held small drums, which they tapped rhythmically to the guitar's sound. Lisette and another girl, a short girl with black hair, the tips dyed a faded red, began humming to the music. I sat patiently, doing nothing but listening. A riff on Morgan's saxophone then joined the peaceful song, and the remaining people began soulfully singing, closing their eyes and swaying.

Zane looked at me, his expression slightly bothered.

"What's wrong?" I asked quietly.

"This isn't normal," he responded. "Criminals singing and making music together in a happy circle of freaking friendship? This is just weird, and I don't trust it."

"Understandable. It is kind of weird."

The group played a few more songs as the members stayed in their sort of mellow trance, until eventually, Morgan stood and spoke.

"Until tomorrow, my friends," he said as he hugged a few of the people nearest him and made his way to the campground.

The people began dispersing—some followed after Morgan, others separated throughout the grotto with friends, and Lisette and Flynn stayed sitting by Zane and I.

"So," Lisette started. "What's your story?"

"Uh," I hesitated, remembering Morgan's advice. "It's a long story…"

"I understand. It was difficult for me to talk about it when I was first exiled too," she smiled sweetly, putting a hand on my shoulder. "I used to live in Rockhallow—"

"Me too!" I interjected excitedly, never having yet met another past citizen of my city.

"What's your name?" she asked. "Do you have any older siblings I might have known?"

"Eos Dawn, and I don't have any siblings."

"I don't think I ever heard anything of you. Did you have a job?"

"I was an in-city messenger."

"Fantastic! How fun! I used to work in the library."

"That explains why I don't recall ever seeing you—I rarely went to the library," I admitted with a laugh.

"Well, I was exiled about eight years ago, so even if you saw me, you probably wouldn't have remembered me."

"Do you mind me asking what your story is?"

"Not at all. Do you remember when Mr. Redelle became the leader? After his father stepped down from the position?"

"Yeah. I was about twelve or so years old."

"And I was about twenty. One of the first laws Redelle had enacted was one prohibiting marriages from citizens of different cities. He convinced the other city leaders that the travel between two cities for such a purpose was 'too dangerous' and a 'waste of resources'. The leaders agreed without a bit of hesitation. My fiancé at the time had been relocated to Eastmeade because he was training to be a driver. He was a driver and he wasn't allowed to come to Rockhallow to get me, and I wasn't allowed to travel to Eastmeade. We had to call off our engagement because of the leaders. We didn't give up right away though. I protested. I posted flyers all over the city, shaming them. I spoke up on the streets, handing out more flyers. I egged Redelle's house once, too. A few days after the egg incident, he sent officials to take me off the streets when I was speaking out against him. They just took me to the courtroom and sentenced me here for being a public disturbance. That was the end of it. Redelle told me he sent officials to Eastmeade to give my fiancé the news. He couldn't follow me and get himself exiled though because he had younger siblings he was helping his mom take care of. Curious, how Redelle would send his officials to another city to break off an engagement, but he wouldn't let me move to Eastmeade to marry my fiancé."

"That's terrible!" I said, shocked.

"What about you?" Zane asked Flynn, who was still picking his guitar softly.

Flynn looked up and stopped playing. When he looked up, I noticed a small golden key on a thin cord of leather around his neck. Zane must have spotted it at the same time—he sat up eagerly, never taking his eyes off of Flynn's neck.

"Well," Flynn started. "I was arrested for having fun. I goofed around in my city—caused too much of a problem, apparently."

Flynn went quiet, looking back down at his guitar as he resumed his quiet strumming.

"We try to make the best of it here," Flynn said. "There's a reason we ended up here."

"He's always saying that. He knows I don't believe it, and frankly I don't think he believes it himself," Lisette complained.

"I do believe it. Everything happens for a reason."

"Yeah—the reason I'm here is because Redelle, the leaders, and their officials are terrible people who ruined my life! It's as simple as that! I was happy—I didn't do anything wrong, I did my job, I had a fiancé who loved me... But they couldn't let someone just be happy! They had to destroy it. Not only that, but they had to destroy my entire life and send me away to live in the freaking woods for the rest of my life! Is that a good enough reason for you, Flynn?"

"That's the surface reason. But there's a greater reason why you're here."

"Oh yeah? Why's that? All this time and you've never given me an answer."

"I don't know what your reason is. You're supposed to figure that out yourself."

Lisette groaned in disgust.

"You love me," teased Flynn, leaning his head on her shoulder and batting his eyelashes at her.

"You're aggravating," she said, her lips turning upwards into a smile as she nudged him.

"Teehee," he said, nuzzling against her shoulder as she laughed.

"I think I'm going to get dinner and then go to bed," Lisette said.

"Carry me!" Flynn shouted, hopping on Lisette's back.

She let out a strained groan as she waddled toward the campground with Flynn on her back, his legs wrapped awkwardly around her.

By the time the two were gone, it was just Zane and I left in the grotto.

"Did you see it? You saw it!" Zane babbled excitedly.

"Do you think that's the key?"

"What else would it be a key for?"

"I don't know. It could be something he brought from home—like something meaningful to him."

"Maybe. Should we ask him the story behind it? See if maybe we can find out that way?"

"Oh, yeah, because that's a great idea. 'Hey, Flynn, where did you get that key? Oh! You found it in a box around Clamorite? Can we take it? Thanks!'"

"Well, we could always steal it," Zane suggested.

"So, we ask him where he got it," I started as Zane nodded, following along in agreement. "And then expect him to not be bothered when he wakes up and it's missing?"

"We will make sure we are long gone before he even wakes up."

"That's a terrible idea. A terrible, stupid idea," I said, glaring at Zane. "Let's try it and see what happens."

Zane smiled, satisfied.

We followed a short trail past the waterfall toward the campground. Many of the people were gathered around a fire, cheerfully conversing as they ate dinner. There were flimsy tents set up throughout the trees, and it seemed as if a few people had already gone into their tents for the night. Zane and I joined up with Lisette and Flynn by the fire without grabbing any food.

"Aren't you two going to eat?" Flynn asked.

"Oh, um, we aren't hungry," I answered for us.

"You really should eat something. We have plenty of

food for all of us—plus we have enough for seconds, some days! Morgan says we get the most rations out of all the exile towns. Here, take my soup—I didn't use the spoon yet," he offered, holding out a bowl of what looked like a creamy tomato soup.

"Thank you," I said, accepting the bowl.

"I'll get you some, too…?"

"Zane," Zane answered.

"Zane. I'll get you some soup as well," Flynn said, moseying toward a stack of bowls on the other side of the fire.

"Lisette?"

"Yes?"

"You know that key around Flynn's neck?"

"Yeah?"

"Do you know where he got it?"

"Yup! He found it near the waterfall one day. He was climbing in trees with me, and he called over to me because he said he saw something shiny in the rocks by the water's edge. When he went to check it out, he moved some rocks around and pulled out this really pretty mirror box. That key was the only thing in it. It was really weird, and we have no idea what it's for, but he's been wearing it ever since. He tries talking about how it's some symbol or some crap like that. Says it represents opportunities or whatever. If you ask me, it's just some weird little useless key that makes for a quirky piece of jewelry."

"That's cool, though. Do you think he's really attached to that necklace?" Zane asked. I subtly elbowed him in the side, and he glared at me in angry confusion.

Eos

"Umm… I guess? I don't know. Why?"

"I was just wondering. You can learn a lot about a person by the things they place value in."

"I suppose."

Flynn returned, handing Zane a bowl of soup. Zane thanked him, and we all began to eat. When we finished, Lisette and Flynn said goodnight to us and made their way to separate tents. We stayed up for a while, until we were the last ones awake.

"So?" I asked.

"You heard Lisette. That's gotta' be the Clamorite key."

"So, we take it?"

"So we take it," Zane repeated.

"You stand guard, I'll grab the necklace," I said, tucking back my hair and pulling up my hood.

Zane stood outside Flynn's tent, nodding to me. I slowly unzipped the tent, careful not to make a sound. I eased myself into the opening, the fabric crinkling with every tentative movement. Flynn lay there, eyes closed and mouth open slightly, peacefully breathing as he slept. I crept over on my hands and knees, looking down at him. *I hate taking this from him if this thing gives him some kind of hope that there's more than this.* I dug out my pocketknife, pulling out the blade.

Please don't wake up.

I delicately lifted the cord from his neck and sliced the leather with my knife. Flynn twitched in his sleep momentarily. I froze, knife in hand, until he settled down again. Steadily, I slid the key from the severed rope. I hurried carefully out of the tent, zipping it shut behind me as slowly as I had opened it.

I held the key up to Zane with a grin.

"Let's go!" he urged, waving for me to follow him as he took off sprinting back toward the waterfall.

We passed the entrance of the grotto, behind the waterfall, and we didn't stop until we made it down the mountainside. Descending the mountain felt a lot faster than climbing it, and after less than an hour of rushing through the trees, we were at the base again. I tried to stop, squatting near the trunk of a tree, but Zane continued to powerwalk through the forest.

"Where are you going?" I called after him, panting on the ground.

"We have to keep moving. Let's get to the truck."

"Zane! Are you joking? The truck doesn't even work!"

"Let's try it again. We have to head that way to leave anyways."

"That's a day's hike away! We have to rest first."

"We can rest when we get to the truck," he said, continuing.

I pushed myself to my feet and trailed after him, struggling to breathe.

"Zane, please! We have to rest. Just for a little while... please."

He stopped in his tracks and turned to face me. His eyes were bloodshot and his hair mussed. It took him a moment before he spoke.

"Eos," he said, his voice sounding gravelly. "We are *so close*. I don't want to waste a minute that we could have that key. I want a moment that we can actually be free again. I don't know where we are going to go when we get it, and I don't know what there is for us out there, but I don't want to be a part of the exile towns anymore. I'm done. I want to get away. This key is our chance to get the things we need to get by on our own with ease, whenever we need. We'll have time to rest when we are free."

I stared back at him silently.

"Fine. Just a couple hours and then we keep moving."

"Deal."

I curled up at the base of a tree, covering myself with my blanket. Before long, I fell asleep.

CHAPTER TWENTY-SIX

We reached the truck by early afternoon the next day. Unsurprisingly, it wasn't working.

"We're going to have to walk, Zane."

"It's too far—it'll take too long."

"We still have Lamb's bag full of food. It's enough food to last us a few days—we'll be fine," I said, making my way down the road and toward the tunnel.

"How do you anticipate getting through the tunnel, E?" he asked, stopping behind me.

I swore under my breath.

"I didn't think about that."

"We need this truck to get us through that tunnel."

"Maybe the truck is just out of gas. Maybe the control panel will still work," I said hopefully. "The tunnel is just over there—I can see it from here."

"What do you propose? Pushing the truck all the way over there? It's just us two, and neither of us is notably muscular."

"Maybe it'll work from over here."

"I guess we can try it," he said, opening a door and reaching over. "Alright. I pressed it. I guess we'll see."

We made our way to the tunnel and heard a pained squeak, followed by a slamming sound. We walked through the tunnel until we saw the gate, still blocking the entrance.

"It didn't work," Zane said, discouraged.

"I heard something though. Maybe it was the gate? Maybe we just need to be faster is all."

Zane sighed as he turned to make his way back to the truck again.

"Let's try it," I said hopefully.

We got to the truck and Zane reached out for the control pad.

"Wait! Let's count down, and when you press it, we run. On 'go.'"

"Alright," Zane agreed. "Ready?"

"Yup. 3...2...1...Go!"

He pressed the button and we both took off sprinting toward the tunnel. The lights along the sides of the tunnel blurred together as I ran, making me dizzy. The gate was still open this time, and we bolted through it. It slammed shut just a moment later.

We both stopped, laughing with a mixture of relief and amusement. After we caught our breath, we pulled out a map.

"There," I pointed to Fallmont.

"Do you think we could make it by this time tomorrow?"

"Probably. We're going to have to stop somewhere to sleep though—we have to be alert if we're going to break into Fallmont tomorrow."

"True," Zane submitted in agreement.

"I guess we go that way," I pointed.

"Lead the way."

Shortly before sundown, we stopped in some ruins, knowing we likely wouldn't find anywhere else to spend the night before dark. We had been walking through nothing but sand for a bulk of the day, but eventually we came across what looked like the remains of a small village. The buildings were charred, and some were nothing but crumbled pieces of rubble. Zane and I picked one of the sturdier looking cottages to stay in, piling our bags near the door when we entered.

"Do you remember when we stayed in those ruins before Delaisse?" I asked, spreading my blanket out on the floor.

"Of course I do, E," he said, looking at me thoughtfully.

"That's about when I realized you weren't a huge jerk," I smirked. "You still are, sometimes."

"I am not!" He laughed defensively.

"Are too. You weren't very nice to Paren back at Bellicose."

"I didn't trust him."

"He was taking good care of me. I was obviously fine when you got there—why didn't you trust him?"

"I don't know… I just didn't! He's too… friendly. It's suspicious."

"So, you think friendly is a bad thing now?" I chuckled. "That explains a lot."

"No! Ugh."

I snickered as I lay down, trying to get comfortable on the rough floor. Zane trudged over and looked at the ground next to me, giving me a pouty face.

"Yes, you may sleep next to me," I laughed, patting the ground.

Zane smiled, his eyes seeming to twinkle for a moment as he situated himself. Already lying on top of my blanket to cushion the ground, I curled up in a little ball to try to keep warm. Zane pulled off his shirt, a simple grey long-sleeved top, and handed it to me, revealing a surprisingly muscular torso.

"Take it," he said.

"Are you sure?"

"Yeah. It'll keep you warm. Then you can use your jacket to cover your legs instead."

I sat up to remove my jacket, draping it over my legs before I put on the grey shirt.

"Better?"

"Yes. Thank you, Zane," I said, hugging him. When he tried to end the hug, I held on for just a moment longer.

"You okay, E?"

"Yeah," I said, releasing him. "Night."

I lay down, rolling over on my side. Zane scooted up

behind me and rested his arm over my waist. A few minutes later, I could hear him snoring softly. For me, sleep didn't come so easily that night.

~

"Wake up," I heard Zane call to me.

I opened my eyes, blinking rapidly as they adjusted to the light.

"I don't wanna'."

"Get up or I'll eat the last muffin," he threatened, digging a blueberry muffin out of his bag.

"Gimme'!" I said, sitting up and snatching the muffin.

Zane laughed as he dug out a biscuit and snacked on it.

"When we get to Fallmont, there's going to be some kind of security there. It's the biggest city in the New Territory. But that also means there are going to be more weak spots that we can sneak through because they don't have enough people to guard the walls of the entire city. That would be impractical. The sun has been up for a while now, and I say we leave at about lunchtime. That way, we will make it there by dark instead. The darkness will work in our favor. We get there, stay close to the walls, and look for a way in. Together. You have the Clamorite, Equivox, and Bellicose keys; I have the Avid and Delaisse keys. We can't get separated, okay?"

"Okay," I repeated.

"Where in the city do we want to look first for the Key?"

"It's probably somewhere that would be fairly high

security because they knew what it could do. Somewhere in City Hall would make sense. That'll probably be near the center of Fallmont. I say we stay close to the walls though as long as we can. When we find City Hall, we pick the lock and both search the inside."

"Someone needs to stand guard," Zane suggested.

"That'll draw attention. Plus, we both need to be looking for the Key because it could be anywhere," I said, digging through my belongings idly.

"What if we get caught?" he asked, twiddling his thumbs as we spoke, as if we were discussing weekend plans.

"You know what to do if we get caught," I hinted, raising my eyes to meet his.

"Okay," Zane sighed in resignation.

"If we get split up, we need a meeting place."

"We could meet where we enter the city. On the outside of the wall, if we have to."

"When we get the Key, I want to find Fortitude."

"I thought you didn't really want to? I mean, I know you agreed to it before, but you didn't sound too thrilled. Why the change of heart?"

"I want to see if it exists, and if it does, I want to help exiles escape to Fortitude."

Zane nodded.

"Alright, that settles it. When we find the Key, we look for Fortitude. That Skylar chick said something about it being between Bellicose and the sea," he said, pulling out a map. "Well, Rockhallow is to the east of Bellicose, so it wouldn't be that coast, or she would have said it's past

Rockhallow. Plus, that coast is really far away. I'm guessing Fortitude is to the west, so when we leave Fallmont, let's head west."

I nodded in agreement.

"I'm going to go look around the ruins while we wait to leave—see if I find anything useful," I said, heading out the door.

I looked around, taking in my surroundings. *This used to be home to someone*, I thought as I approached a heap of black rubble. I rolled the larger pieces of brick and stone aside, digging through the ashes. I felt around blindly, hoping to find something but unsure of what I was searching for.

Nothing.

I migrated to the next area of ruins, rummaging through the remains. I continued idly picking for a few hours until Zane came looking for me.

"Hey," he said, walking over with the Skeleton Key papers in hand. "I did some reading, and it seems like the Skeleton Key has some kind of dial on it that makes it work. I don't really understand the notes on how it works, but from what I understand, you have to put the Key in a lock first, then adjust some little dial on it before turning it."

"So, it's not a key, really. It's a device?"

"Sort of."

"I remember Mr. Montgomery telling me about how it's hollow on the inside and adjusts to locks. Does this change anything though?"

"No, I just thought we should know how it works a little before we go in trying to get it."

"Fair enough. Is it time to head out yet?"

"Not yet. Eat," he said, handing me a simple peanut butter sandwich. "The bread's a little stale. Sorry."

I started eating the sandwich as Zane kept talking.

"I already had lunch while I was reading. Once you finish though, we will get our bags packed up again and head out. If we timed this right, we should get there by sunset."

I nodded and continued eating as we made our way to the house we had spent the night in to pack our few belongings.

"Let's split up our supplies, in case we get separated and something happens. Worse comes to worst and we can't meet near Fallmont, we can meet back here, but this way we at least will have enough to manage on our own if something were to happen."

"Good idea," Zane agreed. "Let's split up the keys between the two of us but keep them in our pockets. If something happens to our bags, at least we will still have the keys."

He took out the Avid and the Delaisse keys from his bag, and I took out the Bellicose, Clamorite, and Equivox keys from mine, and we moved them into our jean pockets.

We turned our bags and Lamb's upside down, dumping out the contents. I began rationing out bandages, food, water, and other little supplies between the two of us, making sure to keep my personal belongings in my pile.

"Should we do something with Lamb's bag?" I asked after we packed our two bags with no leftover supplies.

"I wouldn't feel right just leaving it here," he answered softly, rubbing the fabric between two fingers.

"We don't have room to fit it in our bags, and it'd be impractical to try to sneak through Fallmont with one of us carrying a spare bag."

"I know," he thought for a moment. "Wait... I have an idea."

Zane pulled out his dagger and began tearing into the fabric of the bag. The bag made loud ripping sounds as he cut two, palm-sized "L"s from the burlap, handing me one.

"This way, we can still remember her and carry a little bit of her with us, in a way."

"That's a great idea," I smiled, blinking back tears as I looked over the L, tucking it safely in one of my coat pockets.

Zane picked up the remains of the bag and sat them against the doorframe, giving them a sorrowful glance before turning back to me.

"Ready?" he asked.

"Ready."

We left the brick house without looking back. Ahead of us, all I could see was sand, and the faint image of a city, far in the distance. If I held my thumb in the air, it was large enough to block out the city entirely. We trudged through the sand for a while without saying anything, but eventually I spoke up.

"You grew up with Lamb, right?"

"Yeah."

"What was her story?" I asked. "How'd she end up in Avid?"

"She used to steal even when she was younger. She started stealing when her little sister was born. Her family had more money than mine, so I may have initially started stealing to help my family get by, but her family never had to worry about food. Her sisters and parents were healthy, so she didn't have to worry about medicine or paying for treatments. The money her parents earned was enough to pay for food, new clothes sometimes, school supplies… They weren't rich by any means, but they had enough. But Lamb loved her baby sister from the moment she was born—she had always been the baby of the family and couldn't wait to be a big sister. I remember how excited she was when her mom told her she was having a baby girl. Lamb came to me that day at school with the biggest smile, telling me all about the fun she couldn't wait to have with her sister. From the day Tessy was born, Lamb began stealing."

"Why?"

"She wanted to spoil her. Lamb started by stealing toys for Tessy. Nobody suspected her—young, smart, sweet little girl… a thief? Her parents were busy—they weren't the most attentive couple. They never seemed to notice the new toys. As Tessy and Lamb grew up, Lamb started stealing books, jewelry, girly little accessories, and other things that she knew Tessy wanted. She was caught when she was 15, and so many shop owners had filed complaints against her that the officials had no choice but to do something about it."

"There was nothing else they could do? So they *exiled* a 15 year old little girl?" I asked in disbelief.

"They tried different disciplinary actions. She was on

probation for a year and they had her doing tasks around the city, but she kept stealing. So, when she turned 16, they tried her like an adult and exiled her. That was all about the same time my brother got sick, so needless to say it both influenced me to steal what my family needed and scared me to death to even think about getting caught. But yet, I did get caught. I got cocky about it after a time, thinking that I was good at it, and that Lamb must not have been. Truth is, it wasn't about whether we were 'good thieves' or not—it was about whether we *thought* we were or not."

"I don't understand," I said, looking at him with a puzzled expression as we walked.

"If you get too confident, you get sloppy. You could be the best thief in the world, but it wouldn't matter for a moment if you get too confident. The moment you mess up and get sloppy is the moment you're done for. They'll send you off without batting an eye. A little confidence is a good thing, sure, but what's best is to be a thief who is always afraid."

"Being afraid all the time is no way to live," I argued.

"It is if you want to get away with things. If you're scared, you're careful."

I thought on his words for a while as we walked in silence.

"Eos?" he spoke up. "Why did you decide to trust me?"

"What do you mean? Trust you with what?"

"With anything. With everything. This whole Skeleton Key thing. Why do you trust me?"

"I mean, initially you didn't really give me a choice, honestly," I laughed. "You took the papers and ran, and I wanted them back."

"But you could have taken them and ran off that first night—the one in the house with the ruined roof."

"But I didn't."

"Why?"

"Probably just because you're cute," I joked.

"No, E, I'm being serious."

"I know, I'm sorry. I didn't want to steal those papers, or take off in the middle of the night, or leave you by yourself in the middle of nowhere because I didn't want to be alone," I admitted.

Zane scoffed.

"What?" I asked defensively.

"You didn't leave because you were *lonely*? That's a load of crap."

"It's true! I felt so alone in Avid, and I figured I'd be on my own looking for the Key, but then you said you really wanted to find it, and I saved you so I knew you wouldn't take off before repaying the favor somehow. So, I knew, at least for a while, I could trust you, and I was willing to take the company, even if I hated you."

"You *hated* me?" Zane asked, appalled. "But whoa, wait, take a step back. What do you mean I wouldn't leave before repaying the favor?"

"I knew you may have been a jerk, but you weren't a monster. You gave me that bracelet, you stole my ring back, and the worst you did to me when I hit you was smear pudding on my bed," I laughed. "You were annoying and rude, and I hated you for it, but you weren't beyond forgiveness."

"Somehow I don't believe that you were just such a good person that you decided to forgive me for bullying you."

"Ouch."

"I didn't mean it like that."

"Whatever."

Zane grumbled.

"What's your favorite food?" Zane asked randomly after a few minutes of silence.

I chose to ignore him for a while.

"Seriously? You're going to be like this?"

I looked at him with an unamused face, raising an eyebrow testily.

"The silent treatment? What are you? Five?"

I turned my head back the direction we were headed, still saying nothing.

"Ugh," he groaned. "Fine. I'm sorry. Maybe you're nice enough to just forgive someone. But if you were, you'd forgive me right now and stop giving me the silent treatment... Please?"

"Chocolate pudding," I smiled snarkily.

"What? Oh, come on! You punched me in the face and I was mad! *I'm sorry for the pudding on your mattress.* There, happy?"

I laughed.

"Not what I meant. I mean chocolate pudding is my favorite food."

"Oh," Zane blushed. "Sorry."

Fallmont grew larger in the distance, and I could make out towering skyscrapers that, the nearer we got, the more of the horizon they took up. The sun was beginning to set, igniting the sky in a fiery red-orange.

"It's huge," I breathed, stopping to stare at the city ahead of us.

"Yeah," Zane said softly. "It looks like we are coming at it from the side or the back, so we might have to guess which direction around it to go to reach the gate. Are you ready to do this?" His voice sounded nervous as he looked at me with a hint of fear in his eyes.

"As ready as I'll ever be," I answered.

Zane took a deep breath and continued toward the wall surrounding the city.

"Wait," I said, frozen in my position. *I don't know how this is all going to end. What if something happens to Zane? Or to me?*

"What's wrong?"

I trotted over to him, throwing my arms around him and burying my face in his neck.

"Eos, are you okay? What is it?" he asked, concerned.

"Nothing's wrong," I mumbled.

"Why are you hugging me?"

"I'm just really glad you came with me after all," I said, moving out of the hug and bringing my arms down to my sides.

He smiled, pulling me back into his arms. He hugged me tight around my waist and held the position for a while.

"Please be careful, E. I can't lose you, too. I wouldn't have made it this far without you, and I would have been lonely and miserable even if I had. If you're in trouble, run, and keep running until you're safe. Promise me that?"

"I promise, Zane," I said, my palms flat on his back as he held me there.

"Ready?" he asked, releasing me.

"Yes."

I pulled my hood up to cover myself better as we began running toward the walls of Fallmont. The sun had almost completely disappeared when we reached the wall, but suddenly, there was a bright flash of light as the city illuminated beyond it. We looked up past the wall, seeing advertisements and signs glowing with a rainbow of colors on every building. Some of the lights flashed, others twinkled, and some even moved along to music playing from a speaker.

I stared up at the glowing buildings, stunned. *This is unreal.*

"I've never seen anything like this!" I said to Zane, not taking my eyes off of the lights.

"Me neither. Eastmeade is the second largest city and even *we* don't have lights as insane as these. This is incredible!"

"Come on—let's keep moving," I ushered Zane, still looking to the side up at the lights as we took off around the wall.

Eos

The sand sunk under my feet with every step, and I noticed myself walking in step with the beat of the music blaring from some of the buildings.

"*Get down!*" Zane hissed at me, pointing ahead of him at three guards, armed with guns.

I ducked down, pancaking myself against the sand, hoping the wall would block enough of the city lights to keep me shadowed. The closer the guards were to us, the more I could make out what they were saying.

"What time is it?" one of the men asked.

"Ehh," another answered. "A few minutes until eight."

"Thanks. Mine and Luis's shifts end at eight, so we're gunna' head back inside for the night. Dox and Terry should be here to replace us in a little bit. You good on your own, kid?" the first voice asked.

"Mhmm," a third voice replied.

I could hear two of the men conversing, their voices growing faint as they drew further away. A couple minutes later, there was a commanding shout.

"Put your hands above your head and get on your knees!"

CHAPTER TWENTY-SEVEN

What now?

I held still for a moment, contemplating my options. *From a distance, it looked like those men had guns, and I don't think the guard is close enough to me for me to stand a chance with a knife. I'll just have to do what he says until he gets close enough, then I'll reach for my knife really fast and do what I have to do to get away. He could tell the other guards... He would tell the other guards... I'd have to do more than just injure him.*

I took a deep breath and raised my hands as I slowly maneuvered from my face-down position, sitting up on my knees. As I raised my eyes from the ground, they met those of the guard.

Fabian.

"Eos?" he called, lowering his gun slightly as he stared back at me in shock.

I stared back at his freckled face like a deer in headlights.

"What are you doing here?" he asked. "I thought you were exiled?"

"I was," I said.

"What are you doing here?" he repeated.

"I—" I hesitated. "I'm looking for something."

"What the hell could you be looking for that's in Fallmont? Or is important enough to put yourself in the kind of situation to get caught? You can't be here! The last thing I want is to know my best friend got sent off to live the rest of her days in a jail cell."

"Then help us," I insisted. "Please!"

"'Us?'" he asked, looking behind me until he spotted Zane in the sand a few yards away.

"Yes. Please."

"What do you need help with?" he asked uneasily.

"Help us get into City Hall."

"Why?"

"We're looking for something."

"What are you looking for? You owe me at least that much if I'm going to help you."

"You're going to help us?" I asked, a smile growing on my face.

"I didn't say that!" Fabian said, his lips twitching upwards in a smile as he saw mine fade. "Don't do that!" he said, stifling a laugh.

"Do what?" I asked, dramatically sighing.

"*That!*" he replied. "The guilt trips!"

"I'm not guilt tripping you. I was just really hoping you could help us because we really need to get to City Hall, but it's going to be almost impossible by ourselves."

"Then why are you even risking it?"

"It's just really important."

"Do you understand what you're asking me, E?"

"Yes. I know it isn't fair for me to expect you to risk everything like that. You don't have to help us, just pretend you never saw us and keep walking."

"I'm going to help you, but we have to be fast. More guards are supposed to meet me out here soon to be on watch."

I nodded, scrambling to my feet as Fabian began to walk alongside the wall. Zane and I hurried to follow him.

"There's an entrance specifically for guards," he said, looking at a watch on his wrist. "We have a few more minutes before the other guards should be heading through it, so we can make it in if we hurry. It's safer than the main gate if you catch it between shifts."

As we rushed along after Fabian, we neared a small door along the side of the wall surrounding Fallmont. Fabian pulled out a key ring, fumbling around until he slid one of the keys into the lock. The door unlocked and Fabian opened it, ushering us inside a small room full of weapons and first aid supplies, and shutting the door behind him as he followed us in, locking it behind him again with his key.

"You said you need to go to City Hall?" he asked for clarification.

"Yes."

Suddenly there was a click and I felt cold metal around my wrists.

"Why are you handcuffing me?!" I howled at Fabian.

"This is our best option," he said, handcuffing Zane

288

next. "If you guys look like prisoners, I can escort you to City Hall without raising suspicion."

Fabian pulled out a handgun.

"I have to make it believable. I'm not going to hurt you—trust me."

"I do," I said, looking him in the eyes.

He grabbed the back of the collar of Zane's shirt, forcefully leading him out of the room first, poking me in the back with the gun to lead me out on his other side. We continued like that, pretending to be prisoners caught by Fabian as he directed us out into the city streets.

The streets of Fallmont were unlike any of the other cities for more than just the colorful lights and the music—the streets were full of people. Some carried armfuls of shopping bags, others mingled in talkative groups, and there were individuals who bustled about along the sidewalk. Just from where we stood, I could see multiple carts set up with people frying foods and drizzling sauces on them, filling the air with a sweet aroma. There were lines of people in front of the food carts, eagerly handing over money in exchange for plates and paper baskets full of the snacks. Fabian steered us onwards, turning us down a darker, less populated street.

"It's a few miles down this street," Fabian said quietly from behind us. "Let's move quickly."

"Fabian?" I asked.

"Yeah?" he replied, leading us down the street.

"Why did you become an official?"

"Because of my dad. You remember how excited he was to move here for work with the government. He had been trying to get that job for years. From that point on, he kept pushing me to work for them as well. He put in a good word for me, and here I am."

"Oh, well, I'm happy for you," I said, my voice flat as it trailed off.

We hurried down the street, with Fabian still holding Zane's collar and pressing the gun to my back, until eventually we reached a building wider than many of the others in the city. Most of the buildings in Fallmont were skyscrapers, but this one was shorter, with elaborate marble columns lining a front entrance. Fabian slowed to a casual walk as he ushered us toward the entrance.

"Open the door," he told Zane. "Slowly."

Zane reached forward cautiously and pulled open the door, revealing a large but almost empty room with white marble walls and floors. There was a gigantic, fragile-looking chandelier hanging from the middle of the ceiling, and there were a few people in short lines in front of a counter along the far wall.

"Most of the officials go home for dinner and don't come back until morning," Fabian explained, assuming our curiosity.

"What are these people here for?" I asked in a whisper.

"The people behind the counter are just bankers. These people are just here for personal stuff, more than likely. Don't worry about them—just look like you're my prisoners and you'll be fine. These aren't the kind of people that would question it."

He directed us down a hallway just to the side of the counters. When we were safely out of sight of everyone, he closed a door behind the three of us, released Zane's collar, and lowered his gun.

"So, this thing you need to find so bad, where in here would it be?" he asked.

"It was confiscated from someone years ago—is there a room with confiscated items?"

"I mean… usually when we confiscate things, they just get sent to the dump in either Avid or along the border of the New Territory. If it were something particularly dangerous or useful to the city, they'd probably keep it in room 6A. It's a secure room in the basement level. They keep a few random things in there. I've only ever been in there once, and it was when they gave me a tour of the building when I was hired to be a guard. You need an official ID to open the door to it. It has a card reader. Here," Fabian reached at a cord around his neck, pulling out a plastic card from under his shirt and handing it to me. "I'm not going with you any further. I'm sorry, E. I'm not willing to risk that."

"I know. You always were the goody-goody," I smiled gratefully. "Thank you so much for getting us this far."

"Of course. After I read the letter you sent, I didn't think I'd ever even have a chance of seeing you again. You were my best friend—I had to help, especially because I don't know if I'll ever see you again after this. Use my card to open the door. Remember—room 6A. Continue straight down this hall, take the stairs down, and it'll be on the right side. When you leave, just keep running and don't stop until you're out. My card can't get you out of the guard door—you'll need to pick the lock—but you have to be careful—and very, very fast. Run and don't look back. Stay out of the line of fire too, because depending on who is guarding the gate at the time, some of them might shoot."

It was silent for a moment.

"What? I'm just saying," he said, seeing our looks of fear.

"How will you get your card back once we leave though?" Zane asked.

"Once you run past the gate, drop it in the sand. I'll know to look for it there, if someone doesn't find it and return it first. I can just claim that it must have fallen off my lanyard while doing rounds. I'd much rather get called careless than get called a traitor."

"Fair enough. Thank you again, Fabian," I said with a smile, reaching out and hugging him.

He hugged me back without another word. He gave a solemn but cheesy salute. His brow furrowed as the corner of his lip twitched into a saddened smile as he turned to leave, shutting the door again behind him.

I stood there for a moment, staring at the closed door before turning my attention to the ID card in my hands. It was a thin, flimsy piece of white plastic with a thin periwinkle border. On it was a stiff photograph of Fabian, his strawberry blond hair in tightly curled clumps on his head, his large-rimmed glasses making his hazel eyes look unnaturally small, and his lips turned up in a dorky half-smile. Next to his picture, there were some lines of printed information about his name, birthday, an ID number, and a few other things.

"When you're done staring at that card, we should probably get moving. We don't have much time," Zane said, poking me to get my attention.

"Right," I said, drawing my attention back to the plan. "Let's go."

Zane and I drew our daggers out, holding them steady at our sides as we progressed down the hall.

"Stand over there, out of initial sight if someone is behind the door," Zane whispered, his hand over the doorknob. "I'm going to open it and peek through to see if the coast is clear, but be ready. If there's someone behind it, try to knock them out or something. We don't want to hurt anyone we don't have to, but we also don't want them to go tattling on us."

I nodded, standing guard as Zane made eye contact with me before cracking the door open, barely enough to peer through. He was silent for a minute before he opened the door fully.

"It's empty," he said. "Just the staircase."

He led the way downstairs and into another hallway. This one was lined with closed doors on either side, and each door had an ID scanner fixed on it above the doorknob. As we progressed down the hall, we glanced at each of the tabs above the doorways. The odd-numbered rooms were on the left, and the even on the right. A few rooms down the hall, we saw it. Room 6A.

I fumbled with the ID card for a moment, trying to figure out how the scanner worked. The scanner had a small electronic screen, with a slit in the front. I pushed the card into the opening, and suddenly there was a loud honking sound from the screen panel as the words "flip card" appeared in bold red letters. I pulled the card out immediately and turned it the other direction, pushing it back into the scanner. There was a chime, followed by a deep *thunk* from within the door. Zane looked back at me with matched confusion. He shrugged, held out his dagger, and tentatively turned the knob and opened the door.

"There's no one in here," Zane said, entering the room.

As soon as he stepped foot in room 6A, lights automatically flickered on, revealing metal cabinets along all of the walls. Each of the cabinets had labels taped to them, but the labels made no sense to us—they were seemingly randomized combinations of letters and numbers.

"Remember what it's supposed to look like," I said, digging out the photograph of the Skeleton Key and its box.

We studied the picture for a moment and I tucked it away again.

"Just start looking," I said, pulling open a drawer marked GER534S.

I rummaged through the drawer. Each item in it was sealed in individual bags. In the GER534S cabinet, I found a bag of little white pills, a bag with a pack of cigarettes, and a bag with a syringe.

"Any luck?" I asked Zane, who had started his search on the other side of the room.

"None," he replied, still digging.

We continued searching through the bags in the cabinets, hoping to find something that resembled the Skeleton Key, but then we heard the chime of a scanner outside the door, followed by a *thunk*.

The door swung open, revealing four figures—four officials in uniforms, two of which held weapons and one of which held two syringes. The fourth figure was Fabian.

CHAPTER TWENTY-EIGHT

"Drop your weapons and put your hands in the air!" commanded one of the armed officials.

I looked at Zane, panicked as I saw his palms open and heard his dagger clatter against the tile floor.

"Drop your weapon!" the official repeated, motioning toward me. "I'm not going to say it again!"

I relaxed my hand, letting my dagger fall as I slowly stretched my open palms above my head.

"Are these the criminals that stole your ID?" one of the officials asked Fabian, who looked at me as if we were strangers.

"Yes."

"You are to hold still," the official said, turning back to Zane and me. "If we see you so much as flinch, we will shoot you. Do you understand?"

We stared back at the official in silence.

"Wonderful," he said dryly as the man with the syringes walked cautiously toward me.

I grimaced as he jabbed one of the syringes into my

thigh. He looked at me with a wicked grin as he pushed the plunger, and suddenly everything went dark.

~

When I came to, I began to make out my surroundings. I was in a large, dim room. There was a long, slick black table in front of me, with me at the head seat, and a fair-skinned woman with thick, curled raven-black hair in a pressed suit sat at the far end. Officials sat along either end of the table, and one of them nearest me had mine and Zane's bags and daggers in front of him on the table. Fabian was no longer with them, but my face burned when I thought of how he betrayed me.

Where's Zane?

I sat forward in my seat in panic, feeling a growing tightness around my wrists and hearing the rattle of handcuffs.

"Eos Dawn," the woman started.

"Can I help you?" I asked snarkily.

Her eyes twinkled as she narrowed them, tilting her head slightly as she observed me.

"This is for your protection, Eos."

"My *protection?*" I spat with a laugh.

"Yes. This is your trial. Even though you've broken more laws than the average criminal, the law still states that it is your right to have a trial before you are exiled, though this time it will be a little different."

"Why are you bothering to have a trial if you know who I am?"

"Pardon?"

"If you know who I am, you know what I've done."

"Yes, but we don't know *why*. For all we know, you could have a righteous reason."

I scoffed.

She looked at me plainly and sighed.

"Miss Dawn, you're not doing yourself any favors by not taking this seriously."

"Look, I know what I've done and I know why I did all of it, but I'm definitely not some 'righteous' criminal."

"Are you admitting selfish motivation?"

"Uh. Sure?"

"Write that down," she mumbled to a mousey man on her right.

The man began scribbling away on a notepad.

"Who are you, anyways?" I asked the woman.

"Raine Velora. I'm the leader of Fallmont."

"Okay, look, Ms. Velora—"

"Raine. Just call me Raine. Ms. Velora sounds too much like my mother's name," she said with a chuckle.

"Fine. Whatever. Look, you know what I've done. If you're going to send me off somewhere, why are you wasting your time asking me questions?"

"We can't 'send you off' anywhere until we know exactly why you visited all of the exile towns."

"That's a shame, because quite frankly, I don't want to tell you."

"I'm going to give you one more chance, Miss Dawn. What or who were you after and why? You compromised our entire system by traveling from exile town to exile town, and we need to know the full motivation."

I cocked one of my eyebrows and stared back at Raine, who was growing irritated.

"Bring in Mr. Hess," she called to one of her officials.

Suddenly, two men in HAZMAT suits dragged a sedated Zane into the room, strapping his arms, legs, and torso to an empty chair.

My eyes bounced between the men, Zane, and Raine as I began to panic.

"Tell us why you went to all of the exile towns, and then Fallmont."

"Don't—" Zane sputtered sleepily.

"No," I answered.

Raine nodded to the two men, who proceeded to roll out a cart full of vials of liquid. One of the men steadied Zane's chair, while the other popped open one of the vials, holding it over Zane's arm. A single droplet of the liquid rolled out and splattered on Zane's skin, simmering. He let out a pained yell, shaking in his restraints.

"What are you doing to him?!" I screamed.

"I don't really feel like answering your question," Raine grinned.

"He isn't doing anything wrong—why are you hurting him?"

"He's as guilty as you are, as far as I'm concerned. Answer my questions and they won't hurt him anymore."

I looked remorsefully over at Zane. *I can't tell her. I don't want to be the person that gets the Skeleton Key destroyed, and I don't want to put any of the people that helped us at risk.*

"I can't."

Raine frowned, signaling to the men once again. They poured a few drops this time, but in the same place on Zane's arm. He let out a gravely scream as his skin began to blister.

This went on for a while longer until suddenly, Raine grew tired of not getting her way.

"I'm sick of playing this game," she growled at me. "Plan B!"

The two men looked at her for a moment.

"Ma'am," one of them protested lightly.

"Do it," she commanded.

The man opened another vial, while the other forced open Zane's mouth. The official poured the contents of the vial into Zane's open mouth, and then the official forced Zane's mouth shut briefly as he began to violently convulse. When the grip on his mouth was released, he began to choke. Pink foam oozed out of his mouth as he shook, gasping and letting out gurgled cries.

I wrestled against my restraints, screaming at Raine and her officials.

"STOP!" I shrieked, my eyes welling up.

"Tell me what you were doing outside Avid."

I looked over at Zane; his body was limp as the pink foam dripped from his lips, and he was breathing laboriously.

"Fine," I surrendered.

I paused for a moment as all of the officials turned to look at me.

"I'm here for the Skeleton Key."

"Skeleton Key?" Raine asked, confused.

"It's an invention from a man who used to live in Avid. It's a device."

"What does it do?"

I took a moment before responding reluctantly.

"It's supposed to open any kind of lock."

"Is that so? That doesn't explain why you went to all of the exile towns though, and then to Fallmont. Do you not know the location of this Skeleton Key?"

"I do. But I needed keys from the exile towns to open its box."

"I see. So, is the Skeleton Key supposedly in Fallmont? Is that why you came here after all the exile towns? You found all the keys you need?"

"Yes."

The scribe continued frantically recording our words.

"Where in Fallmont is the Skeleton Key?" she asked.

"I'm not sure. That's why we didn't find it."

"Alright. I believe that answers everything we need for the time being. If more questions arise, Mr. Hess and you will be brought back for further interrogation. Until then, you will be in a holding cell, and you will be brought to Ironwood in the morning."

"Ironwood?" I asked.

"The only remaining prison in the New Territory," she changed her focus to the official with my belongings in front of him. "Bring her to the cell. You two clean up the boy and then bring him down as well."

The official left my belongings on the table as he approached me with a small key in hand. He reached down to uncuff me as he spoke.

"Don't get your hopes up—the cuffs are going to stay on. I only have to remove one hand from them to get you from the chair."

I bit my lip, suppressing a smirk. He released my hand from the cuffs and without a second's pause, I swung my fist around and felt it collide with his jaw. I threw myself across the slick table, snatching up my dagger and wielding it defensively in front of me. The cuffs dangled from my left wrist as I held my dagger with my right hand. I grabbed a handful of hair from one of the official's heads, pressing my dagger to her throat.

"Take off his restraints!" I demanded the men in HAZMAT suits.

They looked at Raine for permission, and she simply nodded her head. They unstrapped Zane, and he fell out of the chair onto his side, groaning in pain. I tugged the official along with me, keeping the dagger at her neck as I guided her toward Zane.

"Zane," I called down to him. "Can you move?"

He weakly nodded his head, shaking as he tried to push himself up into a sitting position. I shuffled until the official and I were blocking the view of the cart full of vials. I released the official's hair for a second, keeping the dagger to her throat as I tucked a couple of the closed vials into my coat pocket subtly, speaking to distract the room of officials.

"You're going to let us walk out peacefully. You will allow me to take mine and Zane's belongings, and you will not stop us," I threatened.

"That is where you're wrong," Raine said smoothly.

As she said this, I caught sight of two of the officials pointing guns at Zane.

"No—" I breathed as one of the officials put his finger on the trigger. "No!"

"You're going to let us take you to the cell peacefully. You will not retrieve your belongings, and you will not protest," Raine said, mocking me.

"Fine. Just leave him alone."

"Deal."

Immediately, guards began surrounding Zane and me, handcuffing us both. They forced Zane to his feet and shoved the two of us forward, turning down a hallway. One of the officials pulled out an ID card and inserted it into a scanner. The scanner chimed pleasantly, and the official opened the large door. Zane and I were pushed inside and without another word, they slammed the door shut behind us.

Zane crumpled over on the floor. He began coughing, spattering blood on the white tile beneath him. He tried to push himself back up, attempting to dig in his jacket pocket but began coughing again.

"Take it easy," I said, sitting on the floor beside him and putting an arm around him.

"I got it," he gasped, spitting up some blood and foam.

"Got what?"

"The Skeleton Key."

"What?" I asked, my eyes wide as my heart began to race. "How?"

"When I heard them unlock the door," he choked. "Pocket."

I reached around Zane's waist, searching the belongings in his pocket. I felt the crinkly plastic of a bag, which I pulled out. In the bag was a shallow, russet-colored wooden box about the length of my hand. I tore open the bag and observed the box, turning it over in my hands. There were five identical locks along one edge of it.

"The keys. Which pocket are the keys in?" I asked Zane.

He rolled over on his other side, making his pocket available.

"Left."

I fumbled around in his jean pocket and pulled out two of the keys. I took the other three out of my own pocket and arranged all of them in a line on the floor.

"Which one is which?" I asked.

Zane shrugged, grumbling.

I picked up one of the keys, taking a closer look at it. They all looked fairly similar, despite some being made with different materials. Upon closer look, I could see a small 'A' engraved on the edge of the key in my hand. *They're labeled*, I thought excitedly, picking up another one of the keys, seeing a 'D' etched on it. Frantically, I organized the keys in alphabetical order.

A.

B.

C.

D.

E.

I put the keys into the locks on the box in order, letting them all stay in place before turning any of them. I looked at the box for a moment and turned to Zane.

"Unlock it," I said, holding out the box.

"What?"

"Unlock it. You were the one who found it. You should get to unlock it."

"You sure?" he asked, turning his head to look up at me.

"Yes," I handed him the box.

He held it, running his fingers over the smooth wood before he turned the locks slowly, one after another, leaving the last one unturned.

"You," he said, holding it out.

I smiled at him. Before turning the final key, I bent down and kissed his forehead. Zane smiled, revealing reddened teeth. I felt a weight in my stomach upon the realization of the physical damage the officials and Raine had done to him.

"What are you waiting for?" He chuckled weakly.

I turned the fifth key and pulled the lid of the box

open. Inside the box was a silver device. The handle was twisted metal, with three circles on it, each filled with a different color stained glass—blue, green, and purple. There was a tiny dial along the metal edging, and the part of the Skeleton Key that was meant to fit into locks was a thin, smooth silver rod covered in tiny holes.

"Zane," I said, staring in awe at the Key. "We did it."

"Lot of good it'll do us here," he said. "They used an ID card to get in."

"I have a plan."

Zane raised an eyebrow and looked plainly at me. I pulled out the vials and his eyes grew wide.

"When they come in to take us, I'm going to throw the acid at them, then we have to run. Don't stop running until we get to the door Fabian brought us through. He used a key on it instead of his ID, so the Skeleton Key should work. Then, we keep running some more until, when we look back, we don't see Fallmont anymore."

"How about those ruins we spent the night in before we came here?"

"Perfect. The main point is—we need to keep moving. Do you think you can?"

"Yes. I just need to rest for a little bit."

"You have time. Raine said they weren't moving us until morning, so we probably have at least a few hours. Get some sleep. I'll wake you up if anything happens."

He nodded lazily.

"Here," I said, sliding next to him on the floor and patting on my lap. "Just lay your head on my lap. It's gotta' be better than the floor."

"Thanks," he said, smiling as he nuzzled his head into my lap and fell asleep.

~

When we get out of here, I want to find Fortitude, and I'm going to release as many exiles as I can.

I kept reciting those plans in my mind over and over for a couple hours until I heard the chime of the scanner outside.

"*Zane,*" I hissed, shaking him by the shoulders. "*Wake up.*"

Zane's eyes fluttered open, and he hurried to push himself up.

"Can you stand?" I asked, pulling out the vials.

"Yeah," he said. "I don't feel quite as bad now."

We got to our feet just as the door swung open. Before I could even make eye contact with two officials, one of which was holding our belongings, I tossed the contents of the vials at their faces, and there was a horrible hissing sound as the officials began to clutch at their faces while screaming.

"*GO!*" I yelled back at Zane. "Don't stop running!"

We took off sprinting through the door, snatching our bags and daggers from the one official and shoving them aside as we ran. The officials began calling for help as we kept running through the hall, turning down another hallway.

"How do we get out?" Zane asked, struggling to keep up.

"I don't know. Just try anything!"

We ran past hallways full of doors with scanners, only going through those without. Eventually, we reached a staircase. *Which floor is this?* I looked around in the stairwell, spotting a plaque with the number 3 on it.

"Down!" I shouted at Zane as I ran clumsily down the stairs.

When we reached the first floor, we burst through a set of doors, setting us in the bank room from when we were with Fabian. There were different people this time both behind the counter and in line in front of it. Some of the people looked at us with fear in their eyes as we stood there, daggers in hand and wild looks on our faces before we took off sprinting out the main doors of Fallmont City Hall.

I started to turn backward to see if the officials were following us, but Zane yelled up at me.

"Don't look back! It'll slow you down. Keep going until we get to the guardroom!"

I kept my eyes focused ahead of me as we ran toward the city's wall, staying close to it until we could see the guardroom along the wall. I pulled out the Skeleton Key and slid it into the lock. Remembering what Mr. Montgomery and Zane told me about how the Key worked, I twisted the dial until I felt that the Key was firmly in the lock. I turned the Key and reached for the doorknob. *It worked.*

I opened the door and ushered Zane inside, closing the door behind the two of us. I dug a water bottle out of my bag and took a swig, passing it to Zane.

"Drink a little. Once we catch our breath, we can head out and keep moving," I said, handing him the bottle as he began to chug. "We'll go to those ruins from last night and figure out where to go from there. We're going to find Fortitude."

Zane nodded.

We were silent for a moment, filling the room with nothing but our heavy breathing.

"Ready?" I asked, standing by the exit door while toying with the Key.

"One second," Zane said, drawing close to me and pulling me toward him.

I looked up at him, his arms around my waist as he learned down and kissed me. I felt my palms and face grow warm as I closed my eyes and kissed him back.

"Ready," he said, a smile on his face as he loosened his grip on me.

I pushed the Skeleton Key into the lock and turned.

Click.

Eos is now available as an audiobook on
Audible & iTunes!

If you've enjoyed this book, please consider
leaving a review. Reviews are the best way to show
your love & support for the author, as well as help
new readers find these books!

Thank you.

**TURN THE PAGE FOR A SNEAK PEEK AT THE
SECOND INSTALLMENT IN THE EOS DAWN SERIES.**

CHAPTER ONE

I distinctly remember the smell of cinnamon.

I remember the sounds of gunshots and yelling.

And I remember the feeling of sweat on my neck.

When Zane and I escaped Fallmont with the Skeleton Key, we sprinted as fast as we could until we had reached the ruins of a blackened village. We managed to find the Skeleton Key box in Fallmont after finding keys to open it in each of the five exile towns: Avid—the dump town for thieves, Bellicose—the caverns for the aggressive, Clamorite—the waterfall grotto in the mountains for the unruly, Delaisse—the abandoned factories for the druggies and vandals, and Equivox—the lake town hidden in a crater for the liars.

It was growing dark by this point, and we hadn't eaten since before we reached Fallmont. Thinking back to the sweet smell of cinnamon and other spices from the food carts of the city, my stomach began to growl angrily. Squatting down on a mound of rubble, I rummaged through my leather bag, pulling out a piece of crumbling, stale bread. Upon closer observation, the bread had tiny specs of green mold. I picked out the moldy pieces and devoured the slice, holding out a second slice for Zane.

"Thanks, E," he said, taking the bread and sitting next to me. He turned the bread over in his hand for a moment, looking at the green specs before biting.

Not wanting to think about anything, I sat there silently, resting my elbows on my knees and my chin in my palms.

"So," Zane prodded awkwardly.

"What?" I grumbled, exhausted.

"Fortitude?" he asked, a little garbled. His mouth was still blistered from the acid the officials tortured him with when Raine had interrogated me.

"Really, Zane?" I scoffed.

"What?"

"Does now really seem like the right time?"

"Is there ever a right time for anything we do?"

I sighed.

"No. But can't we just rest for the night?"

"Of course, but we have to keep moving in the morning. We don't know if officials from Fallmont are still looking for us."

I nodded sleepily as I stood, making my way toward one of the ruined cottages. I peeked my head inside to inspect it, shrugged, grunted, and flopped onto the floor after pulling my blanket out of my bag. Within minutes, I was asleep.

"Wake up," I heard Zane mutter the next morning, prodding my side with a finger.

I threw the blanket over my face as I moaned.

"We have to keep moving," Zane reminded me. "Not only do we not want to get caught here, but we don't have enough food and water to last us forever."

"What's the plan?"

Zane pulled out a map, stretching out on the floor next to me.

"Skylar said Fortitude was past Bellicose, toward the ocean, right?" he asked.

I nodded.

"Didn't she also say something about a purple light?" I reminded him.

"I think so."

"So, where are we, and where are we headed?"

"We are somewhere in *this* area," he pointed to a blank space on the map near Fallmont. "If we head straight west, we shouldn't run into any cities or exile towns. But at some point, we have to work our way south."

I stared at the map, contemplating. While I focused on the map, Zane nuzzled up against me, kissing my shoulder. I turned and looked at him with a straight face before turning back to the map.

"I mean, the map doesn't show much of what's beyond the cities and towns, so I don't really see what other options we have," I said, folding up the map.

After a quick breakfast, Zane and I started the trek to the west. We were silent most of the day, stopping occasionally for breaks in various ruins. Despite the warmth of the air, puffy clouds blocked the sun and spared us of intense heat.

"Let's make sand angels," Zane spoke up during a silent moment while walking.

"What?"

"You heard me."

"What? You mean like people used to make in the snow?" I asked.

Zane and I have never seen snow, at least not in person. The New Territory never gets snow. Before the war, when the country was populated all throughout, there were people who lived in colder areas, and they would get snow. I thought the concept of wanting to play in frozen water to be unappealing, to say the least.

"Yeah! Oh, come on. We could use a break, and our normal breaks are boring! Let's do it!" Zane smiled warmly.

I rolled my eyes and huffed at Zane as he flopped onto his back, sending up a puff of sand.

He began frantically sifting his arms and legs across the fine sand, stopped, and stretched out his arms.

"Help me up?"

I walked over and pulled him to his feet as he turned to admire his work.

"It doesn't look like an angel," I said, squinting at the ground.

"It looks... like a potato..." Zane said, confused.

I grinned.

"It worked!" He beamed.

"No, it didn't! You said it yourself!" I said, pointing to the potato hole, a smug grin spreading on my lips.

"No, I mean my plan worked! You smiled!"

"Okay, fair enough," I said, my smile fading. "Let's keep moving."

After some time walking through emptiness, we came across some ruins, like the others we had crossed before, except in slightly better shape. Some of the buildings still retained the natural red color of their bricks. A couple of the buildings still stood fairly untouched, with fewer crumbling walls.

Curious, I approached one of the buildings with the door still in place. I went to turn the knob, but it wouldn't budge.

"Zane," I said. "This one is locked."

"Don't you have the Key?" he asked. "See if it'll work on that door."

I dug the Key out of my leather bag, turning it over in my hands as light glimmered off of the silver and through the three pieces of green, purple, and blue stained glass at the Key's head. I inserted it into the lock, twisted the tiny dial on the Key, and turned until I heard a click.

The door opened, revealing a room with faded brown couches, a dusty wooden table, and a few dishes scattered around the room. The walls were a pale blue, and the carpet was a stained cream color with sand tracked throughout the house. Zane followed behind me. I turned into the kitchen while Zane brushed dirt off the couch. I looked at the sink, which had water puddled in it.

"*Zane*," I hissed quietly toward the living room.

A moment later, Zane poked his head in the kitchen door.

"What?" he asked as I frantically signaled for him to lower his voice.

"*I think there are people here*," I whispered, my eyes wide.

"*What? Where?*"

I shrugged, pointing to the water in the sink. "*It hasn't evaporated yet. It's recent.*"

Zane pulled out his dagger and I pulled out mine as we split up to search the house. Zane and I cautiously opened doors to closets and bedrooms until suddenly, I heard a shriek.

I turned, the hair on my neck standing on end as I held my dagger out defensively, creeping toward Zane, who stood in a doorway, blocking my view.

"Who are you?" I heard Zane demand of someone inside one of the rooms.

"W-we aren't here to hurt anyone! P-p-please!" a female voice whimpered.

We?

"What are you doing here?" Zane asked, still holding out his weapon.

"Wait a minute… You aren't officials, are you?" The girl's voice grew confident. "You aren't carrying a gun."

"No, we aren't officials," Zane answered. "What are you doing here?"

"We escaped from some of the exile towns. We found each other while looking for shelter in the ruins. We aren't looking for trouble."

"How do I know I can trust you?" Zane asked.

"Why do you *need* to trust us?" a man grunted.

Keeping my distance behind Zane, I could only see beyond the doorframe enough to make out the man who spoke. He was heavy-set, with peppered hair and a bushy beard.

"They don't *have* to trust us, Trent, but there's no harm in allies," the girl chirped.

Trent snorted, crossing his arms.

"Search us! Our bags," the girl continued, and there was a collective *thump* as bags were dropped. "We don't have weapons. We don't have much of anything. The houses here still had some canned food we've been living off of. That's it—I swear."

Zane entered the room, still wielding his golden dagger distrustfully. I could hear him undo zippers and clasps as he searched bags briefly before speaking again.

"Okay. You can't be too sure. I'm sorry for scaring you. My girlfriend and I escaped as well."

Girlfriend? When did we decide this? And why is he willing to trust them so quickly?

"I understand. My name is Cindee—"

"Wait," Zane interrupted, turning to me and beckoning me over.

I stepped into the room, which was clearly an old bedroom, and saw eleven new people staring back at me.

"How…" I trailed off.

"It's a long story," a girl with freckles and two blonde braids replied. *She must be Cindee.*

I looked at Zane, my mouth open in shock.

"I'm Cindee," the girl with braids repeated. She looked about Lamb's age. "I'm from Clamorite."

I looked at the rest of the group. There seemed to be a variety of people—younger and older, male and female.

"This is Bexa from Bellicose, Trent and Persephone

from Equivox, Eve, Braylin, and Gwenn from Clamorite, Yulie and Brenur from Delaisse, and Cameron and Astraea from Avid," Cindee introduced.

"I'm Zane, and this is Eos," Zane gestured to me. "We're both from Avid."

"Why'd you leave?" I asked.

"We could ask you the same question," Trent retorted.

"Yeah, but I asked first."

"We didn't like our situations. I'm assuming it was the same for you. Just because we've committed crimes doesn't mean we define ourselves by our crimes, and it doesn't mean we get along with other people just because they committed the same crimes," replied Eve, a short, thin girl with spiked black hair and notable dark circles under her emerald eyes.

Brenur, a dark-skinned man with wide-set eyes, thick arms, and broad shoulders spoke up.

"Yulie and I left because she—" he started before Yulie, a woman with tan skin, a furrowed brow, and silky brown hair, glared coolly at him. The height difference between the two was so huge that I couldn't help but to stare. I was about average height, whereas the top of Yulie's head hardly reached my nose, and Brenur easily towered over me.

"Did you all expect there to be something greater out here?" I spat bitterly.

"Yes," Cindee replied quickly. "Even if there are

challenges, sometimes change is necessary. Eve, Braylin, Gwenn, and I all left together. We knew we weren't going to be facing it alone. We came across the rest of the group over time. Some of these people were together, some by themselves. But they all couldn't bear being exiled anymore."

"Being out here," I held my arms out, my eyes wild. "Being out here is *worse*. You're safer in the exile towns."

"Safer isn't always better," Astraea cooed softly. She had long, wavy maroon hair and bright eyes. Her gaze seemed to analyze me as she spoke.

"We answered your question, so answer one of ours. What are your plans, now that you're free?" Trent asked.

Zane looked at me, as if for approval, but without waiting for it, he began.

"We're looking for something," he started.

"*Zane*," I hissed, elbowing his side aggressively.

He cupped his hands over my ear, his voice low.

"I searched their bags—they don't have weapons. I didn't see anything on them, either. They don't even have much food. If they really are who they say they are, isn't this essentially what we wanted to do anyways? Guide exiles to Fortitude?"

"Did he just say Fortitude?" asked a tall woman named Persephone. Before she spoke, her posture straightened with an air of superiority, her ginger bob tickling the pale skin of her jaw. Her wide nose was held upwards, but upon the mention of Fortitude, her snooty appearance transformed into one of curiosity.

There was collective conversation from the group of exiles.

"Zane!" I shouted.

"What?" he cried, holding his hands up as if in surrender.

I groaned in disgust.

"I've heard of it!" Bexa spoke up. She had a frizzy brunette bun and colorful tattoos across her arms and chest.

I had to remind myself not to stare at Bexa's numerous piercings covering her ears, her petite pointed nose, and her thin lips.

Those piercings look painful.

"It's a town of escaped exiles. I've heard about it, but I didn't think it was real. Have you seen it before?" she asked.

"No," I replied.

"Do you know where it is?" she asked.

"Not exactly…"

There were shared grumbles from the exiles.

"I mean we have a general idea. We hadn't heard of it until after we escaped, and at that point, we figured it would be worth a shot."

I decided not to mention the Skeleton Key right now, especially with two other thieves joining us. I also figured it wasn't the best time to mention that we planned on eventually going back to break a bunch of other criminals out of the exile towns.

"So, what's the plan?" asked Eve.

"What do you mean?" I asked in return.

"Well, you obviously aren't going in search of Fortitude without a plan. You said you have a general idea of where it is, and I'm assuming you have plans for getting rations?" she replied.

"Umm…" I struggled, looking at Zane for help.

"We don't exactly have much of a plan. We're heading west until we clear the cities, then we will head south a bit until we near the ocean, which is where Fortitude is supposed to be."

"So, you don't have a plan, is what you're trying to say?" Persephone said with an amused smirk.

"We do," I groaned.

"Where do you plan on getting rations?" she pried.

"None of your business," I hissed, thinking about the Skeleton Key.

"E," Zane breathed, looking at me in disbelief. "Sorry, I don't know what's gotten into her. I was thinking we would stop in cities and towns along the way, snag what we can."

"Excuse me?" I growled. "You 'don't know what's gotten into me?'"

Fortitude

"I didn't mean it like that."

"She's upset that you're sharing all of this with strangers," Astraea observed almost inaudibly.

"Honestly, I think our chances are better if you all join us. Safety in numbers, and all that. More people to help with supplies, too, if you want to come with us to Fortitude," he invited, avoiding my glare.

"May I speak with my group for a moment? Privately?" Cindee asked politely.

"Of course," Zane responded, ushering me back into the kitchen with him as Cindee closed the bedroom door behind her.

"*What are you doing?*" I snarled at Zane.

"They're right! We don't have a plan, Eos! I mean, what are we supposed to do about food and water?"

"We have the Key!" I exclaimed in a hushed voice. "We can get in any town or city we want, and we can get all the supplies we need!"

"We can't carry enough to last us more than a few days. Face it."

"And you think inviting *more* people, who *also* need food is going to fix that problem?"

"Some of their group members look stronger than us and can probably carry more. Plus, with a bigger group, we can have people carry extra supplies and we can switch off in shifts, if we get desperate," Zane argued, as if he had calculated all of this carefully. "Or what if someone has a supply that we need, and we have something they need? A bigger group means more supplies available."

"Fine. But how do you know we can trust them? Especially after what happened in Fallmont!"

"They aren't officials, E."

"But what if they report you?"

"That's a stupid question. Do you really think a group of runaway exiles are going to report other runaway exiles? They don't want to get caught. We don't want to get caught. That means everyone protects each other to some degree by default, as a matter of self-preservation."

"I still don't trust them."

"I'm not sure I do either. It's called a leap of faith. Do you trust me?"

"They might steal the Key, Zane."

"I didn't ask if you trust *them*, I asked if you trust *me*."

"Yes."

He smiled at me softly, placing a hand behind my head and planting a quick kiss on my forehead.

The bedroom door opened, and the group flooded out into the main room of the small house.

The corner of Cindee's lips turned upward in a half smile as she nodded.

"You're in?" Zane asked.

"Yup. We've got at least one person from each exile

town, too. We've got everyone we could need to get anything we could need. But first, we have a different plan."

"What is it?" I asked, skeptically.

"We agreed that moving south first, then west, is the best option. South of us is Delaisse, Nortown, and Equivox. If we go south first, we can stock up on supplies, which we might not come across if we head straight toward the west," Cindee offered.

Zane thought for a moment before speaking.

"That's a good point. E?" he asked, turning to me.

"What?"

"I want to know what you think," he said genuinely.

I narrowed my eyes and stared back at him for a moment.

"I—I think that's a good idea," I said, softening my gaze.

"It's settled then. We head south," Zane nodded to Cindee.

"We believe it would be best to visit Delaisse first for a supply run. It's closest. Yulie and Brenur said the rations are easy to access once you're in the town. We just have to find out how to break in, and we can stock up there. If we don't think we have enough to make it to Fortitude with those supplies, we can visit Equivox next. It would probably be safer than trying to sneak into a city, even if that city is just tiny Nortown," Cindee continued to plot.

"Makes sense," I said. "Should we wait until morning to leave? It's getting late, and this is as good a place as any to stay."

"Yeah, that'd probably be best," Cindee answered. "We found some cans of food in the cabinets in the kitchen, if you guys want something for dinner."

"Thank you," I said, staring unblinkingly at Cindee.

What's her motive? She's either planning something, or she's trusting that we can get her somewhere we don't even know exists. Either way, I'm not sure I like it.

The group began to find places to sleep, making themselves comfortable throughout the house as Zane and I dug through the cabinets, picking out a couple cans of beans and vegetables.

"Here," Astraea said, seeming to appear out of nowhere behind me, holding out a metal can opener.

"Thanks," I said, narrowing my gaze at her as her eyes scanned over me.

"You're afraid of us," she perceived, looking into my eyes, her head cocked slightly to the side. "Why?"

"I'm not afraid. I just don't know why you all want to join us."

"We just want freedom. Same as you. We have a better chance of making it to Fortitude if we stick together and help each other. Why do you think we all ended up as such a large group?"

"Look... Astrid," I started.

"Astraea," she corrected under her breath.

"Sorry."

"It's okay. It's a tough one for some people. Ah. Stray. Uh," she sounded out. "You can call me Trae if that's easier."

"Okay. Anyways," I sighed. "We don't even know for sure if Fortitude exists. We've never seen it before."

"So, you're afraid of letting us all down, is that it?" she cooed. "What do 13 criminals really have to lose?"

Their lives.

JEN GUBERMAN-PERRY

Jen Guberman-Perry isn't a New York Time's bestselling author, and she has no critical acclaims, but her mom thinks her books are pretty good. She graduated from Gardner-Webb University with her Bachelor's in Communication & New Media, and she was a member of three honor societies. Jen lives with her husband and their cat in Charlotte, North Carolina.

Made in the USA
Columbia, SC
05 June 2021